MW00682141

Murder on Wheels

Mary Scott

Murder on Wheels

First published in 2000 by
Allison & Busby Limited
114 New Cavendish Street
London W1M 7FD
http://www.allisonandbusby.ltd.uk

Copyright © 2000 by Mary Scott
The right of Mary Scott to be identified as author of
this work has been asserted by her in accordance with the Copyright,
Designs and Patents Act, 1988

This book is sold subject to the condition that it shall not,
by way of trade or otherwise, be lent, resold, hired out or otherwise
circulated without the publisher's prior written consent in any form of binding
or cover other than that in which it is published and without a similar condition
including this condition being imposed upon the
subsequent purchaser.

A catalogue record for this book is available
from the British Library

ISBN 0 7490 0460 6

Printed and bound by Creative Print & Design,
Ebbw Vale, Wales.

To Molly Brown who thought Bryan was a gas the very first time I mentioned him; who endured endless repetitions of John's bad jokes; who contributed umpteen more quips; and who read each chapter, shredded it and suggested how I could put it back together again in better shape. Thanks a bunch, Molly. Oh, and your new novel, *The Aries Grove Centre for Executive Stress,* is sure to raise a storm when it hits the bookshops.

Also to Graham Joyce who gave me a valuable third opinion when I really needed one.

And to Tania Stokes: she knows why.

The telephone box stood on the far side of the cold, rain-streaked, run-down shopping mall. Dark facades of steel-grilled, shuttered shops on either side made the lit interior of the box seem the only place of safety in the grim, deserted, urban scene. No one ventured here alone after dark.

Above the telephone box a single streetlamp flickered. Into its pale pool of uncertain light fled a woman, long dark dress trailing. Her bare arms and one slim, exposed thigh gleamed yellow in the artificial glare.

He called out to her and she turned. He approached her. He had time, as he raised his weapon, arms outstretched above his head, to see relieved recognition turn to sudden, startled fear in the gleaming whites of her eyes.

He'd read somewhere that fear had its own smell. Now he knew it was true. He wrinkled his nostrils as she pressed herself against the phone box, hands flattened on its vandal-proof shell. Sweat. Plus an acrid, almost ammoniacal whiff. Had she, he wondered, lost control of her bladder? He couldn't afford to waste precious seconds wondering. His weapon crashed down with the force of an executioner's axe. And as accurately. It hit her between the eyes, bursting her skull.

Chapter One

'Hi Superman. Been riding any horses recently?'

'Hi cripple.' Bryan removed his large-brimmed black hat – his trademark – manoeuvred his wheelchair sideways in order to lay the hat on a table and grinned at John.

'Not surprised you're late.' John eyed Bryan's studded leather jacket which strained over one shoulder and drooped over the other, the distorted fabric of the waistcoat and black tee-shirt beneath it, the leather trousers clinging to his twisted legs, the boots neatly laced around his wasted ankles. 'Must take you all morning to get into that stuff.' John himself was arrayed in shapeless beige slacks and a yellow crew-necked sweater with a food stain on the front. John's carer was decidedly less meticulous than Bryan's.

'Had a whale of a time last night,' John went on. 'Went to a fancy dress party.' He was lying, of course, he never went anywhere much except to the Centre's Christmas social and for a week at Centreparcs in the summer. But Bryan played along as he always did.

'What d'you go as?'

'Took all my clothes off,' John edged his own chair a little closer as he prepared for the punchline, 'and went as a petrol pump.'

Bryan gave a bark of laughter. He knew full well that absolutely nothing below waist level functioned as far as John was concerned.

'Only thing I wore,' John raised a permanently clenched hand and gestured at his chest, 'was a notice. "Out of Order".'

'Meet anyone?' asked Bryan.

'Absolutely. A dead ringer for Miss Shaggable. Blue eyes, blonde hair, all the right equipment.'

'What did she think of your notice?'

7

'Only went and moved it, didn't she? Want to know where she put it?' He stopped abruptly. 'Hey, hang on. Here comes the original.' He paused. 'I give you,' he flung his hands wide and trumpeted, 'Miss Shaggable of the year. Our Marion.'

Marion swanned across the polished floorboards in immaculate white trainers. She was in her late twenties – a few years younger than both John and Bryan. But instead of sitting in a wheelchair she walked on her own two legs. And what legs! Long, smooth, tanned even at this time of the year. Above the legs a black linen mini dress grazed the surface of her bum. Around her neck was a thin gold chain. Golden hair fell to her shoulders, framing an oval face. Marion, the gorgeous volunteer, had come, as she always did, to brighten their days. And Bryan hated her for it.

How much had she heard of John's remarks? Everything, Bryan hoped, that would be bound to wind her up. But for the moment she said nothing, betraying her distaste for John's sexism by nothing more than a slight pursing of her pretty mouth. Instead she moved across the room, among the other wheelchairs, encouraging their inhabitants to form a circle for the Activity, bending to listen to their often garbled words, demonstrating by every movement of her perfect body the unconscious power the able-bodied wield over the disabled.

'Who does she think she is?' Bryan demanded of John, as Marion, on the far side of the hall, propelled Laura's chair into position with a sweet, compassionate smile. 'Bloody Florence Nightingale?'

'No lamp,' responded John. 'And better tits.'

The Activity Room was the largest in the Centre. Out of the corner of his eye Bryan could see things going on in the smaller, white-painted rooms which led off the central space. Art in one, pottery in another, gardening in a third. In the Activity Room itself the products of some of these sessions – crudely daubed paintings in primary colours and a collection of dog-eared photomontages – adorned the walls. Everything, everywhere, everyone was bright and busy and falsely, determinedly jolly.

It took a while for Marion to have all seven of the group arranged to her taste. She pushed golden-haired Karen into a prime position in the circle. Karen was sweet-natured as well as pretty – pretty from the neck up that is – and could always be relied on to respond with what Marion called 'a positive attitude' to whatever either staff or volunteers suggested. Then she propelled old Mr D, his head nodding like that of a toy dog in the back window in a car, into place.

The worst aspect of being disabled, Bryan reflected with his usual bitterness as he watched the manoeuvres, was not the constant pain, not the inability simply to get up and go where you chose, not the way people trundled you around as though you were a piece of bulky furniture: no, it was the fact that you had, quite literally, been cut down to size. When people – when women – approached, they bent down to you as though you were a child. Your entire life was lived at waist level – *exactly* as though you were a child. He had mentioned this to John once and John had nodded, heaved a deep sigh and pronounced, 'Yeah. Six inches up or down and you'd be at boob or crotch level. Scenery'd be greatly improved.' Bryan had given one of his sharp barks of laughter.

'But,' John had gone on seriously and sadly, 'they never seem to think of these things. No imagination, people with legs.'

Meanwhile, this afternoon, Marion now seemed satisfied with the disposition of her charges. She moved into the centre of the circle.

'Today,' she announced, 'we have a visit from the Mushy Pea Community Arts Group.'

'God, not drama again,' complained Bryan *sotto voce* to John.

'Don't knock it. If it's improvisation and you pick your subject right, you've every chance of copping a feel.'

Neither had spoken loudly enough for Marion to catch the words, but she directed a quelling look at them with her liquid blue eyes. She didn't like whispering in the ranks. What she liked – she now took pains to explain to them – was to offer them an opportunity to explore the implications of their disabilities. She went further than that: to *celebrate* their disabilities. Bryan looked over at Laura, her limbs twisted into their familiar, grotesque shape, her only communication with the outside world a screen on which, after you had asked her something and waited thirty seconds, her response would scroll, letter by letter, slowly across the silver surface. Not much to celebrate there. He didn't know what was wrong with Laura, in fact he didn't really know what was wrong with anyone here. Left to themselves the Centre's users talked about anything and everything – sex, politics, what they'd seen on TV last night – *except* their disabilities. It was only do-gooders like Marion who insisted they 'confront', at every possible opportunity, the way they were.

Now Marion was going on about the positive qualities inherent in being 'differently abled'. Bryan sneered silently. If being 'differently abled' was such a great deal, how come people with legs that worked didn't spend all their time 'confronting' the fact that they could run?

'Which is to say,' Marion was now saying, 'that you all have special qualities which people like myself don't necessarily enjoy.'

'Tell that to my sex drive,' said John, far too loudly, while Bryan wondered why they all had to be lumped together in this way: as though being in a wheelchair, and not the many other complex emotions, desires and interests, was what defined you as a person.

Marion turned to John, an expression of disapproval on her face, tempered by an obvious effort at patient compassion for those less fortunate than herself.

'It's not as if,' she enunciated carefully, 'I haven't mentioned this before. The Activities are for the benefit of everyone at the Centre. Everyone should be free to enjoy them to the full in his or her own way. But if that enjoyment means spoiling someone else's enjoyment . . .' Bryan shot a

10

look at Karen who was now waiting, with an innocent, anxious expression, for the opportunity to show that, in spite of her limitations, she could shine, '. . . then the person who is doing the spoiling must learn to moderate his or her behaviour. And now,' Marion turned to a gap in the circle of chairs, exposing the backs of long, shapely thighs to her audience, 'let's have a big welcome for our guests today.' And everyone made a more or less successful effort at bringing their twisted hands into contact with each other.

The Mushy Pea Company turned out to be a group of obscenely fit young people in skin-tight, tie-dyed costumes of various, bilious shades of green. They came hurtling, somer-saulting and cartwheeling into the immobile circle, energy radiating from their lithe bodies, enthusiasm shining from their faces – as though they believed their efforts could magi-cally imbue their silent watchers with the qualities they them-selves so histrionically expressed. When they spoke, they did so in loud, ringing tones with, after every half a dozen words, a pause which would on the printed page have appeared as !!! or ???.

'For God's sake,' said Bryan to John, 'it's like being back in school.'

'You're just jealous because even your carer couldn't squeeze you into one of those get-ups. Look at the bum on that one,' and John pointed to the nearest Mushy Pea girl.

An hour later. An hour in which they had all strained and struggled. Not just to manoeuvre their chairs in accordance with the movements of the improvisation which they had been required to devise. But with the effort of, as the Mushy Pea people put it, finding something positive to improvise about *being* in a chair. John had ignored all of the Community Arts Group's suggestions and Marion's scarcely concealed frowns and dragooned the uncomprehending Karen into an improv-isation breathtaking in its salaciousness. Bryan looked on with only half his mind on the sequence he was devising with Kenny. Kenny was one of the few of them who wasn't in a wheelchair. He had learning difficulties and recently – as part of his preparation for independent living – had been required to make his way on his own to the sessions at the Centre. Which meant he always got distracted by something en route: which meant he was always late.

'Doesn't it go quick?' he keened at Bryan, as he had, mid-Activity, each afternoon for the past three weeks. Then he carried on waving his arms in a vaguely jangling fashion over his head, occasionally swooping towards the wheelchair and flourishing his open palms in Bryan's face. For some reason (accepted by the green-clad mob as celebrating an alternative mode of movement) he was being the sea ebbing back and forth across a beach.

'I went to the seaside once,' he explained, 'for a whole day.'

Initially Bryan had said that his contribution to 'alternative modes of movement' would be to be a large, black rock, capable of withstanding whatever buffeting the waves threw at him. It would be years, he added, embroidering on his theme, before even minute signs of erosion were visible on his surface to the naked eye.

But both Marion and the Mushy Pea people were united in opposition. He couldn't just sit there! they chorused. He would have to be a pebble – several pebbles if he preferred – and go with the flow. With a sigh he did as they said. He wondered, wearily, for the umpteenth time, as he swivelled his chair right and left, why he came to the Centre. But he knew the answer. At first he had come because they had insisted it would help him come to terms with what had happened; and because there was nowhere else to go. Now he came for a dose – as bracing as a shot in the arm – of John's outrageous, acerbic, over-the-top heckling: for John's undiminished courage in refusing to act the part allotted him. And why did John come? He knew the answer to that too, he reflected as he swung in a parody of a dance around Kenny's agile, but unco-ordinated frame. John came because this was his only oppor-tunity to rebel against his fate. He came because the Centre was a substitute for the family who had long ago abandoned him in a long-stay hospital. He came because here he could rebel to his heart's content; and no one would throw him out. After all – Bryan spared a moment for a fleeting glance at John and nearly collided with Kenny as the latter flung himself over-enthusiastically into an imitation of a bursting breaker – the house John shared with five other people – some with mental as well as physical disabilities – wasn't exactly a bed of roses. Not that John ever complained, in fact he was studious about avoiding any mention of the place. But Bryan could tell.

And now the Activity was over. John was at his elbow, nudging him.

'See that Karen? Reckon she really meant what she said to me in the improvisation? Improvised, yes, but it might have come from the heart. Okay, she's a cripple, but beggars can't be choosers. Be seeing you, mate.' He turned his chair in Karen's direction, then turned back. 'You'll be waiting for the library, won't you?' Bryan nodded. John turned his chair once more and moved away.

The library. For a year now books had been Bryan's major solace. At home, now he *was* at home, his kind, meticulous carer reminded him every moment of his disabilities. He would fetch this, adjust that, stoop with infinite patience to tie Bryan's feet into his black, laced boots. He would lift Bryan onto the toilet, ease him, with the help of the specially fitted hoist, into the bath. Bryan had been lucky with his carer. He had been lucky too to get a housing association flat. The association had fitted all the adaptations so he didn't, as John did, have to live in a shared house. He was lucky with the physical things. But just because you were in a wheelchair didn't mean you'd lost your mind. Nor your appetite for action. So, apart from the diversion of his repartee with John, books had become Bryan's sole source of excitement. Why, then, did he feel a dragging reluctance as he wheeled himself in the direction of the reception hall outside which, in a few moments, the mobile library would pull up?

He knew why. At first his passion had been for thrillers. Frederick Forsyth, Ken Follett, stories whose action took him, as his career once had, across the globe. Then, as he began to come to terms with his own newly limited world, his horizons narrowed to more domestic tales: to whodunnits. He'd read them all. A solid course of Agatha Christie, followed by Dorothy L. Sayers, P.D. James, Ruth Rendell, even an excursion (which he did not enjoy) into the lesbian sleuth novels published by The Women's Press. Once each of them had posed an impenetrable, absorbing puzzle. Now, by half-way through, he always had the villain taped.

Raji was pushing a trolley of books through the swing doors of the main entrance. He stopped when he saw Bryan.

'Got a Patricia Cornwell for you. Or if not, the new Nicci French. Or Reggie Nadelson? Or take all three. You're allowed that many.'

Bryan nodded and thanked him and stowed the books in his lap. Raji turned his attention to helping a couple of other Centre users select videos and CDs while Bryan trundled back into the Activity space where Marion had reassembled her charges after their refreshment break. She always helped with the refreshments; many of the Centre's users were unable to swallow a carton of orange juice without assistance and others of them dribbled. She turned to Bryan with a smile of bright enthusiasm.

'More books? The amount you read you ought to try your hand at creative writing. Especially as you say you can solve all those. Perhaps we should get a tutor.'

Bryan forbore to remind her that she had invited a perfectly good such tutor to the Centre only a month ago, that everyone had enjoyed the tutor's visit and that she was not asked to return because she failed to encourage them to focus, for even a minute of the session, on their disabilities. He also forbore to mention that Marion's idea of creative writing had one thing in common with the other Activities she arranged: they were all pointless. The Centre's users improvised Drama, but none of them had a hope in hell of becoming even amateur actors; they did Pottery and produced lopsided artefacts which no one would ever display, let alone buy; they practised Percussion and achieved the vilest cacophony Bryan had ever heard; and they raised plants from seeds and cuttings for the Centre's grubby garden, which were promptly trampled or uprooted by teenagers from the estate. He forbore to mention these things because he hadn't the least ambition to write about crime. *Reading* about it allowed him a vicarious involvement in dramatic action. To write about it would be to admit that he could never have a slice of that action in the real world ever again. No, if he were to pursue his passion for detection any further – he looked down with apathy at the books in his lap – he would far rather solve an *actual* crime. But of course no one would ever ask him, he would never have the opportunity to do such a thing. But there was always – the idea struck him suddenly – the other side of the coin. He could commit a crime – technically he was already doing so. He toyed idly with the idea. After all, he had the proven ability to plan, to keep things under wraps, to lay a false trail, to fox the opposition. Any crime he committed – he was sure of it – would be perfect, utterly undetectable by the likes of Miss Marple or Chief Inspector Wexford. It would be a crime, he thought, enjoying the sudden, now unfamiliar excitement at a new project, an excitement which had once been part of daily life, that would baffle the best brains which Scotland Yard could deploy in its solution.

But a crime, he reflected, excitement ebbing away, required a victim. Still, no harm in trying on the idea – the first real one he'd had for months – for size. He studied Laura, twisted in her chair, her mouth working soundlessly. Might be doing her a favour to put her out of her misery. Or there was John; after all, if you looked at him objectively, stripped of his bravado, what kind of a life did he have? The same question might be

15

asked of any one of the group, himself included, now gathered, a captive audience, around Marion's perfect form.

It was Marion's voice that intruded on his reverie, brought him back to earth with a bump. Far from being the criminal brain of the century, he was a useless cripple. For Marion was insisting cheerily that he decide in which aspects of making decorations for the Christmas social he would like to be involved. She had a quantity of crepe paper and Sellotape and scissors and brightly coloured ribbons laid out on the table beside her. She was reiterating – he obviously hadn't heard her first time round – that the Mayor would be coming and they must all do their best to put on a good show if they wanted to be sure of next year's funding. And Bryan was back in kindergarten being told over and over – so often that it made a lasting impression on him for years to come – that he must join in, must learn to practise practical skills.

He shot Marion a look of pure, black venom. He'd never learned them. He'd learned to use his brain to earn money, his body to face danger. But he was hopeless with his hands, always had been, couldn't even put up a shelf, always paid someone else to do even the most simple domestic tasks. How many cripples, he thought, a bubble of hysterical laughter rising to his lips, does it take to change a light bulb? He must ask John sometime and see what he came up with.

Luckily for him John had filled the lengthening, expectant silence. 'Not the Mayor again!' he announced loudly. 'It's the feel-good factor. For her, not for us. Laying hands on a few cripples. Have you seen the hairs on her chin? I reckon she's a lesbian.'

Marion opened her mouth to speak, but again John got in first.

'If they really had our interests at heart, they'd hire a few strippers. Chippendales for the girls. And get a licence to sell booze. I can't even remember how a decent pint tastes. And as for getting out of my head, forget it. Tell me this . . .' he paused, tilting his face up towards Marion, his eyes as bright as

16

a bird's, '. . . why is it only people with legs get a chance to get legless?'

He had drawn Marion's fire away from Bryan. She was fully occupied with reproving John. Was that what John had intended, had he read on Bryan's face what Bryan felt? If he had, he'd never say so. In the meantime, the moment had passed and Bryan was agreeing that yes, he thought he was quite up for cutting stars out of silver foil.

The afternoon was over. Disabled transport was at the door. Bryan's carer Edward was there with the car.

'See you down the pub later?' called John as he was wheeled away. That's what he always said when they parted, though Bryan and he never met in any pub and, as far as Bryan could tell, John never had the opportunity to drink any alcohol at all.

Bryan waited as Edward lifted the three hardback volumes from his lap. He settled his black hat on his head and turned to look at Marion shrugging her shoulders into a stylish, maxi-length, black overcoat. Where was she going now, what kind of active, satisfying life did she lead when she had finished with her slumming? He hated her, he thought, as Edward laid a gentle hand on his shoulder. He hated her for being so bright and so beautiful. For being so perfect and so patronising. But he didn't hate her enough to hurt her.

'No more than two children in the shop.' The words were roughly printed on a scrap of card ripped from a cash-and-carry carton, and the card was taped inside the Patels' shop window. Lee and Danny and Rick were all twelve years old, but only Lee could read the sign without pointing to each letter in turn and mouthing the words under his breath. And only Lee had worked out a scam so they could get what they wanted.

This is what they did. Under his instruction they waited until a woman with three small children went into the shop (children with parents didn't count as children), then Lee tagged along as though he was one of the family. Inside, Mr Patel stood to the left, by the till, and Mrs Patel sat to the right; that way they had a clear view along the shop's two aisles. But – Lee had sussed this – there was a blind spot at the further end of the shop where the two aisles met. All he had to do was to get Mrs Patel to follow him along the aisle – he picked several items from the shelves, furtively, as though he meant to pocket them – and entice her round the blind spot and into the left hand aisle. Then Rick and Danny – Lee made sure he never did the actual nicking himself – had a clear field among the alcopops in the right-hand aisle. Meanwhile Lee legged it out along the left-hand aisle, pushing past the toddlers, shouting and waving his hands as though he was running away from something, as though he had something to hide. Which he didn't. If Mr and Mrs Patel decided to call the Bill, they'd find him squeaky clean. But they never did. They just went sadly back into their shop and resigned themselves to a routine of watching the aisles and selling very little of anything.

Lee led Rick and Danny, racing and whooping, to the other end of the mall. They peeled the caps from the bottles with their teeth, drank, then competed at hitting pigeons with the caps. That soon got dull. Lee led them to the Community Centre where they peered through the window and made faces at the people in wheelchairs inside.

But that wasn't much of a buzz either.

'Let's go see if my mum's home,' suggested Danny.

'Let's go see if my sister's got anything to eat,' proposed Rick.

'Might as well go back to school.' Lee's voice was thick with scorn. And then – as always – he came up with the best idea. 'Let's go to the park and burn the shelter down.'

The shelter stood beneath bare-branched trees, lapped by a thick carpet of the leaves the trees had shed. It was made of weather-proofed wood, its roof was painted red. In the spring old men sat there with their grey-muzzled dogs. In the summer couples had it off inside. This autumn someone had spray-canned graffiti all over it.

Lee and Danny and Rick had tried to burn it down several times before. But they'd always ended up with a smouldering, disappointing wisp of dying smoke. This time Lee had the other two kids bank piles of dry leaves around the walls: and this time it worked. The leaves caught, crackling, then ignited the wood of the shelter. Hot flames lapped towards the three of them, warming them. It was nice here. But it would be time, soon, for Lee to order them to go: someone was bound to see the blaze and then the Fire Service would be on the scene.

Rick hummed the theme tune from *London's Burning*.

Danny hummed the theme tune from *Casualty*.

And then they all saw it. A figure upright and incandescent in the midst of the flames.

DCI Dawson closed the file which lay in front of him on the unfamiliar desk, deposited it on the stack of files to his left and opened another. They all made depressing reading. Three officers up on assault charges. One set for a disciplinary for sexual harassment. A serious complaint from leaders of the ethnic minority communities of rampant racism in the force. Community relations in general practically non-existent. Morale and clear-up rate low, bully-boy tactics rife. But then he knew he was on a sticky wicket when he applied for the transfer. That's why he was here, at what was, in his view, the sharp end of the Met's operations – as the new Guvnor of the CID force with the worst record of any in the whole of London.

He sighed grimly as he thought of the sullen response from his assembled team to his initial pep talk. Male almost to a man, they were among the most unprepossessing lot he had come across since he joined the force. Broad-shouldered, thickset, with necks like bulls and brains, he judged, to match. They'd clearly gone out of their way to make the most of the menace of their bulk: crew cuts were the order of the day and their clothes – heavy black leather jackets, boots and jeans – must make them a walking, terrifying nightmare to innocent people on the streets. But he saw behind the facade. They were pot-bellied, they were flabby, lax; soft from years of having it their own way. He doubted any one of them could run a hundred yards without wheezing and certainly they all stood to gain by losing a couple of stone in weight. They soon would. Mentally as well as physically he'd have them leaner, fitter, trimmer within months. As fit as he was. He smiled again as he recalled first the disbelief, then the brutish challenge in their eyes. He knew what a picture he himself presented. Six foot two, yes, but in all other respects as like to them as chalk to cheese. He'd watched them taking the measure of his wiry body, noting the neat, silver-grey suit, the perfectly knotted dark grey tie, the carefully pressed shirt (he, too, dressed for effect) and he knew they'd push him as far as they could. But he also knew – as they didn't – that beneath *his* facade was a core of pure steel.

He wouldn't just change the way they looked, he'd change their attitude. And fast – had to if he was to turn the reputation of the neighbourhood around. Because it wasn't only his team who presented the toughest challenge he'd ever faced. The manor they policed was one of the grubbiest, poorest, most crime-infested corners of the capital. Surrounded on all sides by the affluent suburbs of northwest London, Crandon had become synonymous with urban ills since the 1980s. Poll tax riots, race riots, just plain for-the-hell-of-it riots – Crandon had staged them all. Parts of it had been no-go areas for years and now it was peopled almost entirely by a seedy underclass. He closed another file, rose and looked out of the grime-streaked window of his new office at the grey wasteland below. Tower blocks on the horizon, in the middle-distance a litter-strewn apology for a park with graffiti defacing the walls and derelicts on every bench; closer still a scrap yard, its tatty premises protected by anti-climb paint and razor wire. He shifted his gaze higher and to the left and there was the skyline of civilised London: the Telecom Tower, the dome of St. Paul's and beyond, the glittering apex of Canary Wharf. It might have been a million miles away.

So might New Scotland Yard. He recalled briefly the view from the window there as he had stared out over busy, affluent Victoria Street. His eyes followed a green No. 24 bus as he waited for the panel's decision. Surely they could not refuse his application. It wouldn't be promotion, only a sideways transfer, so it was no skin off the Met's nose financially speaking. And he'd been chained to a desk job for more than two years now.

They hadn't refused. And here he was. He returned to his desk and his reading. Crandon had, in the main, been developed in the sixties and seventies. The local council had poured money for social housing into the area, and had created a ghetto. Benefit fraudsters, drug addicts, sickos, winos, the unemployed, the unemployable, problem families, single parents, extended clans of refugees who spoke no English; all these had been decanted from the better-off suburbs to a place where they would cause no nuisance to their neighbours – because their neighbours were also a nuisance.

A sink neighbourhood comprised of sink estates, and the worst of them all, the scum in the wastepipe, was the Carleton Park Estate. Built as a model community with landscaped lawns and a shopping mall all its own it had swiftly degenerated into a violent slum. The picture was familiar, he thought, as he absorbed the details. Only here it had gone to extremes. Carleton Park Estate had been used in the late eighties as a dumping ground for homeless families. Which meant dysfunctional families. Which meant an intolerably high child density. Which meant – ten years on – an explosively high concentration of teenagers with nothing to do and nowhere to do it. One by one the major chains had deserted the purpose-built retail outlets in the mall. No Boots, no Safeways, not even a Nisa store. No one who lived on the estate had money to buy

21

consumer goods, but plenty of them had the temerity to try to steal them – a perfect recipe for economic decay. All that now remained were a couple of beleaguered, steel-grilled shops run by – he turned the page and found his assumptions confirmed – a Mr and Mrs Patel and a Mr Singh. The seedy pub (which, he inferred from his reading, did more trade in drugs than it did in alcohol) was managed by a Jerry O'Flaherty. The minicab company was run by a Mr Ali. Only the fish and chip shop had a proprietor – one Joe Parker – with an indigenous, family-lived-here-since-the-year-dot sort of name.

So that was it. The Carleton Park Estate was his starting point, the proving ground for his radical, kill or cure tactics. First he'd begin the re-education of his force, then he'd put them all, man and boy, on the case. This time next year, he thought, his enthusiasm rising above the grey pallor of his surroundings, the Carleton Park Estate would be safe for decent people to walk at night. For there *were* decent people there. Pensioners terrified to step outside in case their lives and their savings were at risk. Families struggling to bring up law-abiding kids. Ethnic minority community leaders with the interests of the people they represented at heart. Local councillors who wanted to do the best for their constituents. He would get them all on his side, just as he would the men under his command. The drab room in which he sat – besieged by hostile staff, becalmed in a sea of petty crime – receded as he envisioned a future of ordered, orderly, neighbourly and above all *normal* people going about their normal business. Zero tolerance, he thought. Mop up the winos. Drive the drug users off the streets. Crack down on petty theft. Catch the TWOCers red-handed. Liaise with the council to create defensible space. He would clean this place up if it killed him. For DCI Dawson wasn't just a policeman. He was – that rare bird – a man with a mission. He felt the flush of excitement rise from his neck and stain his face at the thought of the rewards ahead.

A rap on his door.

'Come!' he barked.

The door opened a fraction. One of the most pug-faced, the most bullish of his subordinates inserted his head into the gap.

'Thought you'd want to know, Guv. Report's come in from the Carleton Park Estate.'

'A domestic? Ram raiders?' DCI Dawson was on his feet ready to meet the challenge.

'Actually, Guv,' the man's eyes were thin, black, spiteful pinpricks of malice. 'It's a bit more serious than that.'

Chapter Two

The sirens had ceased. Acrid smoke hung in the air. So did an aroma which, to DCI Dawson who had been too busy at his files to catch lunch, smelt like roast pork. He remembered having read somewhere that cooked human flesh tasted much like a succulent cut of suckling pig. His stomach growled. He ignored it. It was time, now SOCO had taken flash pictures from every angle, to inspect the remains.

It looked, as well as smelt, like a large joint of barbecued meat. Any clothes it might have been wearing when it entered the shelter had been consumed by the ferocity of the flames. Its features were charred, a fragrant, blistered coating of bubbling fat replaced its skin. He couldn't even tell which sex it was. According to the fire officers the blaze could have started as much as an hour ago. It had been reported anonymously – par for the course for the Carleton Park Estate – by a member of the public described as having a high, shaky voice. It would be a public-spirited pensioner, Dawson decided, one of the people he was determined to get on his side. In the meantime there was nothing more to be gleaned until he saw the forensic reports. He turned away.

'Probably a wino, Guv,' suggested Banks, the DC who had first alerted him to the incident. 'Or a junkie. Easy enough to set themselves alight when they're out of it.'

'Or a tom,' added one of the uniforms, stepping forward out of the dark. DCI Dawson knew what the pair of them meant and knew they spoke for the others. They wanted to get the hell out, get home to their wives and girlfriends, get stuck into a decent meal. After all what was one casual, presumably accidental death to the officers of Crandon? They had nothing to gain by taking the investigation further. He thought back to earlier in the day, pictured one of the many, many files he had read: files all stamped with 'Case Closed'. He lifted his chin, felt his jawline harden. This one wouldn't be. It was just the chance he needed to pull his troops into line. And to show the community that he got results. He checked his watch. 6.13. An hour since he had been summoned. His lips stretched in a thin smile as he thought, 'daresay Banks's as hungry as I am.'

'House to house,' he instructed.

'Christ, Guv, can't it wait till morning? If anyone did see anything they won't let on. Stuff going down on this estate, people know to keep their noses well out.'

But Dawson gestured towards the tower block which loomed to the east of the park and from which, on every floor, the windows glowed with light.

'Take a uniformed officer with you. You!' he addressed the other man who had spoken. 'I want a statement from everyone who could have seen or did see anything – and I repeat anything – happening in this park over the last day or so. Concentrate on,' he glanced at his watch, 'activity during the last two hours. Whatever they saw – kids in the playground, people walking their dogs – I want descriptions, I want names, I want times. Got that?'

The dream was always the same. Bryan was lying in the hot, Caribbean sun on a lounger beside a blue pool. On either side of him girls sunbathed, topless. He looked from beneath his eyelids at a particularly attractive pair, one blonde, one dark. They were looking at *him*, but more obviously and giggling a little. Well, why not? He had no illusions about his appearance. He was young, he was tall, he was tanned, he was superfit. He thought of getting up and walking towards the girls, maybe suggesting a drink or two. He had an hour to kill before his hang-gliding session. And he was well enough paid to squander as much money as he cared to on casual encounters. For it *would* be a casual encounter, he was fairly sure of that: girls who giggled and tried to pull strangers were unlikely to have much to speak of between the ears. He ran a hand through his neatly trimmed, dark hair, rose to his feet, took one step . . . and found himself propelled, not towards the girls, but up into the warm, blue sky.

He was thousands of feet high, cruising on the thermals. Like a swift, like a swallow – no, more like a bird of prey, a kestrel, a sparrow hawk. Not a sparrow hawk, he was an eagle, beady eyes sharp as bores fixed on the girls below, his cruel, curved beak an inverted parody of a smile. He was free and soaring. He swerved and dipped, about to make his selection. Then, without warning, he was plunging pell-mell, his wings broken. He was falling helpless, rolling over and over, frantic and tumbling, his desperate fists closing on handfuls of insubstantial air. A strange, garbled, panic-stricken screech, quite unlike that of any bird, stretched behind him like the string of bubbles exuded by a deep sea diver. The screech was his. As he hurtled downwards, the tiny, distant, blue oblong of the swimming pool turned again and again in his vision, like a cough lozenge in orbit. Would he splash into it? But the pool was only six feet deep. Wherever he landed – his mind had time to form a picture of the two girls running screaming – he would be bound to break his neck.

He woke, sweating. His neck was, of course, broken. But now that the dream was receding, his injury was simply a matter of fact, a fact he had lived with for nearly a year. More important was how to get to the toilet. More important were the manoeuvres required to return to bed. More important was the question of how on earth after the familiar – but still utterly terrifying nightmare – he would ever get back to sleep.

He shook his head. He looked at the glowing numerals on his watch. 11 pm. He had gone to bed far too early, often did nowadays in an effort to cut the day short. Which meant – as he should have known it would – that he had prolonged the night. Night was always the worst time and the nightmare had been unusually vivid, had even, he recalled, had a realistic soundtrack. The uproar of horrified voices, the clatter and crash of sunbathers fleeing from upturned loungers and tables and finally – the thing that had woken him – his own screams.

27

No point dwelling on that. He levered himself painfully from bed to chair, from chair to toilet, from toilet to chair. And no point in trying to go back to bed. Resigned, he snapped on the light in the hall, then the light in the living room. He looked around him without interest. It wasn't a bad room: its walls were painted magnolia, its woodwork white and, as the representative of the housing association had taken pains to point out, there was room for him to turn his wheelchair through 360 degrees. But it was a world away from the Chelsea mews house in which he'd once lived, which he'd once owned.

He shrugged. What was the good of a mews house when you couldn't get up the stairs? Here, in this bare room, he had hung none of the watercolours which had decorated the colour-washed walls of his previous home: they'd have looked odd displayed at the height at which he could appreciate their delicate detail. No Persian rug warmed the plain parquet floor, it would have snagged in his wheels. And there was no deco sofa, no frivolous fifties chairs, no chairs at all; *he* couldn't sit in them and the only other person who came here was Edward. Who came here to work, so he could damn well stand.

Bryan wheeled himself past the IKEA coffee table on which lay the three novels he had borrowed from Raji. He had opened each of them earlier in the evening, but none had held his interest. What else could he do to pass the time? The TV? No, he had whiled away too many sleepless nights watching second-rate movies, pop videos and the educational programmes on BBC2. He pressed on towards the only other piece of furniture in the room: the large, black desk on which his PC stood.

He positioned himself in front of the screen and switched on the power. Idly he created a new directory, entitled it 'Crime', created a new file and began to type. 'Motive', 'method', 'opportunity' – he knew all the right headings from his reading. 'Motive' required a good deal of thought. In

fiction people killed on what seemed to him very little provo-
cation. They were jealous because their boyfriend fancied
someone else, they wanted to get their hands on Great
Auntie's money, or they were (a cop-out) psychos or sickos.
But in real life people didn't act like that. Faced with a
personal problem, they took to booze or joined a dating
agency; they went on benefits or fiddled their expenses. That
was what the sane ones did, who could tell about the mentally
unbalanced? He dismissed them, their warped reasoning
offered no logical challenge. But for a sane person to commit
a physical, premeditated crime would require a motive so
overriding it drove every other consideration from his mind.
To the extent that he would not be squeamish about getting
his hands dirty, of hearing the crunch of bone crushed by the
weapon he wielded, of seeing blood spurt like a geyser from an
artery he punctured.

Bryan stopped. God, if Marion could see what he was
producing she'd really think he ought to go in for Creative
Writing. Or perhaps, on reflection, she'd think *he* was a sicko.

He abandoned 'motive'; this whole thing was, after all, an
intellectual exercise, its object was merely to keep him
amused, he didn't have to come up with all the answers. In
other words, it wasn't real work.

He shut that thought from his mind the instant it put in an
appearance. He turned to 'method'. This was even trickier.
Assuming he himself was committing the crime, there was the
little matter of physical strength. Wheelchair aside, a
contender for *Gladiators* he was not. Could have been once.
He shoved that notion aside too. But he did reflect a little on
the upper body strength required in several of the Gladiator
contests – particularly in Hang Tough. Could he, he
wondered, regain that level of fitness in at least some of his
muscles? He resolved – and made a note to that effect – to
instruct Edward to research appropriate training facilities.

Approach to the scene of the intended crime was also a
problem. His existing wheelchair was a lumbering, cumber-

some affair, which he propelled with difficulty and which could, surely, be heard on the move from sufficient distance to allow an able-bodied victim to leg it easily to safety. But there were electric wheelchairs these days, for God's sake, why hadn't he told Edward to look into them? And there were swift, relatively silent ones which disabled athletes used in the London Marathon.

He paused. Christ, he must have been mad the last few months. He'd never thought of anything that might alter the way he lived for the better, he'd left all that to Edward. But now . . . tomorrow . . . he'd make a few changes. He felt pleased and positive for the first time since the accident.

And he felt like a drink. A modest measure of single malt. That was new too. Yet so often in the past he'd returned at the end of a successful day and unwound to the tune of a finger of Glenfiddich. Could he try that now?

First of all, did he have any whisky? After searching the entire kitchen he found a half-full bottle which must have been imported, wholesale, with a load of other stuff from his old home. But there was no sign of any of the heavy, cut-glass tumblers from which he used to drink it. And there was no ice in the fridge. He poured the whisky into a coffee mug and thought he really should get himself better organised.

The alcohol was a shot in the arm as far as his imagination was concerned. The difficulties of committing a contact crime – he'd decided (go for it!) on bashing someone's head in – when you're in a wheelchair became challenges instead of causes for despair. Likewise the business of escaping undetected from the scene of the crime. All you needed was a diversion so that no one noticed what you were doing, then a red herring, something to set the sleuths on the wrong trail. And perhaps – he took another mouthful – he would leave a symbolic, cryptic clue or two: a key ring clutched in the victim's cold fist, a dozen red roses stuffed in her mouth, a medieval scold's bridle snapped over her skull. He laughed to himself – at himself – as he pursued these fanciful notions, entering them all on the screen in front of him. And he wondered: what kind of jokes would John come up with about a crippled, serial killer?

DC Banks was starving, and cold. Accompanied by PC 'Dosh' Jarvis he had slogged up umpteen flights of steps (the lifts were out of order) and tramped along endless walkways in the block of high-rise flats. No joy.

The last 'interview' had been much like all the others. Door opened a fraction. It was on a chain. Suspicious eyes peering out. A young white woman with lank, straggling hair, wearing jeans, trainers, a dirty sweatshirt. Behind her the lingering smell of cooking and the sound of children squabbling. No, she hadn't seen a thing, she didn't get home till six and she was too busy feeding the kids and getting them to bed to bother with looking out of the window, who did they think she was, Lady Muck? She gave, when they insisted, her name, and admitted she worked part-time for Mr Ali's mini-cab business, answering the phone. Then she slammed the door in their faces. Still, she'd been a better 'witness' than some of the others. An elderly Afro-Caribbean man who wouldn't even open the door, just peered through the letter-box and bellowed at them to go away. An Asian man in a dirty vest surrounded by a thick aroma of curry and a horde of wide-eyed, brown-skinned kids. A small, elderly woman with thin grey hair who wheezed and coughed and wanted to invite them in to tea and tell them the A to Z of every minor incident on the estate from the year dot. Banks gathered it was the kids on the estate she was on about, they were making her life a misery, it wouldn't have been allowed in her young days. He'd heard that story too many times before to take a blind bit of notice.

That bastard Dawson, he thought, as yet another tenant shook her head and closed the door. At least at the nick he'll have something to eat. Sandwiches perhaps. His mouth watered. No, he'll have sent out for a takeway. Not greasy chips from Parker's shop. Probably sent someone as far as Golders Green for a decent hamburger and french fries. Or a curry with all the frills. And a cold lager. He shook his head grimly, then spoke out loud.

'Anyone could have told the bastard no one would admit to seeing anything. What say we call it a day?'

Dosh didn't agree. Relations between uniform and CID had never been what you'd call cordial in Crandon – the latter had too many opportunities to take advantage of backhanders, the former too few. And the long, tedious hours the two of them had spent in each other's company hadn't exactly been the quality time of which best buddies are made. So, although a grumbling Dosh followed Banks down the long flight of concrete stairs, he paused at the bottom and pointed to the large, newly converted house which stood on its own to the west of the park. And insisted they knock on the door.

'Place is empty,' Banks protested. 'The contractor's board is still up.'

'There's a blind at the window on the ground floor to the right. And there's a light on.'

'Leave it out. Haven't you got a home to go to?'

'Sure. Want to keep it that way. What d'you reckon he's going to say if we come back with nothing?'

So they knocked at the door.

A guy in a wheelchair opened it.

'Police,' said DC Banks.

'I can see that. You'd better come in.'

'No need for that,' said Banks quickly. 'Just routine enquiries.'

'You may choose to spend a winter evening standing around on cold doorsteps. I don't.' And Bryan turned back along the corridor, gesturing for them to follow.

'It won't take more than a few moments of your time, sir,' said Dosh. Banks cringed at that 'sir'. Dosh was impressed by the guy's accent – which was certainly not your average Crandon one. Christ, sometimes Dosh was a dead ringer for

Reg on *The Bill.* Give him someone to say 'Sir' to and he'd be fawning at their feet like a dog fresh out of Battersea. Banks was made of sterner stuff.

He took in the details of the room in which they stood. God, the way some of these people on benefits lived. You'd think he could have got together at least a few sticks of furniture. Didn't the council run a store of second-hand stuff for people like this? Then his eye fell on the computer at the far side of the large room. Must have cost a few bob. Where had he found the money for that? It was probably hot.

He took a step towards it while Dosh was establishing the man's name, then asked, 'That your computer Mr Greyshott?' and was startled when the wheelchair shot past him and before he was close enough even to see the text, a hand reached out, clicked the mouse twice and the screen was blank.

Meanwhile Dosh, rot his little uniformed socks, had come over all deferential and was explaining the reason for their visit. And being questioned for his pains.

'Any suspicious circumstances?'

'Hard to tell, sir, until we have the forensic reports. But it's always best to get on the case right away before the trail's cold. Just as a precaution.'

'So when did you say the body was found?'

Dosh gave chapter and verse.

'Anyone see anything?'

'Not out of the ordinary. Kids, mums going to the One O'clock Club.'

'Kids? What sort of age?'

'Lads, most of them. You know the sort you get around here, sir. Hardly spend a day in school once they turn eleven or twelve.'

Christ, the guy was acting like *he* was the interrogating officer. Banks intervened.

'We'll ask the questions. If I'm not much mistaken,' he gestured to a cheap blind which covered a third of the front wall of the room, 'that big window of yours gives you a good view across the park. Can you tell us what you saw there this afternoon?'

'No.'

'I'd ask you to remember this could be a murder enquiry. We're not playing games.'

'I can't tell you because I didn't see anything. I don't spend my time looking out of the window.'

Then what the hell did he spend his time doing? There was no evidence of any activity here. Apart from whatever was on that computer.

'I must ask you to help us in our enquiries by accounting for your movements this afternoon. It is, of course, routine.'

'No objection to that. I was at the Community Centre till four. Then I came home with my carer.'

'Your carer? Is she here now?'

'He. No. He doesn't live in. He leaves at five. Neither of us could have seen anything. He was in the kitchen, we both were, organising something for me to eat. By the time we'd done that and he'd left it was pitch dark. So I pulled the blind, and that's how it's stayed since.'

'You didn't look out when you heard the sirens? Or the fire engines?' Even the tenants in the high rise block had admitted to that.

'No.'

'You expect me to believe that with all this going on on your doorstep you simply sat in here and paid not a blind bit of notice?'

'Yes.'

'So what exactly were you doing that was so absorbing?'

'I was sitting in my own home minding my own business. I believe there's no crime involved in that. And, if you don't mind, these "routine" enquiries have already taken considerably more than the few moments of my time you suggested.'

No option but to back off. Banks contented himself with vague warnings about withholding information and wasting police time, then made for the front door. Where Dosh put his oar in again.

'If you don't mind my saying so, you ought to have a chain on this, sir,' he advised. 'All right, so this time it was us. Next time it mightn't be. This isn't the safest of areas.'

'Isn't it?'

'You must have seen that for yourself, sir.'

'Can't say I've looked around much since I moved in. Housing association offered me an adapted place and, far as I was concerned, that was that.'

'Yes, sir. Well you should get them to fit that chain. And a Chubb lock.'

'What the hell was all that about?' Banks demanded of Dosh as soon as the door closed behind them.

'Pleasant, wasn't he? But more Kensington than Crandon I'd say. Funny where people end up living.'

'Fuck "funny". You trying to tell me he really didn't hear a thing? That he was doing something kosher the entire time? I'd like to know what he was so keen we shouldn't see on that computer.' Banks shrugged his shoulders, turned up his collar against the cold and glanced behind him at the top floor of the high rise block to which he had dissuaded Dosh from ascending and which now sported two rectangles of bright light, side by side, in adjacent flats. 'But we'll be back.'

Nice one, thought Bryan, settling himself once more in front of his PC. There he'd been planning a hypothetical crime and the police had turned up to inform him of a real one. Good thing he'd had the presence of mind to close the file before they saw what he was up to. He gave a sudden bark of laughter. God knows what they'd have made of the bit about crunching bones and spurting blood. Probably carted him down to the cop shop forthwith.

He glanced at his watch. It was after midnight, but he wasn't in the least tired. Not mentally. Physically, he had found the interview a strain. His neck ached from the necessity of keeping his head raised so he could look the two officers in the eye. He wasn't used to that, these days people usually came down to his level, but they could hardly have done that short of sitting on the floor. He laughed again. That would be the most unlikely posture for that bulldog of a plain clothes man. Thoroughly used to throwing his weight about, was Bryan's verdict.

He decided on another mug of malt plus the usual remedy for aches and pains. Lucky he hadn't thought of rolling a joint *before* they arrived, he thought, doing so now. They would have been bound to have smelt the stuff and it would probably have made the bulldog's night to pull him in for possession.

He took a mouthful of Scotch and a drag on the joint. He'd intended to return to his notes, but now thought better of it. For, as an aid to planning his perfect crime, what about seeing what he could deduce about the real death? He opened a new file and began to make notes. Not that there was much to go on. Except the kids. Kids got into everything, saw more than most people thought, got up to more than most people thought. Yes, if he were involved in this investigation he'd start with the kids.

Lee had been watching TV for hours. *The Bill,* the news, half-an-hour's channel-hopping, more news, then an American made-for-TV movie jam-packed with the post-watershed sex and violence which kids of his age weren't supposed to see. As he watched a couple of cops gun down a suspect and saw blood spread across the victim's chest, his stomach growled with hunger. Mum wasn't usually home at nights, but she usually left something for him. He went into the kitchen and looked in the oven for fish and chips, hardening in their paper packet. Nothing there. He looked under the grill for fish fingers which would need only a couple of moments to heat up. Zilch. He looked in the fridge. It was empty apart from a carton of congealing milk. He crossed the room, trawled the cupboards, took out a can of baked beans and opened it.

Stupid of him, but he cut his thumb in the process. He licked at the blood. That made him feel even hungrier. Why? Was it possible to want to eat yourself? He shivered. He crossed the small, untidy room a second time, turned on the stove and emptied the beans into a dirty saucepan. The hob was electric. Only one of its rings still worked, and even that took ages to heat up. While he waited he rescued a plate and fork from the mound piled in the sink, rinsed them and stared out of the smeared window into the darkness; stared down from the top floor flat in the tower block in the direction of the park in which they had burned the shed. What were Rick and Danny doing now? Had they eaten and been shouted at and sent to bed? He shook his head. Apart from the TV there was silence around him. Even next door seemed to be out. No footsteps on the steps. No muffled conversations in the corridor. No music throbbing through the walls.

He turned from the window, took his beans from the hob and carried his meal back into the living room. The television blared across an arid space. He dumped his plate on the stained surface of the coffee table. It wobbled. Not again! He'd fixed it last night by sticking a half-full pack of ten Mayfair under one of the table's legs. Mum must have wanted the fags and taken the packet out. There was nothing else in the room to slip into the small gap. He rose, went along the corridor to the front door where a litter of unopened envelopes lay below the letter box. Bills from the LEB, from British Gas, from Thames Water. Mum always managed to pay all those in the end from out of what Lee's uncles gave her. But she didn't take a blind bit of notice of demands for council tax or rent or from Lee's school about his perpetual non-attendance. Lee's mum was an expert at knowing who'd come after what they wanted and who wouldn't. When the council tax people or the rent people came she and Lee simply hid and pretended there was no one in the flat. And no one ever came from Lee's school. Truancy was the name of the game where his teachers were concerned. And if a disruptive kid like Lee failed to turn up, so what? It made their workload a hell of a lot easier. Send the parent a standard letter but take it no further than that.

Lee squatted on his haunches, surveying the mess of mail. Finally he selected a plain brown envelope, took it into the living room and found that, after he had folded it, it did the trick. He settled at the no longer wobbling table and ate his beans.

Chapter Three

The alarm bleeped, a jagged sound splitting the dark. Peter Dawson rolled over and groaned. Mornings were never his best times, but he knew full well that leading from the front was the best way to inspire his troops. He snapped on the light and pushed back the duvet before he had even a second to appreciate the comfort and warmth of his bed. He lowered bare feet to the floor and padded across the wide, sanded boards, switching on more lights. They were spotlights, harsh and bright, and they illuminated a huge, white-emulsioned space. High ceiling, rows of steel-framed windows on either side and, at one end of the rectangular area, the double doors which opened into a large, old-fashioned factory lift. He was in a loft. His loft.

His loft in his building. As he headed for the toilet – which, along with the shower, occupied the only cubicle separated from the main space – he looked about him with satisfaction. The builders had almost completed their work, only a few shiny, chrome shelves remained to be installed. Plus some final touches to the kitchen area.

Within minutes he was in that area, brewing decaf. He carried his mug past the gleaming breakfast bar to the spot where his work-out equipment was set up and straddled the exercise bike for his obligatory ten minutes. The pre-dawn world around him was silent, the bare windows before and behind him were rectangles of pure, velvet black. He contemplated, as he forced his sleep-soft muscles into action, the challenges that lay ahead. Not just in Crandon as a whole, but in this building. The fate of the two went hand in hand.

His mouth quirked into a smile as he recalled the incredulity of the manager of the first building society he'd approached.

'Crandon?' The guy made the word sound like he was swearing. No vision, that was his trouble, common failing of the pen-pushing time-server. 'A derelict factory on five floors plus cellar?' the man went on. 'And you expect me to believe that the upwardly mobile would actually want to buy conversions in such a property, in such a neighbourhood? Oh, no,' he shook his head, 'I couldn't dream of recommending investment of the society's resources in such a high-risk project.'

Which would be his loss. Sure, it hadn't been easy putting a funding package together. Dawson eased himself from the exercise bike, downed a gulp of fast-cooling decaf and slid into the grip of the weight machine which would work his pecs. It had been a matter of a few thou here, a few thou there. And each time he had delivered his crisp, authoratative spiel on why his proposal was a cert. He explained what he envisaged. Cellar to be converted to laundry, swimming pool, sauna and exercise facility – he'd sell the franchise to an established trainer. Ground floor, same deal, only the franchise would go to a seriously up-market restaurateur. The other four floors would be state-of-the art loft conversions – he'd retain the heavy duty lift to give the place character. He'd earmarked the top floor for his own use, but all three of the lower apartments, given Crandon was on a hill, would have uninterrupted views all the way to Hampstead Heath.

But what clinched it as far as his sundry backers were concerned was not the fact that he was prepared to risk his own money (he'd sold his maisonette in De Beauvoir Town for the down payment on the factory building) but his conviction that his campaigning zeal in his career would have a major impact on the desirability of the neighbourhood. He would clean up the streets, he assured them.

'By the time I've done with Crandon, the place will be safe, the middle classes will move in, they'll set up Neighbourhood Watch Schemes and Parent Teachers Associations and a Residents' Forum and . . .' He paused to let his words sink in.

40

He stopped the motion of his forearms, downed the dregs of his decaf and moved to another machine, to strengthen his thighs.

'Because of me, Crandon will soon be a desirable location, will be featured in the *Evening Standard* Property Section as a "discoverable" area. House prices will shoot sky high.' The man's face, the woman's face, the many faces on the other side of polished desks, brightened at the prospect of his success. They would make a killing for their company. And so would he.

As he headed for the shower he thought, with a grim, sardonic pleasure, of the appearance his building now presented. Standing in a sea of industrial detritus, hemmed in by barbed wire, approached only by six-foot padlocked double gates, the windows of the lower floors broken and subsequently boarded. Alongside the building ran the litter-choked course of the Silk Stream, bordered on either side by a tangle of brambles and a cordon of snarled barbed wire. But all that would soon change. He towelled his lean body vigorously, then selected suit, shirt and tie from the simple, functional wardrobe space. He ran one slim fingertip along the black-tiled surface in the sleeping area. Dust! Either his cleaning woman hadn't been doing her job properly or the crap of Crandon was simply too pervasive for her efforts. The encrusted dirt of thousands upon thousands of half-cleaned homes was no more than stirred up each day by half-hearted housewives who harried a few dust motes into the air, then settled onto the sofa to watch daytime TV. He suspected that's what his own cleaning woman did here. Not that she always even bothered to put in an appearance when she was expected to. She hadn't yesterday. He scribbled a swift note to her, then left.

Lee slept in a tumble of bedclothes. The duvet had long ago split and there were feathers all over the floor. Every time he turned in his sleep more feathers drifted up and around him.

Once or twice in the night he woke sneezing, feathers up his nose. And then he woke for real. Mum still wasn't home, he could smell the emptiness of the flat. He kept his eyes pressed tight shut. But he could still hear. Hear – suddenly – the familiar squeak of the front door, the creak of a floorboard in the hall: he knew the sounds, had heard them umpteen times over when Mum crept in with someone. She was back! He opened his eyes. Even when she had someone with her she always put her head round the door, not to check on him, just to say, 'Hi.' Then Lee could go back to sleep or get up, make himself something to eat, listen to the sounds of them doing it in Mum's room or go out. Whichever. And, sure enough, the door opened. Lee opened his eyes. But it wasn't Mum who stepped inside. It was a man, a huge bulk of a man, almost as broad as he was tall. That was as much as Lee could see, the curtains were closed – Mum and he never bothered to pull the ones in their bedrooms open. He lay quite still. Had he been on the street his reaction would have been to run – he was quick, he was agile, that's how he always got out of trouble. But where could you run to when you lived on the fifteenth floor and a guy three times your size was standing inside your bedroom, leaning against the closed door?

But now his eyes were accustomed to the half light and he could see who the man was. 'Oh, it's you,' he said. 'Mum's out.'

'So what's new?' Uncle Jack straightened and opened the bedroom door. 'Isn't it time you were at school?'

'Nah.' Lee grinned and slid out of bed. He hardly saw Uncle Jack these days, even though he lived in the flat next door – not since Uncle Jack and Mum split up. 'School's shit.'

'Don't disagree with you there. Smart lad like you ought to be earning a bit of money by now. Helping your mother out.'

'Can't get a job till I'm sixteen. Anyway, there aren't any jobs.' Lee had slept in his clothes so now he simply pushed aside the duvet, picked a clutch of feathers off his sweatshirt and marched past Uncle Jack into the living room.

Harry was in there, perched on the edge of a wooden chair in front of the cluttered table, his hands between his knees clutching his battered cap, his imitation-leather jeans out at one knee. Lee wasn't particularly surprised to see him. Uncle Jack still had a key to Mum's flat and Harry had probably just walked in behind him. Harry was like that. Harry lived – squatted – in the flat the other side of Uncle Jack. He made his living combing the skips outside houses in Kensington and Chelsea and in Westminster. Said it was amazing the things people threw away. Furniture, carpets, lamps, paintings, mirrors, picture frames, even barely damaged designer clothes. Trouble was they weren't the sort of designer clothes, furniture, etc. that people in Crandon wanted; and the people of Kensington & Chelsea – or more likely of Islington and Camden where second-hand chic was at a premium – wouldn't buy from Harry because he looked as though he'd nicked whatever he had on offer and besides he had no premises from which to sell it.

'What you got this time?' demanded Uncle Jack.

Harry rummaged furtively in a large carrier bag (he looked furtive whatever he did) and produced two crumpled dresses, one short and black, the other long and red.

'Good quality silk,' he said of one. 'And the other's still got the label in. Rifat Ozbek. I thought your mum might be interested, Lee. For fifty quid, say. Only a bit of smoke damage, it'd soon wash out.'

'I'll give you a fiver for the two of them.' A crisp note was already in Uncle Jack's outstretched hand.

'They're worth much more than that! This is designer gear.' But Harry took the money all the same and when Uncle Jack jerked his head and commanded, 'Out!' Harry rose, retrieved his carrier bag and shambled away in the direction of the front door.

'Loser!' Uncle Jack settled himself squarely on the chair on which Harry had perched. 'You know that guy's only a couple of years older than me? Now, be honest, who would you rather be?'

43

That didn't need even a moment's thought. Uncle Jack didn't shamble, he strode. Uncle Jack didn't wear a flat cap and torn jeans: he wore a brand new leather jacket, a gold watch, dark slacks with creases so sharp you could cut yourself on them and leather-soled loafers which must have cost a bomb.

'You,' said Lee, but Uncle Jack hardly registered the single word.

'Look what I've made of myself. Thirty four years old and I can go down Finsbury Park or Camden Town way any time I like and buy Tanya anything she wants. You know, last Saturday, I spent three hundred pounds on clothes for her. Told her to choose anything in the shop. You could be looking at that sort of big time, time you're my age.'

Tanya was Uncle Jack's current girlfriend and Lee knew that what he said was true. Because when Mum was Uncle Jack's girlfriend he had bought all kinds of expensive stuff for her. Only while Tanya always looked great in it (she had shiny black hair which reached to her waist and was as skinny as all get out, but with boobs that could knock you in the eye), Mum always washed things with the wrong other things so they came out peculiar colours. Plus she wasn't very good at ironing. And, though she wasn't exactly fat, no one could call her skinny. That was why, Lee judged, his uncles never lasted long. So it was all true, yes, but he wondered when Uncle Jack would get to the point of his visit.

Uncle Jack drew a finger across the dirty table at which, last night, Lee had eaten his beans. The dirty plate from which he had eaten them still stood on the surface.

'Same old Julie,' said Uncle Jack. 'Never been much of a housekeeper.'

'She's all right.'

'Got some gear of mine. Could have been hers if she'd paid for it. But she hasn't. Know where it is?'

It would be in a tiny plastic bag in the blank envelope he'd stuffed under the table leg, guessed Lee from experience. He reached down, pulled the envelope free and offered it to Uncle Jack.

'Bright kid, aren't you? She leave you alone a lot?'

'I'm old enough, aren't I?'

'Sure. Sure. She's never exactly going to earn a mint is she, the way she goes on? Not enough to get shot of this dump.'

'You still live here.'

'Of course I do, my boy. But I have my reasons. Could move to the West End, Marbella, the South of France if I wanted. But business comes first. Well, you've seen the inside of my place.'

Lee had. Wall to wall shagpile carpet, brand new three-piece suite from World of Leather, gilt mirrors, a music centre to die for. Fitted kitchen with dishwasher, microwave, rotis-serie. Black-tiled bathroom, heated chrome towel rails, a jacuzzi attachment which turned the oval black bathtub into a whirlpool. Fuck knew what the bedroom was like, he'd never seen that. And all this on the fifteenth floor of a council tower block.

'So what?' he demanded.

'So what are your plans? Are you going to be a loser like Harry?'

Lee shook his head so fiercely he felt it might be about to fall off.

'No!' He grinned at Uncle Jack once more. 'I'm going to be like you.'

'Attaboy,' said Uncle Jack, and clapped him on the shoulder.

DCI Dawson was at the nick by eight. He was disgusted, but not surprised, at DC Banks's lack of progress. He would have a word with him ASAP. At least the man had left a report of his fruitless enquiries before leaving the station the previous night. Where he was this morning was another matter. Mean-while Forensic must have been working round the clock – admirable – for here, on Dawson's desk, was a preliminary report.

'Victim Profile,' he read. 'Female, estimated age 25–40. Five foot six. White. Estimated weight 10 stone. Body badly charred. Stomach contents' (also badly charred, Dawson surmised) 'indicate that the subject had last eaten some eight hours before her death. Cause of death' – here Dawson sat up and took sharp notice – 'a single blow to the back of the head at the base of the skull, followed by repeated bludgeoning. Impossible to determine whether the blows or the fire were responsible for the actual fatality.

'Profile of weapon: there were broad abrasions on the skull which would suggest a heavy, blunt instrument as opposed to a sharp one: a sharp one might have penetrated the flesh before making contact with bone.

'Time of death: the same day as the fire. Otherwise impossible to estimate.

'Recommend attempt identification through dental records.'

Attached to the report were details of the state of each of the woman's teeth and an addendum. 'The subject was a heavy smoker.' Which statement was followed by a deal of technical detail about the effect of regular use of cigarettes on the bones beneath the gums. Which reminded Dawson of something he intended to do. He gave his orders pronto. But not to Banks. Where was Banks, dammit? The man was supposed to be his second in command. But he'd make the rest of the team work for their living at any rate.

The next two hours were a flurry of activity the like of which the Crandon nick probably hadn't seen in years. He instructed them to feed the dental records of the deceased into the central computer, in the remote chance they might show up as the teeth of someone already known to, say, a prison dentist. He had them fax all the dentists in Crandon. He gave orders for a further search of the park looking specifically for any blunt object – a fence post, a torch, a frozen chicken, a sockful of sand, a monkey wrench, a desk lamp – he hadn't a clue what he might be after, which is why he suggested such a bizarre list, to inspire the searchers to view anything out of the ordinary with suspicion. Though, of course, had the weapon really been a fence post or a frozen chicken, then it, too, would have been consumed in the fire. And he had them check on missing persons fitting the woman's profile not just in Crandon but London-wide.

It was raining solidly when Banks, a few minutes after ten, arrived at the station. Cold, relentless rain on a raw, grey morning. So why was the door wide open? And why, outside it, was a group of damp, dejected figures, standing, shoulders hunched, raincoats draped over their heads? His colleagues, for Christ sake. People who would normally be inside working. What the hell? He slammed his car door and went to investigate.

'Bastard,' he said when he heard what had happened.

'Insisted on enforcing the no smoking policy.' Dosh looked pathetic, his weaselly white face peering from beneath his coat, a cigarette cupped in his cold hands. A single raindrop clung to the end of his nose. 'Then kept us at it hammer and tongs for two hours at a stretch. Not a hope in hell of slipping out for a fag.'

There was a chorus of pissed-off agreement. Apart from anything else, this wasn't the way to get results. Who on earth could extract a confession from a villain without the promise of a fag – which had been withheld for hours – as a reward? Or without pushing your own packet of twenty across the table as a way of making the suspect relax? No smoking building! Fuck that! Could they take it up with the union, someone wondered? Nah! Someone else turned away and ground his damp stub into the tarmac. It was policy, it was just that until now, no one in Crandon had cared a toss about putting the rule into practice.

'Tell you something else,' said Dosh, with a sneer, lighting a fresh cigarette from the butt of the last, 'he's been asking where you were ever since he came in. On the dot of eight. Wouldn't choose to be in your shoes.'

'Bastard,' said Banks again and strode inside. After all, he knew a thing or two which would change Dawson's tune.

Why was Edward peering into Bryan's eyes, his face as close as a lover's about to instigate a kiss? It was a pink face, young, rounded, slightly podgy, with a lock of brown hair, à la Hugh Grant, drooping across the brow, and it wore a look of furrowed concern. Bryan tried to move his own head out of range of the face, and pain stabbed at his neck like the blade of a knife. He groped for his hoist, but his hands met only thin air. Christ, it was like a repeat of his accident. He grappled for a moment with panic, then realised from the lack of a pillow and from Edward's troubled murmurings that he was still where he had been in the small hours of last night. In his chair in front of his PC.

The sharp edge of agony dispersed into a generalised, just tolerable ache – like a giant bruise. How the fuck had he managed to fall asleep in his chair? And what the hell had he been thinking about indulging ridiculous, impossible plans in the middle of the night? After all, what was he but a cripple?

As usual, he took things out on Edward.

'What the fuck do you think you're doing leaning over me like that? When I want your sympathy I'll ask for it.' And he wheeled his chair, wincing, in the direction of the loo.

At least Edward, unlike the nurses at the hospital, Bryan reflected as he lowered himself over the toilet with the help of the hoist, had the decency to stay outside. But then anger welled up in him again. What able-bodied specimen of humanity had ever to be thankful for the fact that he was allowed to take a dump without someone watching?

By the time he had trundled into the kitchen his fury boiled like the water in the small saucepan in which, courtesy of Edward, two eggs swirled and bobbed.

'You know I like my eggs done for three minutes only,' he announced, well aware that he had spent longer than that in the loo.

'Sure. I timed them.' Edward was as mild as ever. He lifted the eggs from the pan with a small spoon.

'Well, today I want them hard-boiled.' Bryan could hear that his tone of voice was that of a fretful invalid, to be humoured. Or that of a tyrannical boss whose word was law. The contrast between the two roles fuelled his fury.

'Oh, sod off. I'll eat them as they are. You didn't finish the washing up before you left. I want that done. After that you can make my bed. And clear up in the bathroom. It isn't as if I don't pay you enough.' He smiled with satisfaction as Edward set off to undertake these tasks then, just before Edward reached the kitchen door, shouted, 'Stop!'

Edward turned back.

Bryan had a pretty good idea of how he looked, stuck there in his wheelchair, his face as yet unwashed, his teeth as yet uncleaned, brandishing a spoon, like a petulant child in a high chair. But he pressed on just the same.

'I don't want you going into the living room. You hear me?'

Edward nodded.

Bryan spooned egg into his mouth – and dropped a fair amount on the napkin which Edward had tucked around his neck. After a night like last night he couldn't rely on his hands not to tremble. Damn his weakness. He remembered his dreams about training for Hang Tough, his thoughts about a new, smooth-running wheelchair and thought, fool!

He abandoned his losing battle with the eggs and wheeled himself into the living room. Thank God. Not a thing on the screen of his PC. He must have closed the file. He didn't remember doing so, but he must have been pretty out of it with the dope and unaccustomed alcohol, given he couldn't even remember falling asleep. The bottom line was that he certainly didn't want Edward to see what he'd been writing. But he did want to see the scene of the real crime.

DCI Dawson had put a rocket up Banks's backside, made it clear that while a murder investigation was underway he expected all his officers to be on the case for as many hours in the day as it took. No lolling in bed half the morning just because you'd been making enquiries late the previous night. He called Banks soft, called his record unimpressive, called his attitude slipshod. And he ridiculed Banks's attempt to deflect his, Dawson's, attention to other matters.

'What do you think you're playing at?' he demanded. 'If you think I'm pulling in the ten-year old son of the Mayor of Crandon Council for questioning in connection with a protection racket on your say-so, then think again. What are you trying to do? Sabotage every chance I have of getting respectable members of the community on our side?'

Dawson was deliberately making an enemy of the man, he had no option. It was nothing personal, not exactly. He knew he was going to have to make an example of one of them and best to come down hard the instant the very first of them put a foot wrong. He dismissed Banks to join the search for the murder weapon – another succession of tedious hours of routine enquiries, pounding the pavements. Then he sat back and asked himself what, exactly, had he got?

A youngish woman, killed violently. Presumably the fire was started intentionally. Which indicated that whoever started the fire was either ignorant of what forensics could achieve these days or was someone who knew at first hand the laxity of Crandon CID in pursuing a case on which they had little to go and from which they stood to gain little kudos. An ignoramus? he asked himself. Or a known criminal? That would mean going back through the files for similar cases, similar causes of death. It would also be worth checking the records for all cases of arson – indeed all recent fires, however minor. But Christ – he struck his forehead with one hand as the thought struck him – it was mid December. There had no doubt been umpteen reports of fires which had got out of hand in the last month; there always were after November the fifth. Still, he assigned three more officers to these painstaking tasks.

50

The manner of death had not been sophisticated, this was not a contract killing involving a single neat bullet to the heart or head. So the killing could be unpremeditated. It might be a simple matter of a lovers' argument, followed by an outburst of rage (cause of?), followed by a desperate effort to cover the killer's tracks. Or it could have been planned. In which case the perpetrator must have arranged to meet the woman in the shelter, or enticed her there, must have brought along the blunt instrument with intent to kill. In which case the instrument might be any one of a number of household objects. But some objects would look odd – even to the inhabitants of the Carleton Park Estate – if carried without any covering into the park. He made a note to order a further house-to-house with specific questions re: anyone carrying anything unusual into the park yesterday afternoon, or anyone carrying a large bag. He checked his diary. Lighting-up time the previous evening had been 5.10. The 999 call had been received at 5.21. The fire had then been burning for anything up to an hour. So at the time of death it would have been light enough for any witness to spot someone toting a bulky bag, or toting anything else.

Who could be relied on as witnesses? He was fully aware that most local residents would prefer to keep quiet, whatever they might have seen. So it would be worth getting on to the council, check if a park keeper, dog warden, street sweeper had put in an appearance at the relevant time.

Was that it? No. So far he had only considered the perpetrator. But what of the victim? Who was she? And why was she in the shelter? All he knew about her was that she was a young(ish) woman, fairly tall and plump for her height. She smoked heavily. She hadn't eaten for a while. That might mean a tom, a junkie, a single mother who paid for her kids' food before she bought any for herself. He paused and crossed the latter off his list. A mother on a budget who had her children's welfare at heart wouldn't spend her money on cigarettes. DCI Dawson rose to his feet and went into the outer office to give his instructions to his remaining staff. He'd better get them cracking. After all, he had a wasted afternoon ahead. Not wasted in terms of future relations with the community, of course, only wasted as far as the investigation was concerned.

An hour later, washed and meticulously dressed, Bryan was being wheeled by Edward around the small, grimy park. He hadn't really registered before how grimy it was. What had that policeman said last night about the neighbourhood? That it wasn't the 'safest of areas'. Bryan could see by the amount of litter, the broken fences, that it wasn't exactly what he'd been used to. But it was no more than he deserved. He'd ended up here quite simply because the housing association had offered him a place. Said they always converted a quota of their properties for people with disabilities. But people with disabilities – he should have realised this at the outset – aren't usually rolling in money. In fact, they tend to be on benefits. So no wonder the housing association had welcomed him with open arms when he offered to buy equity in a shared ownership, adapted flat. He would have bought the flat outright, but they said that was against the rules. So he bought fifty per cent and rented the remaining fifty. What other option was there? Okay, so in theory he could have had a private flat converted to his specifications; but when you're fresh out of hospital and not sure you're going to make it, you're not exactly in the mood to settle down with an architect to draw up a load of plans. So when he saw this flat – the first he saw – he decided it would do. Plus it had the advantage of being miles from all his friends from his previous life, all those people who had loomed over his bed when he was in hospital, their falsely encouraging smiles failing to conceal their pity. He didn't need their pity, he was quite capable of pitying himself, thank you very much. So, with Edward's help, he simply disappeared, leaving no forwarding address. And gave no thought at all to choosing a home which was set in a pleasant neighbourhood.

Rather the reverse. He knew full well he'd have nothing in common with people who lived in Crandon. He knew he would find nothing to interest him in the area's surroundings. That was his punishment. For his foolhardiness, his stupid arrogance, his crass belief in his personal invincibility. Because it wasn't as if anyone else had broken his neck, he'd done it himself. Now he deserved no better than to be a cripple among cripples, in a place which held for him absolutely no allure at all.

But today, like a man reprieved from a death sentence, he took in his surroundings with greed. To reach the park they had had to negotiate a complex series of obstacles on the pavement. Roadworks were going on, though he hadn't noticed them before, it looked as though they had been going on for some time. A long, muddy trench bisected the pavement: for what purpose Bryan could not imagine. No one was at work on it, it was empty, surrounded by cordons, but it appeared to be heading in the direction of his home, rather than running harmlessly away in the other direction.

'Make sure you write to the council,' he told Edward. 'So that they install a ramp wide enough and solid enough for my chair.' Edward nodded.

Now, in the park, Bryan looked around him: at cracked, tarmac paths, a few beleaguered shrubs making a sad effort at growth. An encrustation of diamonds of broken glass. Graffiti (competently executed, though derivative) on the walls of the One O'Clock Club. The heap of ash which was all that was left of the shelter. The police tapes which surrounded it. Uniformed officers on hands and knees, practically combing the grass. And then, at the far end of the park, its – presumably habitual – users creeping in, anxious to witness whatever action there was. A couple of winos. Several skinny, raucous mothers with kids in buggies. A young Chinese woman with a terrier straining at the end of a flexi-lead. An elderly man in a tweed trilby and wrapped in a huge scarf like a character out of Dickens calling, 'Henry! Henry!' after a stout, waddling dog. How come he hadn't registered before all this activity taking place just outside his door?

There was something else he hadn't registered. Shit. Dog shit. It was everywhere. If you were able-bodied you'd scarcely be able to put a foot between the piles of it. And when you were in a wheelchair, well, the stuff clung to your tyres and simply rolled round and round. He watched a smelly smear of it coming up for the umpteenth time and was glad that he wasn't, after all, in a disabled athlete's chair: in those chairs you got to push the wheels with your hands. Remind Edward to buy several pairs of washable gloves before he, Bryan, opted for that sort of change in his seating arrangements. In the meantime what to do about the unwanted passenger, the shit? He instructed Edward to push the chair swiftly back and forth across the cleanest piece of grass he could find.

During manoeuvres Henry's owner approached. He had a mild, sandy, whiskery face, a bit like his dog's.

'Morning,' he said, then, 'nice one, isn't it?' though the day was palpably grey, the grass wet from earlier rainfall. Of course, the old guy merely wanted some sort of opening gambit, any excuse to talk. Bryan decided that talking to him would be the way he would start investigations (had he been starting any). For while kids did everything, got into every-thing, elderly people saw them doing it and were only too ready to chat to a sympathetic person. Which kind of person – judging by the bulldog last night – was hardly likely to be the police.

'Heard what happened yesterday?' the man continued.

Bryan nodded.

'Thought you must have. Henry, leave that! Of course, news gets around. They say it was a woman. My last dog was a beagle, you know. Henry's half. They're the devil for getting into things they shouldn't. They say she was knocked on the head first. Henry, I said leave! Some drunk been sick by the look of it. Don't spare a thought for the dogs, do they? Could pick up any number of things. Not to mention chicken bones. Stick in

54

their throats, you know. You new here?' He was looking from Bryan to Edward, but Edward knew better than to open his mouth.

'Yes. Just moved into one of the flats.' Bryan waved a hand at his home. Even for him it would be over the top to leave Edward standing there unacknowledged. 'This is Edward, my carer. How did you hear about . . . ah . . . what happened last night?'

'Nice to meet you, Edward. I remember when that was a house. Had half the park for its back garden. One of the uniforms let something slip.' He jerked his head at the police officers on their hands and knees in the damp winter grass. Hands and knees deep in dog shit too, Bryan guessed. 'Can't keep a thing to themselves. Not if you know the right way to go about asking them.' He gave a conspiratorial wink. 'It was different in my day. Help Dad. Keep Mum. That sort of thing.' And Bryan realised, with a shock, that to Henry's owner he was someone to be welcomed, someone who had time on his hands to stop and chat and listen. That was down to him being in a wheelchair; and it was the first time the wheelchair had ever been an advantage. If he was careful and didn't rush things he could use that realisation to find out more.

'He's a nice looking dog,' he said untruthfully. 'Have you had him long?' Edward bent to pet the creature and the dog growled.

'Leave, sir! Yes, years. Strictly speaking he's not mine. It's a scandal the way the kids go on. They've been trying to burn that shelter down for months. And as fast as the council put up fences they rip them apart.'

Kids, thought Bryan. Keep him talking. 'So whose is he?'

'As good as mine these days. She's too old to cope with him. Fellow needs his exercise, though. Besides he's a man's dog. Never been the same since Ron died. Her husband that was. That's when I took him on. She pays for his food, give her that. But you see she hardly ever goes out.' He paused and waved a hand at the higher reaches of the tower block. 'Sits up there all day looking out of the window. What kind of life is that for a dog?'

What kind of life was it for a person? Bryan shivered. Since his accident even the thought of being more than a few inches off the ground turned him rigid and sweating with fear. He who had once climbed sheer rock faces, piloted a glider, would now be unable – even if he'd been able in the physical sense – to tolerate ascending to the upper floor of a double-decker bus.

'None at all,' he replied, thinking, but she might have seen something. Could I do it? Should I try it? And for what? The frail chance that an old woman might know something pertinent to an investigation in which he was not in any way involved? Who the fuck did he think he was? Of course, in the old days he wouldn't have thought twice, would have taken up the challenge at the drop of a hat. But in the old days he wasn't a cripple. He scowled down at his useless feet, splayed motionless on the foot board of the chair in their expensive, black, polished boots.

The old guy had changed subject seamlessly and was rabbiting on about TV programming. Vaguely, through the now familiar blanketing haze of self-pity, Bryan caught the end of a series of dismissive comments.

'. . . too many of these soaps. Women's rubbish, they are.

'. . . not enough sport. That's what we want to watch.

'. . . and all those politicians. Making out they can change the world for the better. Makes no difference to the likes of you and I, does it? You've only got to look at the National Health Service. Daresay you know more about that than I do.'

Bryan switched off. He was wrestling with himself. Could he face the ordeal of rising in a lift as he had once faced rising on the thermals? Of looking down on this park as he had once done on the swimming pool seconds before he plunged? His heart was hammering as it hadn't for months. He was used to the feel of this, the adrenaline rush which made him feel tinglingly alive, which enabled him to confront challenges in both his work and his leisure. And the feel of making them look like he was doing nothing out of the ordinary, of playing a cool hand.

He looked up at the old guy who was now holding forth about inflation and how little his pension would buy him in the shops. And he nodded to himself. Yes, he damn well could. It was time he faced up to his fears. He steadied himself before trying his voice.

'Does she have many visitors?' he asked in so level a tone that he surprised himself.

'Who? Oh, you mean her up there. Not that I know of. Except the Social.' He turned again in the direction of the uniformed searchers. 'God knows what they think they'll find. Anyone with any sense would take the evidence with them. You see, she talks too much about the old days. People can't be bothered.'

Bryan thought, yes, old people might see things, but could they make sense of them? You'd need a sieve the size of a trampoline to sift the pertinent from the dross in what this old guy said.

'D'you think she'd mind if I dropped in?' he asked with studied vagueness. 'I'm quite interested in hearing how people used to live.'

'Each to his own, that's what I say. Mind? She'd be over the moon. Not that you can just drop in. Not up there.' He bent and peered closely at Bryan. 'Not from the Social, are you? Or one of those media people? No, of course you're not. They wouldn't send someone in a wheelchair. She'd prefer to invite you properly, I daresay. To tea, that's what she likes.'

'So, suppose I came to tea . . . perhaps tomorrow?'

Henry's owner guffawed. 'You'll be lucky with them wheels of yours. Lifts are out of order. That's why *she* doesn't get out at the moment. Hard enough on my legs. The lifts and the boilers,' he added. 'If it's not one it's the other. Always on the blink. Whole place ought to be pulled down. Which it will be in a manner of speaking.'

'How come she keeps a dog anyway in a high rise block? I wouldn't think it was allowed.'

Whisker face dropped the lid of his right eye in a slow wink. 'There's a lot goes on up there that isn't allowed. But who's telling? Anyway, you might be in luck. They've stuck up a notice saying the engineers are due tomorrow. Take that with a pinch of salt, I would. Might be next week, might be not. Of course, I'd have to come with you.'

'Couldn't I just turn up? If you said I was coming?'

'Lot of good that would do you. Henry, leave! This minute!' The terrier on the flexi-lead had dragged its owner into the vicinity and Henry, exhibiting a massive erection, was attempting to mount the smaller dog's rear. Its owner hauled the terrier away again and Henry – and his erection – subsided.

'He's getting on a bit these days,' said Henry's owner. 'Like most of us. Long in the tooth. Of course, you can't be too careful.'

'Of unwanted pups?' asked Bryan, thinking surely a tatty little mongrel like Henry ought to have been castrated years ago. After all, who on earth would want to reproduce more of his kind? Though he supposed the same could be said of most of the shabby specimens of humanity dotted about the park. That filthy wino sprawled on a bench, for instance, bottle of Thunderbird at his feet; might have been better for the future of the human race if he'd been destroyed at birth. Same went for the squalling toddler with a face like an anaemic rat. Ditto the child's mother, lank ringlets of dark hair drooping on either side of a pinched, angry face. And that scrawny, shambling man in a flat cap clutching two bulging carrier bags who had sidled up to Edward and appeared to be bending his ear about something. But Bryan had, once again, misunderstood the train of Henry's owner's thought.

'Fathered umpteen litters in his day,' the old man announced proudly. 'No, it's her.' He gestured towards the tower block again. 'Amount of hardware she's got on her door, it takes her a good five minutes to get it open. Chains, bolts,

Chubbs: you name it, she's got it. And she has to know who you are before she'll even make a start on unlocking one of them. God knows what would happen if there was ever a fire up *there*. Emergency services'd never be able to get her out. What sort of time were you thinking of?'

'Would four o'clock be all right?' And Henry's owner nodded.

'What did the guy with the flat cap want?' Bryan asked Edward as they trundled out of the park.

'Tried to sell me two dresses. Blue one and a yellow one. They were in the bags.'

'Took you for a cross-dresser, did he?' Bryan sneered.

Lee was clear about his instructions. Uncle Jack had delivered them like a general directing his troops. And explained why he needed to recruit Lee.

'It's not that the gofer I usually use has been nicked. Too careful for that. Too many friends in the Bill. But he's been fingered. Can't use him once they have their eyes on him. Know what I mean?'

'Sure.' No one would ever finger Lee. He was far too quick, knew the estate far too well, could wriggle through any of its tight spots far too fast for anyone to catch him. And this was his big chance. He stood, poised on the balls of his feet, waiting for the off.

'One more thing. The less your mum knows the better. Sooner you start pulling in the money, less she'll have to be doing with those uncles, eh?'

'She doesn't have to.' Lee had been on his dignity. 'She likes them.'

'Oh yeah? Daresay she enjoyed her spells in Holloway on the drugs raps too? Who looked after you then?'

'People,' said Lee. 'Mum's friends. I have aunts as well as uncles.'

'Not too many of them, I hope. In this trade you want to keep your biz close to your chest.'

59

'Goes without saying.' Lee had rapped one fist on his breastbone. 'You want to tell me what I have to do?'

The deal was fairly simple, nothing heavy. And now he was paying a visit to the Patels' shop. They would let him in this time, legit, because he was on his own. After that he'd be heading for the Singhs, then Joe Parker and Mr Ali. There wouldn't be anything heavy at all, just a kid enquiring whether they had what they owed his uncle. Nothing for anyone to see that was out of the ordinary. Lee sped on his way.

Later in the day, when Bryan and Edward drove to the Centre, Bryan saw that, too, in a new light. Saw it properly for the first time. A dingy, red brick, unlettable retail unit in a shopping mall which managed to support only two run-down shops. The mall itself was bleak, windswept, litter-strewn. Most of the streetlights were on the blink. Outside the Centre was a tiny, grubby garden. Two teenage boys perched on the low brick wall opposite – he supposed it was supposed, in the mind of some demented social housing architect, to be decorative – and shouted at him as Edward wheeled him in. What the fuck was he doing here? He had enough money – he knew that now that he was beginning to come to his senses, to see beyond the end of his nose – to live in far more salubrious surroundings of his choice. But other people didn't. John didn't. Kenny didn't either. For them it was like it or lump it. For them it was abuse from kids half their age every day of their lives. He squared his shoulders (he could still do that) and ordered Edward to push him through the glass door.

John was waiting for him inside. Today he wore a grubby blue sweatshirt with 'University of Illinois' in white letters on the front of it. Bryan doubted John had been within spitting distance of a university. He had certainly never been to Illinois.

'Hi, cripple, you're late,' announced John. 'What kept you?'

'Dog shit on my wheels.'

'What's the difference between a car on a cross-Channel ferry and dog shit on your wheels?'

'Pass.'

'One rolls on and rolls off. The other rolls on . . . and on . . . and on.'

'Which reminds me. Something I meant to ask you. How many cripples does it take to change a light bulb?'

'Cripples don't change light bulbs. Light bulbs don't change cripples either. If you don't get your skates on we'll miss whatever treat Miss Shaggable has in store.'

They were soon all assembled in a circle. All except Kenny, who would no doubt turn up later. Marion made an entrance into their midst. Today she was wearing black leggings, black ankle boots, a black and grey flecked baggy sweater and great, hooped earrings which looked like real gold.

'Nice to see her bum, pity we can't see her boobs,' was John's comment.

'As long as it's not drama again,' said Bryan.

It was and it wasn't. Later on, Marion announced, they would all have a chance to practise their improvisations so that they would be perfect for performance at the Christmas social. But in the meantime, she had a very special guest: the newly appointed Detective Chief Inspector Dawson who had generously given up his valuable time to talk to them about personal security for the vulnerable in the 1990s.

'Personal what?' demanded John loudly. 'Wouldn't mind giving you a personal one, Miss Shaggable.' Marion frowned. Then, as a man took his place in the centre of the ring of chairs, John said loudly, 'Pig!'

'Cool it,' said Bryan. He looked at the police inspector, taking his measure. Sharp dresser, obviously worked out, probably kept his mind in good shape too. About the same height as he himself had been in the days when he could stand. Same colouring, same neatly cut dark hair. They could have been brothers. Except that Bryan, bitter, sedentary Bryan, was confined to a wheelchair and the other guy wasn't.

Still, this afternoon the other guy *was* confined to the Centre. Looked entirely uncomfortable about it too. Had he been expecting a different audience? Surely not, a man of his rank must have sussed beforehand what he was letting himself in for. More likely he was here because he knew it was his duty, but he'd rather be out catching criminals, getting a piece of the real action. Who wouldn't? Although there did seem to be a lot about pensioners' fears and racial harassment in his talk, which was hardly appropriate, apart from Mr D they were all in what would be called in other people their prime. And none of them was black. Still, he seemed to know his stuff. He was explaining to them the facts behind the myths about street crime. A minority of muggings were perpetrated against vulnerable people, he told them. Most victims of casual crimes were active young men; and the criminals who attacked them were other active young men.

'Lucky sods,' said John.

The man continued. He advocated wearing nothing worth stealing whilst on the street. No obvious jewellery, for instance.

'What jewellery?' demanded John. 'Who can afford to ponce about in medallions and Rolex watches? D'you know how much a week we get in benefits?' Marion looked reprovingly in his direction.

He advocated never going out unaccompanied.

'Chance'd be a fine thing.' John was getting thoroughly stoked up. 'You see me pushing my own chair?' The Chief Inspector pressed on. He was talking with passion now – about making the streets safe for decent people. That would be his hobbyhorse, Bryan judged. Man like him, obviously ambitious, had to have something driving him. Should have had the nous to realise though that his speech would have been more appropriate addressed to a line-up of local dignitaries. He was quoting PACE, referring to community policing policies, treating them to the ins and outs of Operation Bumblebee. Bryan found it all quite interesting, but as for the others . . . Mr D had nodded himself to sleep, Karen was gazing at the

Chief Inspector with a puzzled, eager smile and Laura was off in a world of her own.

And as for John: 'Hey, Bryan,' he demanded, 'why did Jesus tell the cripple to take up his bed and walk?'

Bryan shook his head abruptly, three times, in warning. What the fuck was the matter with John? He was being over the top, even for him. Had something untoward happened in the shared house? The more likely eventuality was that John's mother had been in touch, that always pissed him off. Either way it was time he shut up. No point in riling the guy unnecessarily. Besides, he, Bryan, wanted to hear what he had to say. Why? Because he knew the man. Not him personally, knew his type, had come across him time after time in boardrooms and in business deals. He was always on the other side of the table, clued-up, sharp, ready to pounce on any loophole in the contract which Bryan had prepared. He was a man of Bryan's sort. But even had Bryan not been in a wheelchair they would never have been mates, there would always have been a competitive edge between them.

'Because the skip outside his house was already full of old mattresses!'

The policeman paused. Had the heckler been anyone other than John, Bryan might have left him to it; for the pleasure of seeing what he felt sure would be the man's authoritative deftness in crushing what was after all such a pathetic attempt at opposition.

Instead: 'I wonder if you could tell us, officer,' he asked in the smoothest voice possible, 'what our best course of action is if we *are* attacked? Would you recommend complying with an assailant's demands? Or having a go?' And he looked the man directly in the eye.

The policeman returned the look blankly. It was clearly beyond his imagination that someone in a wheelchair might fight back.

'Who was the first person to be guilty of able-ism?' demanded John into the silence.

63

'Or making a run for it?' Bryan pressed on loudly. 'Metaphorically speaking, of course.'

'Fucking filth, brainless fuzz,' announced John, abandoning any attempt at humour. Out of the corner of his eye Bryan saw Marion leave her seat and head for the Centre's office. That meant she was bringing in the heavy mob – the jobsworth of a Head of Centre who had the power to make whatever decision he liked. And to make it stick.

'As I was saying, officer . . . ' Bryan smiled, 'although, as you have amply demonstrated, statistics prove that the victims of most violent crimes are active young men, just suppose I came across the unusual scenario of an elderly woman being mugged by a group of teenagers. Should I, as a member of the public, intervene? Make a citizen's arrest? Perhaps you could explain the procedure I should follow in that event? Also under what circumstances – it would be useful to have references to the relevant case law – would I be justified in acting in self defence?'

Sparks of anger as well as disbelief in the man's eyes. Bryan was more than ever convinced that the audience this guy was expecting wasn't the one he'd got. He hadn't expected to be heckled. And he certainly hadn't expected some cripple – hadn't expected Bryan – to take him on. He opened his mouth to speak. But again John got in first.

'Poofter plods!' he shouted, and they were his final words. Marion, the Head of Centre and two carers simply descended on him and wheeled him away. Just like that. You can't stand your ground when you're in a wheelchair. Not unless you have one with in-chair user powered steering. Which John didn't. Couldn't afford it.

Bryan spun through 180 degrees and tagged after the little procession. He was at the door of the Centre before he caught up, such had been their rush to remove John. Marion and the Head of Centre had peeled off – presumably to placate the policeman – and now only a single carer, a stocky young man with bushy eyebrows, stood beside John, hands clenched firmly on the handles of his chair as if in expectation of some further attempt at insubordination.

'I'm banned for the next two weeks. So what? So I'll miss the Christmas social?' John's bravado was a cocky, but, Bryan knew, thin veneer. 'Plenty more going on in my life.'

'Sure,' said Bryan. 'When you draw breath between other engagements I'll have something for you. Christmas present.'

'What?'

'You'll see. So who *was* first guilty of able-ism?'

'Cain.' And John was wheeled away.

Bryan went back to the Activity Room. The Inspector and Marion were commiserating. Well, she was apologising, damn her.

'No, no, entirely understandable,' the policeman was saying. 'I expect my talk was rather over their heads. In fact, I believe there must have been something of a mix-up by my staff. Our fault entirely. Inefficiency. The sort of thing I'll take steps to stamp out. Still, I was under the impression that I was to be addressing *leaders* of the vulnerable community.'

Arrogant bastard! He was making a show of shaking hands with all and sundry, but you could see he hated it. Not that most people could shake hands. Kenny – who'd finally turned up – made up for them, pumping the man's arm up and down. Old Mr D sat nodding. Karen smiled her beatific smile. Laura contorted her already twisted limbs and appeared to be about to 'say' something. But the man paid her no attention. As for Bryan, the Inspector didn't even glance in his direction. In spite of the fact that he'd made no attempt to answer his questions. Thought a man in a wheelchair was beneath his notice, did he? That did it! If Bryan ever did commit his hypothetical perfect crime, this was the guy he would want detailed to detect it. The man he would choose to be his adversary.

Fat chance of that. In a few moments all was back to normal. Marion had them settled in a circle. She wittered on about spraying gold glitter paint on pine cones then about tying red satin ribbon round cotton reels: for all the world as though she were a *Blue Peter* presenter. After that she instructed them to polish their improvisations. So they did. But as Kenny rushed round Bryan making whooshing noises in imitation of the sea, Bryan watched Marion as she dipped graciously to hear what Mr D was trying to say. She was tall, she was slim, she was beautiful, she was able-bodied, she was perfect. And she had banned John. She deserved to be taught a lesson. That's when Bryan decided he *would* plan the perfect crime. And that Marion would be its victim.

Chapter Four

Rick and Danny were sitting on the low wall outside the Centre. Without Lee they had no way of getting alcopops from the Patels' shop. They had no bottle caps to throw at the pigeons or, later, at the people in wheelchairs as they came out of the Centre. And without Lee they hadn't a good idea between them as to what to do next.

'You seen him at all?' asked Rick.

'Yeah. Went up to his place yesterday. He was there but he weren't coming out. Said he had a job and didn't need to nick nothing no more.'

'A job? What job?'

'Didn't say.'

Rick nodded. It made sense. If anyone could get a job it would be Lee. And if he was making money, he'd never let on what the deal was. Not even to them. Rick drummed his heels on the wall.

'So what shall we do?' he asked for what seemed like the thousandth time that afternoon.

'Dunno.'

They thought of going to look at the remains of the park shelter, but what was the point? The park would be crawling with police who would chase them away, or demand to know why they weren't at school. They thought of going – as they sometimes had with Lee – to the play area on the Mandela Estate a few streets away from Carleton Park, and bullying the littler kids there, maybe getting a football away from them and kicking it about? But without Lee could they be sure of getting a rise out of the kids? And could they be sure of making a getaway if the gang of older kids from the Mandela Estate turned up? Then they thought of going to Carousel near the bus terminus and playing the slot machines. But without Lee they had no way of getting any

67

money to play with. Without Lee there was zilch they could do. They vented their boredom in an attempt at fighting each other but, after a short scuffle, gave up. Their hearts weren't in it. In the end, they fell back on the idea of throwing things at the people in wheelchairs. The pair of them wandered round the mall picking up potential missiles and piling them in a stack beside the low wall. Rick was bending to snatch up a beer can, when:

'My, my, it's like bob-a-job week. Of course, you wouldn't remember that.' A stupid old bag leaning on a stick stood smiling down at him. 'Not many children these days would take a day off school just to clear up the litter on the estate. Or perhaps it's a project? That's how you're supposed to learn things nowadays, aren't you?'

Rick swore at her and lobbed the can in the direction of the stack, but she didn't take a blind bit of notice.

'Doesn't matter why you're doing it,' she went on. 'It's a treat for my old eyes to see. Here, I can't afford it, but you deserve it.' She pressed a ten pence piece into Rick's hand. 'You too, dear,' and she pressed a second into Danny's hand. 'And look,' she continued brightly, 'you couldn't have timed it better. There's the man from the council.' Rick and Danny followed the sweep of her hand and saw – rare sight on the Carleton Park Estate – a guy with a barrow, a shovel and a broom, descend on their hoard, scoop it up and trundle away.

'Shit,' said Rick as the old bag limped off.

'Shit,' said Danny.

'Still, we got ten pence each.'

'So what? What could we buy with that?'

'Nothing.'

'Tight-fisted old tart.' Danny aimed a kick in the air as if at the old woman's bum, although she was now out of sight behind the brick facade of the Centre.

'Tell you what, though.'

'What?'

'There must be some other shit around we could throw. Stuff the guy with the barrow wouldn't touch.'

Which, sure enough, there was.

An iron bar bent as though Uri Geller had practised on it. The remains of a computer keyboard. A heavy-duty plastic toy pickup truck with no wheels. Half a rusty car radiator. A length of copper piping with a knob of a joint at one end. A broken brick. A large frying pan with a residue of congealed foodstuff adhering to its battered surface. A piece of varnished chair leg. A gas meter. A tangle of components from the interior of a defunct TV. A chunk of concrete. A length of chain. A mustard-coloured loo seat. A pink conch approx. nine inches long and smeared with white paint. A Chubb lock. A rock – many faceted, brightly coloured – the size of a man's fist. A bin liner holding ten pounds in two pence pieces, all neatly parcelled up in bags from a bank. Two metallic tubes attached to a gilt frame – door chimes, wind chimes? All these objects lay, tagged and bagged in clear plastic, on the table in the incident room. Dawson had to hand it to the uniforms who'd searched Carleton Park and its surrounding streets. They hadn't found any frozen chickens, but they'd certainly used their imaginations in the stuff they had spotted and seen fit to retrieve. Good!

'Christ, Guv, where is all this junk supposed to be leading us?'

Dawson looked up from his prizes in irritation. It was DC Banks who had spoken. The rest of the team looked on eagerly, clearly hoping for a showdown between the two of them.

'It's just a pile of crap,' Banks went on. 'You could pick up stuff like that any day of the week in any patch of the manor. In any skip for that matter. When are we going to get on with the real job?'

Dawson felt rather than heard a rustle of agreement from the others.

'Which is?' he demanded coldly.

'We all know that, Guv. Catching criminals, not busting our heads in over some domestic. For instance, this protection deal I was telling you about. Set up a stakeout of the Patels or the Singhs and we might just get a result.'

'The Patels? The Singhs?' Dawson was incredulous. 'Have you looked at either of those shops recently or have you been resting on your laurels for so long you can't see the evidence in front of your eyes? Not enough legitimate turnover in either of them to pay the bills let alone protection money. Besides, what makes you so sure it was a domestic?'

'Stands to reason. No one's reported her missing, means no one wants to report her missing. Got something to hide. Take it from me, if we do pull a body in, it'll be some toe-rag of a wife-beater. This is Crandon, Guv. We don't get none of your fancy *Murder She Wrote* kind of crimes here. People get on the wrong side of each other, they do each other in. End of story.'

'Would it be beyond the bounds of possibility,' Dawson kept his voice level, 'to come up with other reasons why no one has reported her absence?'

'Oh, sure. Piece of cake. Crandon people don't exactly keep regular hours, have regular jobs. You might see someone the same time every day for a couple of months – at the shops, say, or in the DSS office – and then they're gone. Maybe the council got after them, evicted them for not paying the rent. Maybe they and the kids got put in a B & B someplace else. Maybe they went and stayed with a sister or whatever for a few weeks. Maybe they went on the streets. Maybe they even got a part-time job somewhere. That can happen, even in Crandon.' He paused and smiled. 'Though not often, mind you.'

'So that's your theory, is it?'

'Not so much of the theory, Guv, more a matter of practical experience. Easy come, easy go, that's Crandon. Daresay we'll soon identify her through the dental records. Find she's a tom or a junkie. Probably no fixed abode – could be another reason why no one's come forward.'

Banks was sure that, whatever Dawson thought of him, he, Banks, now had the troops on his side. He pressed his advantage.

'After all,' he added, as though offering a valuable piece of advice, 'I know the manor like the back of my hand. Can't expect you to have the same feel for it after a couple of days. No one would. That'd be aiming for the moon.'

'You recommend we aim for the gutter instead? No, no,' Dawson brushed aside any further contributions to the debate. 'This is a murder inquiry and I expect it to be treated with the seriousness the crime warrants. And I expect you to remember,' he raised one slim hand, quelling opposition, 'that effective policing is achieved by solid groundwork. And by being seen by the public to be carrying out that ground-work. Incidentally,' he paused once more, 'my congratulations to the uniformed branch for their search of Carleton Park. It must have been of great reassurance to members of the respectable, law-abiding community to see such diligence at first hand.'

Dosh, encouraged by the compliment, chose this moment to speak up.

'Like the guy in the wheelchair,' he said. 'Delighted to have my advice on personal security, he was.'

'What guy in a wheelchair?'

'The one we questioned. With a computer. DC Banks thought it might have been nicked. Lives on the edge of the park. It'll be in DC Banks's report.'

It hadn't been.

Banks started blustering. 'Just part of routine enquiries. No call to give him special mention. Especially not the time of night I filed that report. Transcribe every single irrelevant remark of everyone we interviewed and I'd have been here round the clock.'

'Which would have had the advantage of your being on time for your duties the following morning,' said Dawson. The omission of the interview was another black mark against

Banks, even though it had no bearing on the case. What guy in a wheelchair would have the strength to smash someone's head in? Even in the unlikely event that the woman sat down next to the wheelchair and presented her skull to her assailant it was simply beyond the bounds of possibility, the weapon had been a heavy one. Ergo, it must have been wielded by healthy, muscular arms.

'And now,' Dawson gestured to the bagged-up items on the table, 'I want each and every one of these traced to its source.' He headed for the door, then turned, a hand on the handle. 'One other thing. New duties. The rosta's posted up in the canteen. I expect every man and . . .' he shot a look at WPC Jones, the only woman on the team, '. . . woman to report in good time.'

The door flew open. Not because Dawson had turned the handle, but because one of the uniforms – a fresh-faced young lad, looked like he was hardly old enough to leave school – had burst in from outside, breathless.

'Incident on the Carleton Park Estate, sir,' he managed. 'Came straight to alert you. You said to keep you informed of all developments there.'

'Good man.' The uniforms were coming up smelling of roses every time, thought Dawson, casting a look of disgust at his plain clothes team. 'What have we got this time?'

'A disturbance. Some kids causing havoc at the Community Centre. Not much more than that to go on, I'm afraid, sir. The informant seemed reluctant to go into details. Shall I say you're on your way?'

The Community Centre, thought Dawson: the Centre in which he had given the wrong speech to the wrong people only the day before. To people in wheelchairs. The Centre and wheelchairs were becoming a double motif in Crandon. Was that altogether a bad thing? After all, the Centre was on the Carleton Park Estate, the focus of his operations. And besides – admit it! – what he'd seen of the woman who worked there didn't exactly make him reluctant to stage a return visit. Not that his interest in her was purely personal. She was – undoubtedly – an example of Crandon's respectable citizens and, as such, merited the most senior police presence possible. He grinned. He was kidding himself, he knew that. She was a stunner.

'A hundred quid!' Lee could hardly believe it. It was more than Mum sometimes managed to pull in an entire week. But there stood Uncle Jack, his bulk filling the living room doorway, peeling notes from a bulky wad. Behind Lee, Harry sat perched on the edge of a chair, a couple of carrier bags clutched in his fists.

'You did the biz, my boy. Told you you could make it big time, didn't I? Well, you just got yourself started.' Uncle Jack grinned and flapped the notes in Lee's face. 'Anyone does what I say, they get what they deserve. Now what are you going to spend it on?'

Trainers, thought Lee. A puffer jacket. An Arsenal sweat-shirt. But no, the trainers he wanted – the trainers which would drive Rick and Danny wild – would knock him back at least eighty quid. Only twenty quid left. You couldn't do nothing with twenty quid. Not even buy something really special for Mum.

He shook his head. He recalled how the Patels, the Singhs, Mr Ali had become suddenly so polite to him, after years of chasing him out of their premises. The Patels had practically cringed as they explained that they didn't have the full amount this month, but they'd have it next week, certainly they would. Cringed because they knew he had Uncle Jack behind him. Uncle Jack had power. Because he had money. Lee raised his head to Uncle Jack. 'I'll save it,' he said.

'That's my boy.' Uncle Jack tucked the wad of notes into the pocket of Lee's worn anorak. 'Now, you look after it. And don't be letting that down-and-out Harry milk you of a penny of it.' Harry stirred on his chair as though he would have liked to have protested, but didn't.

'Mum not home yet?' Uncle Jack went on.

Lee shook his head.

'She sometimes isn't. If she meets an uncle she likes. Doesn't bother me. Uncle Jack?'

'Yes?'

'When can I work for you again?'

'You up for something a little more hands-on?'

Lee nodded.

'Then it just so happens that there's something going down tonight. Ideal job for a bright lad like you.'

Bryan had just finished cutting out his twenty-seventh silver foil star when the commotion started. He'd already spent over an hour at the Centre. As usual Kenny hadn't turned up yet. Marion had set the others to polishing their improvisations ready for the Christmas social. At first she had suggested that, now John was no longer with them, Bryan join forces with Karen and they work out a new routine between them. But for once Bryan stood – sat – his ground. He elected not to do a heavy number about John being his friend and he, Bryan, not being willing to take his place. Instead he said, quite mildly, that Kenny and he had practised being the sea and the pebbles and he was convinced it would be a step backwards on Kenny's road to independent living to deprive him of a public performance of the finished piece. Marion frowned – a charming pucker of her faultless eyebrows – but allowed him to trundle away to a table in the corner of the Activity Room; she supplied him with a pair of blunt-ended scissors and left him to it.

Bryan snipped and trimmed at the silver foil. It was the devil of stuff to work with, even had he been good with his hands. Time and time again, the foil crumpled, or he tore a point off a star and had to chuck the whole caboodle into the waste-paper bin which Marion had placed – thoughtful as ever for the needs of the disadvantaged, damn her! – just to the right of his wheelchair. He glanced down at the bin. More foil in there than there was on the table. And the results of his

74

labours – the 'stars' which lay in rows on the table – were no better than the clumsy efforts of a child in kindergarten. Certainly no better than the cack-handed things which the other Centre users proudly produced. He imagined his 'stars', come Christmas, mounted on a sheet of crimson card (as he was sure they would be) his name written – by Marion – at the bottom of the card, for all the world as though he'd be delighted to be the author of such a paltry, such a useless 'achievement'.

He raised his eyes. Marion was doing her Lady Bountiful act, slipping between wheelchairs, dancing around them on her long, perfect legs, encouraging everyone to exert themselves to the full in yet another pointless activity. Bryan was almost sure it was all too much for old Mr D. Not only was his head nodding, his tongue was hanging out to one side like that of a panting dog. Marion had instructed Karen to devise – in John's absence – a solo routine. That was, Bryan judged, beyond Karen's scope. He watched her pathetic manoeuvres, saw her face raised to Marion in a timid, avid plea for approval and thought: Christ, I could kill that woman.

He thought of the stuff he had written that night about crushed bones and severed arteries and thought – yeah, I could do that – then felt Marion's eyes on him and bent once more to his task. Why? He didn't have to do this, did he? Yes, he did. Not for his sake, but for the sake of John, the sake of Karen, of old Mr D. They deserved better than to be badgered and bludgeoned into activities in which they did not want to take part, when they'd rather be sitting, dribbling, in a quiet corner. God knows why people couldn't be left to dribble if that was the career path they chose. He looked at Marion again and decided – garrotting, hanging, shooting, stabbing, they're all too good for her. What she needed was to be taught a lesson, a lesson which would teach her to look at a man in a wheelchair with respect. And, as he thought that, he realised that his hatred of her physical perfection was only the other side of the coin of his hatred of his own imperfection.

Which was when Kenny burst in. Dishevelled, panting, his eyes rolling in his head. He was crying, great gusty, painful sobs. Bryan spun his chair towards him, but, of course, Marion got there first. Got there, and recoiled. When Bryan reached the scene he could quite see why. Smell why. Kenny was spattered in dog shit – Bryan knew the distinctive, repulsive stink from yesterday's excursion in the park. Shit on Kenny's jogging bottoms, shit on Kenny's t-shirt, shit in Kenny's hair, shit on Kenny's eyebrows, even – Bryan imagined the assailants had congratulated themselves on a direct hit – shit spilling from Kenny's open mouth.

'Call the police,' he instructed Marion. He reached out a hand to Kenny. 'I'll take him to the loo.'

DCI Dawson thought, here we have really reached the pits. Kids pelting loonies with dog shit, no less. And no trace of the kids. The uniforms had given chase, but the kids had legged it. All that was left was a clutch of plastic bags which, presumably, the kids had used to pick up the shit and throw it at the half-wit.

Bryan thought, that arrogant bastard's back. Why didn't he send one of his minions? Might have been a touch more sympathetic to Kenny. No way I'm letting him anywhere near him. No way I'm letting him question him. Kenny's frightened to death.

But the arrogant bastard didn't even try. Wasn't bothered, by the look of it. Spent all his time talking to Marion. And then the penny dropped. The bugger had come here to ask her out. To take her to dinner or whatever. He watched as the couple went, at a distance, through the familiar moves. An inclined head here, a flutter of the hand there. Yes, he was certain of it, they were arranging to meet. And, in spite of Marion's supposed 'caring' attitude, in spite of the policeman's supposed concern about security for the vulnerable, when it came down to a choice between Kenny's welfare and the chance to chat up a bit of a looker, then Kenny, Bryan was sure, could go hang. He was sure because once – before the accident – his own priorities would have been the same.

It wasn't as if Bryan didn't like women, he reflected, as he stared, furious, at the pair of them getting it together. Wasn't, either, that he didn't like good-looking women. It wasn't as if he'd ever looked down on them either, wasn't guilty of being macho; he'd had women colleagues who were as sharp as all get out. Sharper than him, tell the truth. It was just that he expected – no, assumed – that they would find him attractive, would at least want to flirt with him, even if they didn't want to take things further. And they always did – flirt with him, that is. The only ones who didn't want to take things further were the ones already in a rock solid relationship. He recalled umpteen occasions after a serious battle over the boardroom table – a battle which was as good as a flirtation, as good as foreplay – agreeing to meet a sharp young woman in a sharply cut suit that night. Sometimes the suggestion was his, sometimes it was hers. Same difference. These days no woman would make such a suggestion. Nor would he.

Kenny was still crying. Bryan touched him on the hand. And Kenny, seated now on an upright chair in the Activity Room, leaned on Bryan's chest like a child seeking comfort. Yeugh! Because Kenny, though he now looked reasonably clean, still stank. Bryan's nose wrinkled as he looked up again at the tableau of the perfect woman and the perfect man arranging an assignation. While as for him – it was only a matter of timing that he, too, hadn't been pelted with dog shit by kids less than half his age.

DC Banks was sweating like he'd never sweated before. Rivers of sweat pasted his damp hair to his brow and cascaded into his eyes in what seemed to him like torrents. A sodden t-shirt clung to his wet, wobbling paunch. His jogging bottoms were soaked through. His legs felt like pieces of chewed string, his arms trembled uncontrollably, muscles stretched beyond endurance. His breath came in short, painful gasps, his heart hammered as hard as a pile-driver. He lowered his head like a bull, shook it like a dog and droplets of sweat sprayed into the air, splattering the men on either side of him.

'Rest!' bawled the instructor. Banks stopped and bent, head down. He rested his hands, palms open, on his shaking thighs, then rotated his left wrist and glanced at his watch. Christ, it was six-thirteen which meant they'd only been at it for thirteen minutes and he was wasted; but the bloody instructor, even though he'd taken them through the work-out step for step, was as dry and spruce as if he'd stepped out of a fucking commercial. This fitness session was, Banks knew, nothing more than a direct challenge from that bastard Dawson. The others knew it too.

It wasn't a challenge Banks could afford to ignore. His standing in the nick had gone down by leaps and bounds ever since that bastard arrived. Plus the bastard was his senior, had the power to hire and fire. No way could he, Banks, refuse to work out with the others when that was what Dawson decreed. It was like being in the bloody army. Okay, so he'd had it pretty much his own way with the previous DCI, man was a time-server, turning a blind eye, sticking it out for the sake of his pension. Still, Banks'd built up a pretty solid reputation over the years as the hard man of Crandon nick – among colleagues and villains alike. And here he was now: stripped of his usual heavy gear, exposed as a soft, shaking, blubbery mound of flesh. He glanced to right and left. Christ, even the uniforms were taking the punishment better than he was. Dosh, for instance, had no more than a film of sweat glazing his upper lip. But he knew they all hated it, looked to him to put a stop to it. Did they think he couldn't? And, as he looked at Dosh, Dosh smirked.

That did it. Time for a serious heart-to-heart with Jack Noble. Okay, so their first minor effort to put Dawson in the shit – to have him pull in the Mayor's kid – had backfired. But between them they had plenty more where that came from. Thing to do was to give the guy serious egg on his face over the murder inquiry and take him down a peg or two in a couple of other departments as well. Yes – he nodded his head, feeling dried sweat itch along his scalp – soon as this was over he'd hotfoot it (that was a joke, crawl more like) down to the Icicle Club on the pretence of making further investigations into the park shelter murder. Jack usually put in an appearance at the club around six. He'd be counting up last night's takings, having a leisurely drink perhaps. Any rate, he'd be sure to offer Banks a pint of the best. Might go some way to replace the fluid he'd lost in this session. Banks ran his tongue around his salty lips. And besides, if they didn't, between them, cook Dawson's goose, the bastard might soon get much too close for comfort. But not if he, Banks, had anything to do with it. And not if he and Noble put their heads together ASAP.

'Stomach curls!' shouted the instructor, fitting action to words. And Banks, with the others, followed suit, lowering himself painfully onto the floor.

'Fuck!' It was seven thirty. DCI Dawson sat, in solitude, at his desk. But by next morning the news would be all around the nick. The dental records had arrived by fax. They had been brought to him by the uniform on the outer desk, who had undoubtedly read them. They had come from HMP Holloway. The victim of the park shelter murder had, as DC Banks predicted, been a frequent recipient of Her Majesty's hospitality. She was a junkie, she was a tom, she had a string of petty offences – shop-lifting and the like – on her record. Worse – he took a sharp intake of breath as he read the name Julia Stone on the report – she was his cleaning lady. So he himself was one of the people who – as Banks had also predicted – simply didn't think anything of a Crandon woman's disappearance. Thought it was par for the course for the place. Dawson read on through the report, swearing under his

79

breath. Why the fuck hadn't Holloway come up with the goods on the first day of the investigation? He knew for a fact that they had enough IT capacity in the place to achieve a response time of fifteen minutes. Christ, if *he'd* received a fax in connection with a murder investigation he'd have had his staff up all night until they got results. In fact he *had* had his team up half the night, had Banks and Dosh pounding the streets. And for what? For a seedy, sordid, Crandon killing of one of the underclass presumably by another of its members. Hardly the stuff of which reputations are made or neighbourhoods redeemed. Was he imagining it, or was there some sort of conspiracy at work here? He probably was imagining it. A fuck-up theory seemed more on the cards than a conspiracy theory. For as his eyes reached the bottom of the list of the deceased's minor felonies, they registered the words, 'Please accept our apologies for the delay in responding to your request. This is owing to staff shortages and an unavoidable failure in the computer system.'

Unavoidable, be damned. Sounded like the sort of guff you got from BT or British Gas or LEB when their computers made a balls-up and billed you for the wrong amount. Like as not, if he rang the prison in the morning, he'd get some half-wit announcing, 'This is Helen – or Tracey, or Laura or whatever – how can I help you?' What did it matter what the woman's sodding name was when she – no, not her, someone else in the organisation – had just achieved a monumental cock-up? And put his reputation on the line.

Bugger it! But at least the woman, the victim, now had a name and a last known address at which he could make further enquiries.

Dawson buzzed for one of the uniforms.

'Oh no problem, sir.' It was the fresh-faced youngster. 'That's the flat over the Icicle. The club,' he explained. 'On the Mandela Estate. Actually DC Banks said he was going there more than an hour ago. Must have had a tip-off, don't you think?'

Dawson rose to his feet, ready to renew the investigation. But before he could so much as call for transport, for back-up, Banks appeared, his thick lips stretched in a sneer.

'Got a result, Guv. One of my snouts came through with the goods. Got a guy banged up in one of the cells ready to make a confession. Told you it was a domestic, didn't I? Get him put away for a stretch and we might be able to get on with some real police work. Interview Room Two's free.'

Dawson nodded. He rose from his desk. Banks stood aside in a parody of politeness to let him through the door first. But the pair of them got no further than that. The fresh-faced uniform was back, bursting with news.

'It's the Carleton Park Estate, sir!'

'What this time?' Dawson was unwilling to credit that the place could come up with anything more than dreary violence perpetrated by its dreary inhabitants against people who – to be honest – deserved no better.

'A fire, sir! Spreading by the minute according to the emergency services. And they say there might be people inside.'

The Crandon bush telegraph had done its work. On the pavement outside the blazing Patels' shop a mob swarmed: teetered on its toes, speculated, demanded information, obstructed the fire brigade and the paramedics. Danny and Rick hadn't a hope in hell of getting a look-in. They darted this way and that, trying to dodge past the adults, without success. But at least they could see the flames.

'Awesome,' said Danny.

They thought of Lee.

'You reckon he started it?' asked Rick.

'Might have. Seeing how he got the shelter going. Reckon we can get round the back and lift some stuff?' The pair of them set off along the mall, heading for the service road at the back of the shops.

It was amazing there. Great, grey paladin bins on wheels clustered together, rotund shapes looming in the dark. As Rick and Danny darted between them, the contents of one bin burst into flames. It was better than Guy Fawkes night. Way better. It was even better than the day they had burned the park shelter down. This would show Lee! Show him they could be in on stuff without him here to tell them what to do. Danny skidded to a sudden halt and side-stepped, tucking his feet well under him. A rat. No, not a rat – rats! Hordes of the little buggers, pouring out of the burning paladins. Didn't faze Rick or Danny. They ran on towards the store at the back of the Patels' shop.

The door was locked, of course, they hadn't expected anything else. But inside – they peered through the window to the left of the door – Christ, there was enough booze to keep them out of it for a month. Enough booze, but was there enough time? Flames already licked at the edges of the room, reaching with long tongues for the shelves of wines and spirits. Danny turned back, grabbed a length of wood from beside one of the paladins, thrust it through the window and – oomph! – flame burst out and engulfed them both.

It was the same aroma which DCI Dawson had inhaled at the scene of the crime of the park shelter murder. The aroma of suckling pig. The smell of roasting human flesh. He questioned the Patels urgently. Were any of their children unaccounted for? Was there any way anyone else could get in?

They shook their heads dumbly, then Mr Patel ventured, 'If only you people had taken what we said as a serious complaint.'

No opportunity to get to the bottom of that now. Dawson's mission this second was to save lives.

'Round the back,' he urged the fire crew. 'Try there.'

Which is where they found Rick and Danny.

This time Rick didn't hum the signature tune from *London's Burning*. And Danny didn't hum the signature tune from *Casualty*.

As for Lee, he was in bed, still alone in the flat, hugging around his thin shoulders a duvet which had now lost so many feathers it hardly provided any warmth at all.

It was a long night at Crandon nick. Statements from the Patels, the neighbouring Singhs, from every member of the watching mob who had teetered, on tenterhooks, on the edge of the pavement. Periodic reports from the hospital about the condition of the two boys. Not good. Demands from their families about how the boys came to be at the scene of the fire and what the police were doing to find out who started it. Tearful episodes. Harrowing episodes. The kind of thing DCI Dawson had hoped to stamp out by his presence here. Then, eventually – when the mob, the bystanders, the parents, the sisters had all gone or had subsided into a tearful heap in the waiting room – there was the prisoner in the cells to deal with. DCI Dawson gave orders to have him brought out.

The absolute epitome of Crandon's most seedy specimen, that was DCI Dawson's first impression. A small, skinny man in a flat cap, a shapeless waist-length coat with sagging pockets and torn, imitation-leather trousers. His shoulders were hunched, he refused to meet their eyes. Probably had a record of petty offences as long as your arm. Ask him to admit to any minor misdemeanour going down on the Carleton Park Estate – or, for that matter, the Mandela Estate – and odds on he would. Odds on he would turn out to be implicated in those misdemeanours too. They cautioned him.

'Name?' demanded Dawson, then recalled that DC Banks had been the one to bring him in. Whatever he thought of Banks, fair was fair. He nodded in Banks's direction.

'For the benefit of the tape,' said DC Banks, 'it is now 11.40 pm. We are questioning the suspect, Harry Green. Is that your name?'

'Yeah.'

'And you admit to the murder of Julia Stone?'

'Yeah.'

83

'Your motive?'

'She was going with other men.'

'Can you tell us why she is last known as living at 2A Freedom Close on the Mandela Estate?'

'It's the flat above the Icicle. Jack Noble let her stay there sometimes when she had nowhere else. He's good like that.'

'And later she had somewhere else?'

'Yeah. She was with me.'

'Where?'

'Here and there. Nowhere in particular.'

'And you say you killed her?'

'Yeah. Sure.'

'Why?'

'I was out of it, wasn't I? Some geezer gave me a joint as thick as your thumb. With a load of charley in it.'

'Who gave it to you? Where?'

'Can't remember. Somewhere outside. Think it was raining. But I was well out of it before that. Put back at least six pints.' He paused. 'Bought them for me, didn't he?'

'Who?'

'No idea.'

Harry Green stopped contemplating his fingers which were twisting together in his lap, like a bunch of pink worms dug up by a gardener's fork. He raised his eyes – not to Banks, but to DCI Dawson. Eyes which revealed he wasn't in the least fazed by the prospect of going down for a long, long time. Eyes which held a weariness beyond the man's apparent age. And held an animal's instinct for survival.

'My dresses,' said Harry Green. 'Where are they? They're worth a few bob.'

Dawson *was* fazed. 'Dresses?' he asked. 'What dresses?'

'Sergeant at the desk's got them. Insisted I check them in. They're my property. What'll happen to them while I'm inside? Okay, so one of them's got a tear in the hem. It's a purple Jean Muir. Not to everyone's taste, but someone'll buy it, mark my words. Cut on the bias, it is. Could suit a brunette with a very slim figure. The other one's in mint condition. Designer label and all.'

'They'll be taken care of,' Dawson told him wearily. 'We follow all the proper procedures here.'

'Chance'd be a fine thing.' Harry Green's eyes were narrow and cunning now. 'Since when?'

Banks intervened. 'Enough questions! To return to the matter in hand, to the killing of Julia Stone.'

'Said I killed her, didn't I?' Harry Green dropped his eyes again.

'How?'

'Bashed her head in.'

'What with?'

'Big piece of wood. It was lying around in the shelter.'

'And you set fire to the shelter?'

'Must have done. Suppose I threw the wood back onto the fire. Covering my tracks and that.'

'Christ,' said Dosh later, 'you wouldn't think a little creep like that could get it up, never mind do someone in.'

2 am. Peter Dawson sat alone in his loft. The rectangles of black on either side of him – his windows – seemed to be made now not of velvet but of some much more harshly abrasive stuff.

Another file stamped 'Case Closed'. At least this time there had been a result. But it was Banks's result, not his. Banks had been proved right. He knew his patch better than he, Dawson, the newcomer, did. All he had done by pursuing the park shelter murder was to alienate respectable members of the community. He had blown it. He had only himself to blame. If he'd been less sure of himself, if he'd listened to his subordi-nates . . .? But, no, he was sure he was right. There was some-thing unexplained about the park shelter murder, something that he couldn't put his finger on. He recalled Dosh's remark after Harry Green had been returned securely to his cell.

85

Dosh was right, Dawson was sure of that. Green wouldn't have the bottle to commit a murder. Hot blooded murder, cold blooded murder, didn't matter which. He simply wouldn't have the bottle.

What to do about it? Dawson toyed with the idea of going back to the nick, rousing Green from sleep, questioning him again. He imagined the scene of his arrival, saw the sleepy desk sergeant occupied with taking far too long over the details of some tom or other. Saw him raise his eyes to Dawson, incredulous that so senior an officer had turned up, unannounced, in the middle of the night. Sniggering behind his hand at that same senior officer who'd already got things so seriously wrong, both about the murder and the protection racket. No way would he, Dawson, compound his humiliation like that.

Nor would he admit defeat. Not yet, not by a long chalk. Crandon had driven him out once and he was damned if it was going to do so again. Not after all those years in which he had put his life on hold; years of studying, of working his way up the force – all so he could return to Crandon and, by cleaning it up, lay his personal ghosts to rest. He looked up, once more, at the impenetrable darkness outside the windows. He wasn't a child any more, terrified of the dark corridor along which he had to grope his way at night to the lavatory they shared with so many other people crammed into rented rooms in the squalid, crumbling house. Even now he could still feel beneath his fingers the join between the dark, blistered wood panelling and the peeling wallpaper above. But the journey *to* the toilet was not the worst terror. Far more petrifying was what he might find when he reached it. An ominous clank and rumble of the old lavatory chain, the door flung open and . . . sometimes it was the huge drunk from along the corridor who tottered out, retching and reeking of beer; sometimes it was the ancient smelly crone who leered at him and touched him in a way he hated; sometimes it was one of the younger women, her arms around a man, trousers crunched around his ankles; sometimes it was a cripple, heaving himself onto his crutches. The Crandon nights of his childhood had been peopled by, dominated by grotesques: twisted, misshapen phantasmagoria. And the most twisted, the most grotesque of all of them had been his father, his head lolling sideways, his blue tongue, his bulging eyes, his feet dancing above the open, stinking, toilet bowl as his corpse swayed on the end of a noose in the yellow gleam of the bare electric bulb.

Crandon had done that to his father. It wasn't about to do the same to his son. The adult Dawson squared his shoulders. It didn't do to look back on the dark past. For years he had suppressed those memories, disciplined himself to banish all thoughts of them even from his dreams. And he'd always succeeded, his willpower was like a rod of forged steel. Besides which, what he must do was find a solution for the future. For that, he turned, as usual, to his books. Over the years he'd assembled quite a collection on the theory and practice of policing – especially inner city policing. He trawled the spines of the volumes on his – now slightly dusty – chrome shelves. And selected Beatrix Campell's *Goliath:* an investigation from a feminist perspective of the riots of the 1990s. He leafed through the pages. Did he have something to learn from them? Certainly he was willing to entertain almost any point of view which would give him a better handle on the most effective tactics for policing the place.

When, finally, he was tired enough to go to bed, he thought, briefly, of the date he had arranged with Marion. An outing to the West End, no less. A return to civilisation. A decent restaurant with proper food, not those ghastly, greasy chips someone had brought in from Parker's place on the night of Julia Stone's murder. He embroidered his vision further. The pretty woman on the other side of the table. Linen napkins. A single rose or a fuschia perhaps, in a specimen glass vase in the centre of the table. Subdued conversation from the tables on either side. A decent wine list. A proper menu, presented by a waiter who was properly deferential. What would he choose to eat? Stuffed artichoke hearts, he rather thought, his mouth watering. Then rack of lamb with rosemary. And perhaps zabaglione to finish. He wondered what Marion would choose.

His thoughts moved smoothly from his civilised date with Marion to the civilised future of Crandon. He imagined the Silk Stream cleared of detritus, flowing swift and clean. He slipped into a dream which inhabited some region between sleep and wakefulness. On either side of the fast-running brook wasteland had been replaced by meadows. Meandering paths undulated through the long grass from which colourful butterflies rose in fluttering clouds. Fragrant wildflowers tangled the hedgerows which bordered the meadows: honey-suckle, daisies, purple vetch. Ornamental, rustic footbridges humped their backs over the clear water; ducks swam therein. It was midsummer. The sun shone. People in shorts and summer dresses strolled without fear of molestation or mugging in this charming, idyllic, linear park. Laughing children fed the ducks. A family picnic was in progress on a smooth stretch of sward. There was no litter. Even the people walking dogs had brought plastic bags issued by the council with which to clear up after their charges.

He *had* been asleep. He woke with a start in the dark night, his purpose renewed by the vision his unconscious had showed him.

Chapter Five

Twelve days had gone by and it seemed to Peter Dawson that he was no nearer getting either the community or his troops on his side. In spite of the number of spectators on the night of the fire, not a single witness had come forward to report anything of note. Even Mr Patel, after his initial remark about having made a complaint, shook his head sadly when asked to make a statement and melted into the background. Dawson had the files checked, but there was no record of Mr Patel having made any complaint in the first place. He ordered a round-the-clock vigil beside the hospital beds of the two kids who'd been injured in the incident and who were now on their way to recovery; but they too had their mouths clamped firmly shut. He was up against a wall of silence.

The only people singing out loud and clear were the community leaders. Dawson sighed as he looked down at the latest copy of the *Crandon Courier*. Some joker on his staff had seen fit to wield a highlighting pen over the weekly rag before leaving it in the centre of his desk. The *Courier* was a freebie – Crandon's economy didn't run to a paid-for publication – delivered door-to-door to every household in the manor. Which meant that every inhabitant of the place – at least, those who could read, he reflected sourly – was aware of the ignominy which was the current state of play in his now decidedly less than brilliant career. Didn't help that the reporting wasn't exactly quality broadsheet standard. The *Courier* went for tabloid headlines, pulled at tabloid heartstrings. He read, once again, just a few of the highlighted phrases. 'New broom in Crandon Police sweeps muck under the carpet . . .' 'racism rampant in the Met . . .' 'send him back where he came from . . .' ' do they want another Broadwater Farm? . . .'

The long and the short of it was that the community leaders felt they had been sold down the river – as they had been for years in Crandon. The Met had promised them everything would change, and what had they come up with? A middle-class white man fresh out of a pen-pushing job in the Yard and without a clue about policing Crandon's streets, protecting the interests of minorities, understanding racial tensions. In short, thought Dawson, they were convinced he was a dead loss. Exactly the opposite of what he had hoped to achieve in his first weeks here.

Thank God he'd had one night's respite from what seemed an endless string of setbacks. His dinner with Marion had thoroughly lived up to expectations: had been a charming, civilised interlude in a routine of constant challenge and sordid petty crime. Surprising, though, that she came onto him so strongly afterwards. Still, gave him an opportunity to show off his loft – she was, barring his now deceased cleaner, the first woman to set foot in it since he had moved in. And what man would turn Marion down?

Hadn't had a moment for anything further in the way of a social life. He'd been mending fences fast as he could. Meeting after meeting: with the Bengali Action people, the Afro-Caribbean Alliance, the Asian Community Federation, the Irish Pensioners Group, the Senior Citizens' Forum. A charming smile for all of them, a warm handshake, cups of tea or coffee all round. Didn't cut much ice with them. Pretty soon it dawned on him that their antipathy wasn't solely down to the torching of the Patels' shop. Turned out that the speech he'd wasted on the disabled people at the Centre should have been delivered at that same venue the following day; to the seemingly endless procession of people who now tramped in and out of his office and voiced their grievances in the loud, angry tones of those who know they have right on their side. He placated, he conciliated. Then he made the mistake – could he be losing his touch? – of pleading staff error for his having turned up on the wrong day. The assembled company rounded on him. Was he in charge, or was he not? He admitted that he was. In which case he was responsible for ensuring that his staff got it right, the buck stopped with him. He lowered his head in a bitter, unfamiliar gesture of humility and took the rap.

It soon became apparent that one thought was uppermost in all their minds: the peaceful success of the forthcoming Carleton Park Estate Fun Day. This event was clearly so important to the community he should have been thoroughly briefed on it as soon as he took charge, but he hadn't been. He flannelled his way uncomfortably through initial references to it, it wasn't his style to flannel. He assured everyone that he'd do everything in his power to minimise petty crime on the day, to ensure an adequate but sensitive police presence, to pour oil on the troubled waters of racial tension. Then he took the bull by the horns and proposed that the Organising Committee – of whose existence he had swiftly been made aware – should meet in his own office the following afternoon.

This time he made sure that a proper briefing was prepared pronto. The Carleton Park Fun Day was, it seemed, a new initiative funded by the council at the instigation of the Mayor. It was intended both to 'dramatise the oral history of life in a tower block' and to encourage residents to 'envision' and 'celebrate' their low-rise future. Because the tower block to the east of the park was to be demolished – blown up, in fact, in a controlled explosion – which occasion would be the focus of a second Fun Day. But this, Dawson gathered, wouldn't take place until well into spring, by which time some of the new low-rise houses would be completed and the tower block empty, those of its tenants for whom permanent homes were not yet finished being accommodated in short-stay homes.

The purpose of the Fun Day in terms of social policy was to develop a community spirit well before the new estate was constructed. Which was entirely laudable, thought Dawson, but he could have done without a meeting about a Fun Day right now, he had more important matters on his plate.

Odd time of year to hold such a Day too – he knew these things usually took place in the summer when everyone could be out of doors long into the evening, but this one was scheduled for the Saturday before Christmas. He turned the page of his brief and found that the idea was to capitalize on the festive spirit. Apparently few of the residents of the tower block even knew who their neighbours were. The Day was to get them out and about, meeting each other on neutral ground and generally socialising preparatory to more formal consultation, the formation of a Tenants' Association etc.

On a more technical note he registered that the Day – like the new estate itself – was jointly funded by the council, two housing associations which provided affordable homes to rent and one which specialised in shared ownership and that the official title of the whole scheme was the Carleton Park Housing Action Trust. In terms of numbers upwards of 500 people lived in the block itself, many of whom were large families; but, of course, people from all the surrounding streets would be welcome. A major turnout was anticipated at the event.

Dawson couldn't fault any aspect of the entire Trust. It had all the right elements to create a thriving, balanced community for the future. Careful forward planning; built-in consultation; and the design of the new estate itself was, according to the plans laid out before him, a veritable model as far as social housing was concerned. Family houses, each with its own small garden, smaller units for single people, sheltered housing for the elderly; it was exactly the kind of initiative which formed part of his own vision for Crandon. He smiled grimly. No matter that he had a murder inquiry, two cases of arson and a possible protection racket on his hands: he must give this project all the backing he could.

The meeting of the Organising Committee turned out to be the most difficult meeting out of a series of meetings, none of which had been a piece of cake.

Chaired by a tall, stout, forceful, middle-aged, bearded Asian who was addressed by all and sundry as Rashid and who was, Dawson judged, a professional on the equal opportunities circuit, its members also included Crandon's Mayor, Anne Thompson, fat, white and belligerently working class; a dapper, sparky young man in a suit (Steve Ainsworth) who was the Chief Executive of Oblong 22 Home Ownership Housing Association; the Head of the Community Centre, Charles Mendip; Mary O'Hara, representative of the Irish Pensioners' Group; Shauna Dunn, Mediation Outreach Worker; and three other people of ethnic minority origin whose names Dawson had, for the moment, difficulty in getting his tongue around. Not like him not to have had time to do his homework. Alison Speir, a neat young woman from the council's Committee Secretariat, her brown hair caught back in a black ribbon, was on hand to take notes.

The meeting began with a generalised discussion about defensible space, adequate kick-about areas, child densities, mixed tenure, the lessons learned from rejuvenation else- where of the sink estates of earlier decades.

Dawson stuck his oar in.

'You are, I understand, going for pepper potting?'

And was rewarded for this display of knowledge of social housing policy by a glance of approbation from Steve Ainsworth.

'Absolutely. Dotting shared ownership homes among new social housing always gives a fillip to the community. Brings new skills. New life. And the purchasing power which can turn a neighbourhood around. Always assuming,' his mouth turned down, 'that we can persuade economically active people to part-buy in an area like this. Still,' he brightened, 'my sales team have never failed yet.'

Dawson was about to reply when he noticed that Alison Speir hadn't written a word on her notepad and that Rashid was sitting silent as a ceramic Buddha, his hands settled on his paunch. Of course! The design of the new estate – though of enduring interest to this committee – was down to the architects concerned who answered to some other, more powerful committee. What was at issue today was the peaceful and harmonious conduct of the Fun Day.

Rashid came to life and gave an outline of the programme for the day. There was to be painting for the kids. Drama and creative writing for the adults. The council grant would cover the cost of hiring two bands. It would also pay for tea and coffee. Those attending would be invited to bring their own food – the thinking was that that, too, would help to foster community spirit.

'We have to recognise,' said Steve Ainsworth, 'that few of these people have ever exchanged more than a couple of words with each other. Except insults. That's what happens when you're stuck in a tower block. After all, none of those flats is designed for the lifestyle expectations of the 1990s. No adequate soundproofing. How would you feel if you could hear every detail of your neighbour's love life? Had to listen to them going to the loo?'

'A recipe for neighbour to neighbour disputes,' agreed Shauna Dunn. 'But the potential for neighbour to neighbour interaction in the new environment is exciting, not to say limitless.'

'They'll be able to talk to each other over their garden fences,' put in Charles Mendip. 'What a radical departure from the isolated lives they now lead.'

'In the meantime,' added the Mayor, 'if we get the Fun Day right, they might even send each other Christmas cards.'

Everyone beamed at this heart-warming thought.

Dawson ventured an intervention.

'In what way, exactly, can we help with the festivities?'

Rashid recommended that Crandon police put as many officers from the black and ethnic minority communities as possible in the field on the day. And women. And younger recruits. Commit a really strong presence which would visibly demonstrate solidarity with the community. After all – Rashid spread his hands as he made his point – that could only be of benefit to the Met in terms of the improved community relations in which Dawson had expressed in previous meetings so enthusiastic an interest. Indeed, it could be said – Rashid nodded his head – that the Fun Day was a chance for the police to get on a better footing with the people they served.

He meant, Dawson knew, that it was a chance for the new CID Guvnor to redeem his earlier 'mistakes' and to achieve what he had assured them all were his goals. He nodded his head. He smiled. He racked his brains. There weren't many black faces in Crandon nick. Except amongst the cleaners. But he nodded again, with vigour, in agreement.

'Get them to enter into the spirit of it,' enthused the Mayor, 'take off their helmets, boogie on down to the music.'

Dawson nodded again.

'You have it on my authority,' he told them all, 'that the policing of the Fun Day will be accorded the highest priority possible. There will be a substantial presence, but it will be unobtrusive, non-provocative. But, on a lighter, more positive note, I wonder if you'd like us to be involved more closely with some of the events? For myself, I'd be delighted to judge one of the competitions, if that would suit? Perhaps we could get up a collection at the station for one of the prizes? Or maybe some of the uniforms could be involved in activities in the run-up to the event? I expect there'll be sessions in school, won't there, to prepare for it? And creative writing classes? I could send some of my men – and women, of course – along, not as observers, but as participants. That should help to break down barriers.'

There were delighted nods all round. Dawson had them eating out of his hand now, he knew it. Time to show them that he was streets ahead of them in the field of community involvement. 'Out of interest,' he asked, 'you talked of envisioning the future as one of the functions of the Fun Day. What role will the residents have in the layout of the estate?'

'Oh, none,' the official from the Housing Department said airily. 'The plans are all signed and sealed. But we thought they might be consulted,' he laid heavy emphasis on the final word, 'on what shrubs we select for planting in the central open space. We see it,' his voice rose an octave with enthusiasm, 'rather in the nature of a village green. There'll be a notice board encased in vandal-proof glass. We'll post up meetings of the Neighbourhood Forum there; also where to get advice on benefits, council tax rebates; who to complain to about abandoned cars or stray dogs. Everything people in the community need to know. Added to which,' he went on, 'they'll be able to choose the colours of their front doors. From within the range specified, of course. There'll be a newsletter telling them what to expect when – the date we require them to move out, the location of their temporary accommodation, the standard to which they are obliged to maintain their gardens. Oh and,' his face brightened at this final thought, 'we're going to hold a competition to decide the name of the new estate.'

After Dawson'd ushered all the Organising Committee out there was the little matter of putting his own house in order, of dealing with the climate of dumb insubordination which now pervaded the entire place. When he'd called for tea or coffee for a meeting they'd made sure there was one cup too few, so he had to go without in deference to the community leaders. When he gave instructions for the urgent unearthing of a file it turned up an hour later with some mumbled, lame excuse. Worse, the new regime he had introduced was falling apart at the seams. Numbers were dropping off at the daily work-out class. And when he opened his door into the open plan office there was an unmistakable whiff of tobacco and a series of not quite furtive enough movements as everyone stubbed out his or her cigarette in the nearest waste paper bin. Christ, the way they were all going on, there'd be a fire in the nick, never mind anywhere else. For which – given the way his luck was running the last few days – he would probably be blamed. But now wasn't the time for a showdown with his subordinates, not when he was on a losing streak. He had to do something to regain the upper hand, the high moral ground. But what?

Bryan chuckled a little as he read the headlines about Dawson in the *Courier*. Serve that arrogant bastard of a policeman right. He turned the page idly. A picture of a man whom he vaguely recognised. From where? Sad, defeated eyes, a weak, receding chin. Hadn't he been wearing a hat when he saw him? Wasn't like Bryan to forget a face, he never would have in the old days. Nor would he now. He placed one thumb across the image of the man's brow to simulate how he would look with some sort of head covering, and got it in one. It was the seedy guy in the park who'd tried to sell Edward a couple of dresses. His mug shot was superimposed on a study of the spot in the park on which the shelter had stood. Photograph wasn't much cop. Didn't think he'd have made out what it was supposed to be, had the scene not been on his own back doorstep. Taken in fading light, by the look of it. Poor definition, fuzzy focus, seriously under-exposed. It wasn't a competent photo-journalist's pic, it wasn't even a good happy-snap. But then a freebie weekly in Crandon was hardly likely to attract the David Baileys of this world.

He read the story below the picture. The man – name of Harry Green – had been charged at the local magistrate's court with the murder of Julia Stone – a murder known locally as the Carleton Park shelter murder – and remanded in custody. There was a picture of Julia Stone too. Plump faced woman with rabbity teeth. Green was understood to have made a full confession, including to the lesser charge of damage to public property – i.e. burning down the shelter. So that was that. Bryan was surprised by how disappointed he felt. He'd wanted it to be a complex crime, one which would really be worthy of the exercise of his brain. He wondered whether to give up on what he'd intended to do today – perhaps stay home, entertain himself with the three crime novels which he still hadn't read? Or embark once more on the fantasy of planning his own perfect crime. No! The months of babying himself, of shutting himself away and refusing to engage with his surroundings or the people who occupied them were over. He'd made his plans for the afternoon and he was going to stick to them. Particularly because it seemed that if you were in a wheelchair gaining admittance to the local tower block was near as dammit as difficult as getting invited to a garden party at Buck House. No, more difficult – he'd been to one of those garden parties when he still had the use of his legs. As difficult as – he decided a clichéd comparison would do, he had other things to think about – breaking into Fort Knox.

Because it had turned out that Henry's owner – Mr Tozer, 'Gerald, to you lad' – had been more than overly optimistic about the speed at which the lifts would be repaired. Repaired permanently, that is. It seemed they'd worked for one day the previous week, then gone on the blink again. So it wasn't until earlier this morning, on Bryan's now daily outing to the park, that Gerald had reported the all clear, and that Mrs Corke would be expecting him at four.

He'd have to give the Centre a miss, but what the hell? Visiting the tower block, even if nothing came of the interview, was a major step forward in his own rehabilitation. It had become a personal challenge. Besides, he'd cut out way more than his quota of silver foil stars, tolerated far too many of Kenny's inept impersonations of the sea. And he'd be at the Centre soon enough: this evening for the Christmas social.

Without John. Bryan frowned, suddenly furious, then put in a call to the shared house. Took whoever answered it ages to bring John to the phone. Daresay the staff there didn't mean to patronise their charges, but that was as sure as dammit the end result. He said as much.

'Don't knock 'em,' responded John. 'Where would I be without 'em? Do their best, don't they?'

Not with getting you dressed and keeping your clothes clean, Bryan thought, but didn't say.

'Latest news here is we've got a new recruit,' John breezed on. 'Single white female. Nose ring – must be into self-mutilation – and scraggy, dyed hair in bunches. Reckon she's got nipple rings, too? Anyway, you should see her body. If Miss Shaggable is a ten, then I'd put Shelley on a score of at least nine and a half.' He paused. 'As in *9½ Weeks*.'

'Getting to know her well, are you?'

'Do chairs have wheels? Highlight of her day when she trundles me to my room of a night. You should hear her bedtime stories!'

'About Miss Shaggable,' Bryan said. 'Going to give her a taste of her own medicine. Cut her down to size.'

'What? Take a chainsaw to her legs? That'd be a serious waste of the best of British thighs.'

'No. Something else. While you're on, remember I told you I'd have something for you? To make the festive season go with a swing?'

'Sure.'

'It'll be with you this evening. Edward's bringing it.'

'Cheers, mate. Got something for you, too. So what you doing for Christmas? Nothing much, I bet.'

'Spot on. You?'

'Usual stuff. Umpteen parties in the run-up to the festivities. Or roll-up for the likes of you and I. We've had a do at the shared house already. Made a speech, would you believe it? Told the staff here beforehand that I had some ideas I wanted to share about self-help for people with disabilities. Didn't realise until too late I meant sexual self-help. Anyway, most of the others probably didn't understand a word. Not too clued-up on the contents of the Kama Sutra. Still, Laura took the time to tell me – via that screen of hers – that she'd be quite interested to know more. Funny how the quiet ones are always the ones to watch. Any case, I got a sitting ovation. Think Shelley got a kick out of it too, though she didn't let on. Actually, I'm getting a bit of a name myself for entertaining the crowds. Been asked to a kids' party Christmas Eve, planning to pull off a few magic tricks for them. Know what you get when you saw a cripple in half?'

'What?'

'A bleeding dwarf.

'D-day,' John pressed on, 'I'm going to Christmas dinner at an old people's home. As an alternative Santa. Okay, so it's a bit of a come-down compared to what I could be doing.' He paused again and drew breath, 'Only got myself invited to a swingers' alternative Yuletide, didn't I? Everybody throws their car keys onto the table beside the turkey. After you've eaten you pick up a key at random and hotfoot it to the bedroom with whoever owns it.'

'Or in your case, hotwheel.'

'Still,' John said, 'wouldn't do to deprive the old biddies of my charismatic presence. I'll maybe catch the other party later. Know what?'

'What?'

'Think I'm cut out for an actor. Only thing is I wouldn't need a stand-in. What I'd need is a . . .'

'Sit-in,' they both said together. Then Bryan said goodbye and put down the phone.

The *Crandon Courier* was the means by which Lee, too, found out about Harry's confession. And about who his victim was. It was lunch time and Lee was coming home, cock-a-hoop, from the shopping expedition of a lifetime. None of your po-faced I'll-save-it for-the-future-Uncle-Jack stuff this time. Christ, in one night the other week he'd earned more than Mum ever did in a month. And for what? Pouring half a can of petrol through the letter box in the Patels' front door, striking a match to a page of last week's *Courier* and sticking that through the letter box too. Then scarpering, fast as his legs would go. Piece of cake. He grinned to himself, then stopped in his tracks. Rick and Danny! He hadn't meant for nothing like that to happen to them. They were his mates, the three of them went way back, since they were little kids. For a moment tears smarted at the backs of his eyes. But he wasn't a little kid no more. He blinked the tears away and pressed on. Like Uncle Jack said, he was old enough to make something of himself, old enough to help Mum out. Besides, it wasn't his fault. They should have known not to get involved in a scam without him there to direct operations. As Uncle Jack always said, when you're in business you take a risk every time you turn a corner. Lee shrugged his shoulders and hefted his laden carrier bags. Maybe if he and Mum had something left out of all this stuff, he'd take it round to Rick and Danny.

He wondered, vaguely, as he crossed the park, where Mum was. She wasn't usually gone this long, even if she really liked a new uncle. But it didn't matter. He had plenty to show her when she did get home. He'd spent a fortune. Legit shopping, all paid-for stuff, he didn't need to rob no more. He wriggled his shoulders in the brand-new puffer jacket which warmed his back. In strained fingers he clutched four plastic carriers crammed with other goodies. Trainers to die for. GAP jeans. An Arsenal sweatshirt. Perfume for Mum. And food. Pizzas, pop-tarts, pork pies, pot noodles, packets of bourbon biscuits. Mum liked bourbon biscuits. Mince pies, a mega Christmas cake, two M & S turkey dinners. While he was in M & S he couldn't resist swapping the labels on some crackers and getting a box of super-de-luxe ones for half the price. He'd bought booze too. Two bottles of wine for Mum, from the pub. Jerry O'Flaherty didn't dare refuse him after Lee's last visit and the fire at the Patels. Lee himself preferred alcopops, so he bought some of those too. He even bought Mum a bunch of flowers. He had everything they needed for Christmas, the kind of Christmas they had never had before. He crossed his fingers as he crossed the park. Because surely she'd be home soon. She'd never leave him alone on Christmas Day.

He entered the tower block and pressed the button for the lift. No need to worry about some smart-arse trying to relieve him of his consumer goodies. He had Uncle Jack to protect him now. Lift took a while to come. He read a poster taped to the wall about the forthcoming Fun Day. Little kids' stuff! He grabbed a copy of the *Crandon Courier* from the pile beside the entrance to the block. People who were paid to deliver it always dumped loads there, couldn't be bothered to carry them upstairs. If they were working for Uncle Jack they wouldn't dare bunk off like that. First page of the paper was a boring load of crap about some high-up in the Bill. The lift arrived, Lee stepped inside and pressed the button for the fifteenth floor. He dumped his bundles on the floor and turned the page. Bit of a surprise to find a pic of Harry there. What was he supposed to have done? Couldn't do anything much – the loser! Certainly couldn't do what he, Lee, had accomplished over the last few days. Then the words on the printed page sunk in. Harry had confessed to murder.

The lift stopped. Lee gathered his parcels and stumbled blindly out. Because the person Harry had confessed to killing was Mum. It was Mum that he and Rick and Danny had seen in the blazing park shelter. Mum that Lee had ordered them all to set alight.

Chapter Six

Bryan was ready for the off. It had taken him ages to decide what to wear. Ages for Edward to dress him in the outcome of his decision. Not black jeans, not his wide-brimmed black hat. What an affectation those were, Bryan thought as he discarded them. What kind of statement did he think he'd been making all these months? In a way, he'd been as bad as Marion, creating a facade which set him apart not just from the other cripples in the Centre, but also from the people in the estate, who couldn't afford to consider their image. Still, old habits die hard. In the end, his version of dressing down consisted of a pair of dark blue corduroy trousers, a pure cotton dark shirt (which Edward had to iron before Bryan was satisfied) an oiled-wool Guernsey sweater, desert boots and a dark green Burberry – in case it rained on the way. He surveyed himself in the mirror in the bedroom. For once he didn't think about how his clothes looked draped about his twisted body. He thought, did he look right for a visit to a tower block? Could he cope with a visit to a tower block? God knew, he reflected, as he instructed Edward to start the ball rolling. In other words to wheel him out of the door and across the park.

They negotiated the roadworks. Bryan was pleased to find that, as a result of Edward's letter to the council, he had a ramp all of his own (made of some sort of stippled metal) which enabled his wheelchair to cross the chasm which now separated his flat from the street. It was dusk. The nights were still drawing in. Come Christmas they'd start to lengthen again and that would be a plus. Or would it? What did it matter whether the evenings were light or dark when you had nothing of interest to occupy them? Which wasn't true. This afternoon – this evening – Bryan was sure as hell interested in what lay ahead.

They halted in the entrance to the tower block. A mean, concrete, inhuman, unfriendly space. Cold. Smelly. Dogs like Henry had probably urinated here. People had too, more than likely. Litter – beer cans; bottles; used condoms; infestations of paper; the remnants of discarded fish and chips; the polystyrene cartons which had once held take-aways – silted the corners of the place and contributed their own odour to the overall stench. No flats on the ground floor, apparently. Instead, heavy-duty metal double doors sporting a broken padlock and a notice on which Bryan read, 'Staff Only'. Below this apparently permanent warning was a more ephemeral message: 'The council apologises for the current non-functional situation in respect of your boilers. It is hoped that the situation will be rectified shortly.' Which must mean that those doors led to the boiler room, whose inanimate inhabitant, according to Gerald Tozer, was on the blink almost as often as the lifts.

Next Bryan's eyes lighted on a stack of *Crandon Couriers*, probably dumped. He had Edward wheel him over to the pile and took the top one. Given his hostess couldn't get out much, he'd be doing her a favour to deliver the paper. Oh, all right, admit it! anything to keep his mind off the ordeal ahead.

The lift stank worse than the space they had left. It was just big enough to accommodate Bryan's wheelchair and Edward, but Bryan pretended it wasn't. He had no intention of taking Edward along for the ride, having Edward witness whatever gutless reaction he, Bryan, had to the ascent.

So he instructed his carer to summon the other lift and set off on his ascent alone. As the door closed the last thing he saw was Edward's pink face screwed up in an all-consuming expression of concern.

As well it might be. The journey was a nightmare. The stinking walls pressing on either side of him, the roof seeming to bear down on him. It was interminable, it was intolerable. Only plus was that Edward wasn't there to observe his fear; Edward who had presided over all the most vulnerable moments of his life – and there had been many such moments – for almost a year now. This one he would endure alone.

But there was worse to come. The lift stopped at the fourteenth floor. Bryan was in a long, dark corridor. Alone. At the end of the corridor was a window, shielded by steel grilles. Through the reinforced glass he could see the green postage-stamp of a park below. He reeled in his chair, clutching its arms. He had been a fool to force himself to come. Apart from the involuntary dizziness from which he was suffering, what of the practicalities? Suppose Edward was stuck in the lift? Suppose he had been mugged on the way up? No one else knew Bryan was here. How on earth could he face the descent on his own? In the meantime he was horribly drawn, like an alcoholic to drink, to the window with its vertiginous view. He rallied himself by imagining what John would do were he in these circumstances. Make a joke about wishing his legs had enough feeling to be able to turn to jelly, he reckoned, and gave a swift bark of laughter which sobered him somewhat. But still the window exercised an inexorable pull. He trundled towards it.

The door of the second lift opened and, in an instant, Edward was at his side.

'Where the fuck have you been?' demanded Bryan.

'The lift stopped. Apparently it happens quite often. Kids stick things in the outer doors and then it won't let you out at the floor you want. I've been up to the top one and had to come back down.'

Gerald appeared in the corridor. Beaming. Bryan made an effort to conceal his fury. And his fear. He tried for the mundane.

'Where's Henry?' he asked.

'Had to go to the vet. Problem with his unmentionables. Comes to all of us. This is her place.' He banged hard on a red door from which the paint peeled. Number eighty two, Bryan registered, reading the two gilt numerals on the door.

A voice from within. 'Is that you, Mr T?'

'Yes, Mrs C,' trumpeted Gerald. 'She's a bit deaf,' he confided.

A clanking of chains. It was a good two minutes before they were all drawn back. But the elderly woman inside was wreathed in smiles.

'Come on in. Gerald has told me all about you. So good of him to look after Henry the way he does. You want to hear about the old days, don't you? I've got the kettle on.'

Bryan turned to Edward.

'I'll expect you back in an hour and a half sharp.'

'Oh but surely the young man,' protested his hostess, 'deserves a cup of tea. So nice to have *two* young men coming to see me.'

Bryan shook his head. 'He's got other things to do.' Which was true. Of late Bryan had become more independent around the flat, had accomplished the boiling (and timing) of his own eggs, for instance. So, over the last few days, he had set Edward to the task of cutting out silver foil stars which, unlike Bryan's efforts, actually looked like stars. Edward's mission this afternoon was, under cover of helping with preparations for the social at the Centre, to substitute Edward's perfectly executed stars for Bryan's lopsided ones. So that come the evening Bryan would not have to suffer just the indignity of being patronised because he was in a wheelchair but also the – somehow much greater – indignity of not being able to cut out proper silver foil stars.

Gerald said he'd be off as well, talking about old times wasn't his cup of tea.

Only problem was, Bryan realised as soon as the pair of them had left, the door wasn't wide enough to admit his chair. Should have realised that councils wouldn't build with the disabled in mind, not in the 1960s at any rate. For a few frustrating minutes he struggled, trying different angles of approach as though manoeuvring an awkward piece of furniture through an impossible gap, while Mrs Corke fussed around like a chicken. Finally he recalled – thank God! – how

106

Edward folded the chair when he lifted Bryan into the car, and risked half-folding it. He managed to effect entry. Mrs Corke led the way along the corridor. 'I mightn't be the best person to ask, either,' she confessed. 'I'm a bit forgetful.'

Bryan found it difficult, given his recent ordeal, to make soothing noises, but he did. And then he registered the room into which she ushered him. It was like a room in a country cottage, inhabited by one of Miss Marple's retired house-maids. There were huge, overstuffed chintz chairs. A patterned sofa deep enough to wallow in. Little tables and whatnots here, there and everywhere, their surfaces teeming with photos in frames, cottage teapots, china shire horses with chains around their necks, crude pottery dogs with thin leather collars, bowls, toby jugs, shells, bits of rock, sundry other artefacts all labelled with a present from somewhere or other. On the walls were framed tea towels. 'A horse's prayer', he read on one of them, 'A dog's dream', on another. The other things on the walls were decorative plates bearing legends about leprechauns and Devon pixies. The place reminded him of that of a godmother he'd last seen way back when. But she'd had a spacious flat in an expensively converted Tudor mansion. And her stuff was for real, was insured for umpteen thousands. The tat on display here couldn't be worth, in total, more than a couple of hundred at a push.

'What an amazing room,' Bryan managed. 'I'd never have believed anyone could make it so homely up here.'

'Of course, it's warmer when the heating works. It's on the blink at the moment. But that doesn't worry me too much. The electric fire,' she pointed to a two-bar job, 'keeps this room cosy. Thank you, dear,' she went on. 'I'm very fond of it myself.' She poured two cups of tea. Bryan took a sip from his. It was strong and dark and bitter, as though it had been stewing for far too long. 'All my little treasures,' Mrs Corke went on. 'And the view from my window. I could look out there all day and never be bored. It's such a pity we're in a hat.'

He looked at her silver wisps of uncovered hair. 'In a what?'

'Short for a Housing Action Trust. Means they're going to move us all out. Pull the block down. Build us little new houses with gardens. I'd hate to have a garden. What would I do with it?'

'Well,' supposed Bryan, 'you could always grow plants.'

'Oh, stop it! Me? Never had a garden in my life. Don't want one either. Messy things, full of worms and pests.' She shuddered. 'They're decanting us, they say. Turning us out of our homes. Floor by floor. Top floor was scheduled to be empty months ago. But there's still,' she stopped and jabbed a finger at the ceiling, 'people up there.'

'Who?'

'You can bet your bottom dollar the council don't know they're there. Have a piece of bread and butter.' He took one. 'Must eat your bread and butter and your sandwiches,' she continued, 'that's what my mother said, before you take any cake. Mind you, she always served cake on a stand. With doilies. Can't run to doilies these days. We used to have iced fancies on Sundays and plain cake every other day of the week. Is that the sort of thing you want to know?'

'Absolutely. About the top floor. Wouldn't the utilities have been cut off? And the doors boarded up?'

'Utilities? Oh you mean the gas and the electric. There's ways round that. Almost anyone on this estate would know how. I've seen 'em at it. And as for a bit of board, that never stopped 'em. Of course, in those days we didn't have the electric, only the gas. Used to have to share a bathroom with five other families, would you believe it? I went into service when I was sixteen, the first of us to bring in any money. Six of us in one room. Wasn't a patch on what I've got here. Can I give you a refill?'

Bryan shook his head.

'You're allowed a sandwich now you've finished your bread and butter. They're fish paste.' Bryan took one and swallowed it hastily, hoping his distaste for the nasty little morsel didn't show on his face.

'Won't you find it easier being on the ground floor?' he persisted. 'So that you can get out and about?'

'So nice to see a young man with an appetite.' She pressed the plate on him again. 'Go on, do. No, I'd much rather have my view. Mind you, I do get out sometimes. When the lifts are working. Of course, we didn't have lifts when I was a girl. But then there weren't so many stairs.'

'What sort of thing d'you see from the window?'

'All sorts. You wouldn't imagine the comings and goings. Kids mainly. Make my life a misery, some of them do, pounding up and down the stairs at all hours, banging on my door and then running away. You'd think they'd have something better to do. I blame the parents. Take my mother. She didn't have an easy life. Father died just after the miners' strike. But she brought us up strict, she did. That's what I told the police when they came here. But they didn't want to know.'

The miners' strike? Had she got her dates mixed up? Surely her father couldn't have been alive in the 1980s?

'1926,' she announced with sudden, startling precision. 'I was lucky that way myself, didn't lose Ron until a few years ago. Went right through the war without a scratch. He was an air warden. Up all night putting out fires. Could have done with him the other week.'

'You saw the fire in the park? Did you see who started it?'

'That's what I'm saying. The kids. Nice lads at heart. Those two, anyway. I told you, didn't I, how I went out?'

'What, before the lifts broke down?'

'No, after. Just the other day really. The one day the lifts did work. Took the opportunity to get a few groceries. They won't deliver these days, you know. Can't say I blame them with all these stairs. Anyway. Reminded me of the time we used to do Good Deeds. Miss told us about that in Sunday School. We used to sit in rows on wooden benches, very hard they were on your backside. Sometimes we were allowed to colour in pictures of people from the Bible. I liked the ones of the baby Jesus best, but we only got those at Christmas. And a toffee each.'

'What sort of good deeds?'

'Helping elderly people across the road, that's the thing I remember.'

'Is that what the boys did for you?'

'Oh no.'

'But it was a good deed?'

'Oh yes. There's good in everyone, I always say.'

'And they started the fire?'

She nodded. 'Just like the Germans. But that was different. You could see the whole of London lit up. I used to hold my little Violet up to the window to watch. Not this window, of course. I didn't live here then.'

'D'you know where *they* live?'

She shook her head. 'You don't know your neighbours like you used to. Now what else can I tell you?'

Bryan recalled that he was supposed to be interested in 'the old days', asked a few questions about life during the war, listened patiently to the rambling answers, then returned to the real subject of his interest.

'What about their names?'

'Whose names?'

'The two boys who started the fire.'

'I didn't say it was two of them.'

Impatience rose in Bryan's throat like a high tide. He swallowed it. Okay, so in his previous life he'd have had anyone with Mrs Corke's magpie mind for breakfast. But his current line of enquiry required rather different skills.

'So was it a gang?'

'That's what they call them nowadays. Call themselves it, some of them. Makes them feel braver, I daresay. My mother always said there was safety in numbers. Used to send our little Frank out with me and Dora. One of us would hoist him on our hip and we'd be away. It was down to the Silk Stream in those days. Used to do pretend fishing for hours.

110

With a branch and a piece of string. Or just lie in the long grass and look at the sky. Never caught anything, of course. But we'd come back tired and happy with little Frank asleep.'

'Did the two boys have a smaller one – like little Frank – with them?'

'Like Frank? He's never like Frank.'

'Who isn't?'

'Him. Mother's no better than she should be either. Leaves him alone all hours. They should put a stop to it. After all, there's enough of them poking and prying.'

Bryan decided to ignore the extra characters – the 'they' – who had muscled in on a narrative already peopled by a bewilderingly large cast of characters. Presumably 'they' were social workers and the like. 'So you do know who he is?'

'Of course I do. He lives up there.' And she jabbed her finger once more towards the ceiling. Bryan began to wonder whether anyone actually did live on the fifteenth floor or whether she was referring, with olde-worlde delicacy, to people who had ascended rather higher, to meet their Maker. Or whether she was simply off her trolley.

He coaxed her back onto the subject. He tried to get her to say if she'd seen anything untoward earlier on the afternoon of the fire. But she interpreted 'earlier' as 60-odd years ago and started telling him stories of laying fires in living room grates and of a cast-iron kitchen range which had to be black-leaded every day and which, if the chimneys weren't swept regular, could 'catch' and belch clouds of smoke. Not to mention burning the missus's dinner.

Bryan tried another tack. He produced the copy of the *Crandon Courier* he'd brought up in the lift. Did she know the sad, seedy man in the picture? She nodded. 'There's another one of them as is upstairs. Or was.' Which was beginning to sound like a standard reply to anyone he asked about. Fair enough, one of the protagonists in the drama in which he was interested might be lurking, illegally, on the supposedly empty fifteenth floor of a tower block. But not practically everyone who was in the frame. He'd take everything Mrs Corke said with a pinch of salt. And then some.

Lee was still crying, knuckles pressed into his eyes, body curled into foetal position. He hadn't switched the light on when he came in, not even the TV, just dropped the stuff he was holding and collapsed on the sofa. Great, painful sobs spasmed his chest like hiccups. He was bawling out loud; the sound of it filled the room, it seemed to come from someone else; and every new assault it made on his ears triggered a fresh onslaught of hysteria. Then he was screaming like the tabby cat on which he had scored a direct hit with a sparkler on Bonfire Night.

Bonfire Night! Fires! The vision of Mum upright in the park shelter, flames crackling round her figure, flashed across his retinas. He crammed his right fist, hard, into his mouth and bit on it. The pain sobered him, exhausted him.

He must have fallen asleep. Because it was pitch dark. For a moment he lay peaceful and warm, making a silent inventory of the goodies he had bought, anticipating the Christmas he and Mum would have. He listened to the familiar creak of the front door opening. That would be her! He'd known all along that she wouldn't stay away for Christmas. Then he remembered. Mum was dead. And he had killed her.

This time, no wracking outburst of grief followed that thought. He felt sick. He wasn't warm, he was deathly cold. He didn't move, though he was panicky and desperate to escape. Escape was what he always did when there was a ruck going down. Scarper. Leg it. That was the way he operated. He stuffed his knuckles into his mouth again. Fresh tears, silent ones this time, spilled from his eyes, ran across his nose and soaked into the already damp cushions. There was no one to run to now.

The light snapped on, a sudden glare, making his eyes smart.

'Well what have we here?' Uncle Jack loomed over him, then crossed the room and switched on the TV. A swaying row of black people in red robes swam into focus. They were singing Revivalist renderings of Christmas carols.

'Got the right idea about what to do with your earnings, haven't you?' Uncle Jack was eyeing the bulging carrier bags strewn around the room. 'Going to have a cracking Christmas by the look of it. Mum still not home?'

Lee managed to shake his head.

'Not to worry. You can have Christmas dinner with me and Tanya. Tanya always does us proud. Brandy butter, the lot. All the trimmings. Are those crackers?' Lee nodded.

'Bring 'em with you when you come. Someone to meet you,' Uncle Jack went on. 'Policeman. Heard quite a bit about you. Could be quite a fan of yours if you play your cards right. Always pays to get on the right side of a policeman, know what I mean, Lee?'

Lee nodded again. He tried to focus on the man behind Uncle Jack. He was the same height as Uncle Jack. He was as heavily built as Uncle Jack. He wore the same sort of clothes as Uncle Jack. But his features were hazy, fogged by the film of Lee's tears.

Lee struggled to sit up. 'Mum's not coming home. Ever. I killed her.'

Uncle Jack raised his eyebrows at the man behind him. He laid a large, warm hand on Lee's shoulder.

'Whatever gave you that idea?'

'It was in the paper. Mum's dead.'

Uncle Jack raised his brows again. 'Fraid she is, lad. Would have told you before, but Tanya said better not. Women know more about that sort of thing. So I didn't.'

'It says Harry killed her. Harry couldn't hurt a fly.' Which was true. Lee'd come across Harry often enough, down in the park, poking at a beetle or a ladybird that had got stuck on its back, trying to turn it right way up so it could fly away. Lee always went up and stomped on the insect before it had a chance to escape. 'Besides, it was me.'

The policeman muscled in. '*I* say he killed her. Your Uncle Jack says he killed her. And that's got to be good enough for you. Right?'

'Lay off,' said Uncle Jack, 'the kid's upset. Get your arse next door, there's beer in the fridge. Now then,' he turned back to Lee. 'I'm sure Tanya'd know what to do, but I sure as fuck don't. And she's out. Christmas shopping. Women! Oh, sorry, lad.' He gripped Lee's shoulder tightly in his fist.

'Got any booze in all this lot?' he went on.

Lee nodded. 'Wine. For Mum.' He gagged over her name.

'So what we'll do is we'll open it. I bet you even thought to buy a corkscrew.'

Lee nodded again. Uncle Jack found the corkscrew and did the honours. He folded Lee's fists around a coffee mug full of wine.

'Not my normal style, encouraging under-age drinking.' Uncle Jack, Lee realised, was trying to make a joke. Not funny. But he took a gulp of wine. Felt weird. Bitter. How come Mum liked it? Mum, he thought, and the tears pricked at his eyes again.

He tried to speak. His voice came out as a whisper. 'I burned up the shelter. She was in it.'

Uncle Jack's hand was on his shoulder once more. 'You heard what the man said. Harry confessed. Doesn't matter what you burned, she'd already snuffed it. Thing about Harry is that, even on a good day, he can't remember half of what he's done. Now is that booze going down the hatch or what?'

Lee nodded again. The wine was fire in his throat. But if Uncle Jack said he ought to drink it, then he supposed he should.

'Hey,' said Uncle Jack, 'know how old your Uncle Jack was when he lost his mum?' Lee shook his head. He didn't care. He took another gulp of wine. At least he wasn't cold any more.

114

'Let's say a damn sight younger than you. And what did he do about it?' Lee didn't know. 'He got on with things, that's what. Didn't pussyfoot about thinking what might have been. Looked to the future. Made himself serious money. Could have bought his old woman everything she wanted if she'd had the sense to stay alive. But she didn't. In the end, lad, it has to be water under the bridge.'

The policeman returned with a six-pack. He and Uncle Jack took one each and cracked them open.

Lee's stomach was warm now. A fuzzy warmth which crept all over his body.

'No need for you to worry,' Uncle Jack told him, 'I'll see you right, no problems. We'll make a man of you yet. Want to be a man like your Uncle Jack, don't you?' And Lee agreed.

He sat on the floor. The wreckage of his Christmas was spread out around him. Didn't matter. He took another slurp of wine. Uncle Jack was going to look after him, wasn't he? Nothing mattered. He leaned against the sofa and listened to the two men.

'So,' said Uncle Jack. 'Looks like we've got your bastard of a Chief Inspector sorted.'

Banks laughed. 'After tonight he'll pack his bags and get back to where he came from. Here's to us. Which mob are you getting to do the dirty?'

'Less you know, less likely you are to let anything slip.'

'Would I hell?'

'Let's just say it's all fixed. Job for bigger boys than our lad here. Should cause a major dust-up. Not just in the *Crandon Courier*, either.'

'You're not getting involved yourself?'

'Won't be anywhere near the place. Cast-iron alibi. And you'd better be down at the nick.'

They drank another can each. Uncle Jack told Lee to keep his pecker up. Said Tanya should be home any minute, he had only to go next door. He treated Lee to another squeeze on the shoulder. Then the two men left.

5 pm. DCI Dawson had finally got a handle on what to do next. In his years at the Yard he'd dubbed it the 'on the side of the typist' style of management. Get to know the people at the bottom of the pile, get them on your side and you're laughing. Well, even if you're not laughing, you'll find out everything you want to know. And you'll get routine tasks accomplished far more quickly than if you issue instructions through the proper chain of command. So he'd arranged to replace Dosh on evening patrol. He was going out with Constable Paul Hindmarsh, the newest recruit in Crandon, the fresh-faced youngster. Dawson planned to show Hindmarsh what real policing was; let him see how to do things Dawson's way and eventually high standards would percolate their way up the ladder.

'What have we got on tonight, lad?' he asked as he slid into the passenger seat.

'We're to demonstrate a visible presence in the mall, sir,' Hindmarsh announced, in a tone loud enough for a concert hall, 'at the scene of the prior incident at the retail outlet owned by the Patels as a deterrent to further crime. We're to make ourselves further visible by a slow patrol of the entire estate. Then we're to drive past the Community Centre. There's a Christmas social on there. Vulnerable people. We are to patrol in the vicinity of the premises on two occasions during the course of the evening. In between we're to proceed in a south-westerly direction and patrol the perimeter of Carleton Park.'

In other words, a routine Crandon night, Dawson decided, as he clicked his seat belt closed. Which should give him plenty of time to get to know Constable Hindmarsh.

5.30 pm. Lee was alone. He was restless. Uncle Jack had assured him he'd look after him, so that was all right. But there was a cold void in his stomach which might be hunger – given he'd eaten nothing all day. But he didn't want to eat, not alone. He wanted to show someone all the things he'd bought,

bought with money he'd earned for himself. He wanted someone to envy what he had, to ooh and aah, to be impressed. Tanya? He tried her door, but she was still out. Rick and Danny? Nah. It would have been all right to go round bearing gifts like one of those sodding kings in the Bible. But he didn't feel like a king. Felt like shit. Besides, last time he'd knocked at Danny's door Danny's mum peered out of the window, saw who it was and made threatening gestures for him to clear off. Rick's dad had done the same at his place. Rick and Danny wouldn't have squealed, Lee knew they wouldn't dare. Nor would Danny's mum or Rick's dad go to the police, no one did in Crandon. But Rick and Danny must have said just enough for the families to make sure Lee came nowhere near them. So where could he go? Lee thought for a moment. Aunt Suzy's, that's where. Aunt Suzy was Mum's best friend and she lived on the other side of the estate. He remembered his last stay – when Mum had been in Holloway – in Aunt Suzy's warm, bright, untidy flat. This time of year the flat would have a Christmas tree with winking, wonky lights. It would have paper chains and tinsel and Aunt Suzy would be run off her feet, or so she said every couple of minutes. What would she be doing? She might be painting her nails, he decided, or drying her hair. Or ironing; the scent of warm, damp fabric overlying the persistent, homely smells of food and nappies and chocolate and cheap perfume. He would show her his new clothes, he would take her a present, perhaps even something for the younger kids. She would bawl at all of them to be quiet while she admired what he had brought. She would feel the warmth of the puffer jacket, smooth the expensive fabric of his sweatshirt. She would run a hand through his hair and say what a big lad he was these days, earning his own living, would you credit it? Then she would clear a space on the crowded kitchen table and fry up a huge panful of luscious, aromatic chips. Crisp and brown on the outside, soft and hot and white inside. He licked his lips. At Aunt Suzy's he would want to eat.

He dressed quickly in his new gear. He trawled the litter on the floor for the second bottle of wine and the perfume. He tucked the box of M & S crackers inside his jacket. Then he sped away across the estate. It was freezing cold, but he was warm in the comfort of his new clothes and in the certainty of the welcome which lay ahead.

6 pm. Bryan hadn't bothered to change his clothes. Figured what was good enough for braving a tower block was good enough for the Centre's Christmas social. He did change his wheelchair, though. Figured the new one Edward had ordered to his specifications could have its first outing. It was a chair for a disabled athlete – he wasn't in that league yet, but no harm in aiming high. It had a narrow, lightweight frame, slim, relatively quiet rubber-clad wheels and was easy to propel under his own steam, particularly since he had been working out over the last couple of weeks and had a good deal more strength in his upper body. Wasn't up to the strength he would have liked, but he was certainly strong enough to propel himself around the Centre for a few hours. At the door of the Centre he said goodbye to Edward, giving him strict instructions to return by 8 pm.

The Centre was decked out with Christmas finery – which wasn't all that different from its usual, depressing 'displays' except that everything today was red and gold and green and silver instead of its everyday hotchpotch of clashing colours. Plus there were twisted chains of crêpe paper hanging in uneven festoons from corners of the room. The end of a red one had come adrift from the piece of Sellotape with which Kenny had anchored it in place; the length of chain dangled forlornly like an outsize, detumescent penis. None of the Centre users took much notice of the festive decorations, they'd spent too many hours forcing their cramped fingers to make the damned things in the first place. But everyone else – the guests – oohed and aahed and generally expressed admiration as though this bunch of cripples had achieved an effect

118

worthy of a photo-feature in the *Sunday Times* Style section. They were particularly impressed with the neat silver stars mounted on a red board and labelled with Bryan's name.

Marion was presiding over the refreshments. She was wearing a long, dull-red dress which clung to her figure. It had a low, scooped neck which showed off the curve of her boobs, and the fluid drape of expensive fabric which drifted round her ankles was split on one side to reveal an expanse of thigh every time she moved. In her ears were small gold hoops. Her slim fingers flashed gold and emerald rings. Elizabeth Hurley, eat your heart out! The contrast between Marion's perfection and the twisted shapes of the Centre users couldn't have been more dramatic. Bloody bitch did it on purpose, was Bryan's view.

Marion was serving curls of cardboard sandwiches, slices of shop-bought Christmas cake, reheated Mr Kipling mince pies and polystyrene cups of tea. Not much of a treat when you're accustomed to expense-account French cuisine and decent wines. Besides, Bryan had had enough of scraps of pappy rubbish masquerading as food during his afternoon with Mrs Corke. He shook his head at Marion and turned away.

Didn't take long to suss what his role – the role of all the Centre users – was at this affair. Marion had informed them in advance – in her most serious voice, with her most po-faced expression – that they were to be the hosts and hostesses and added what a great responsibility that was. More like an honour really, given the Mayor was coming. Honour, fuck! The Centre users' role this evening was to provide living, breathing, crippled evidence of the generosity – in terms of time, money, career choice, whatever – of all those others present. Their role was to sit submissively, smile when spoken to, and to praise the facilities and the activities on offer at the Centre to all who asked about them. Bryan watched Marion introduce Karen to some condescending git in a suit with smarmed-back black hair. Watched Karen look up at him with her sweet smile and felt the same black, venomous hatred towards Marion as he had on the day she first asked him to contribute to the making of the Christmas decorations. But he said nothing untoward, he smiled and nodded and shook hands just like all the others. He was biding his time.

The important thing about his perfect crime, he thought as he watched Marion drift around the room doing her Lady Bountiful act with all and sundry, was not to implicate anyone else. Or, at least, if they were implicated, they must be able to be cleared of suspicion quite quickly. If the police were bright enough, they ought to be able to follow the trail to Bryan. He wouldn't cheat, he would leave enough clues. That guy – the DCI who had given the talk at the Centre – ought to have the brains to suss the whole thing out. And what if he did suss it out? Bryan recalled that day in the Activity Room at the Centre when he had looked round the group of Centre users and thought that anyone of them – himself included – would be better put out of their misery. So what did it matter if they tracked him down? His life couldn't be much worse than it was now. After all, people didn't get hanged these days. Going to prison could hardly be more of a culture shock than the one he had already suffered. He wondered if there were many people in wheelchairs in prisons. Didn't seem to be in any of the news footage he'd seen. So, would there be lifts? If not, he expected they could accommodate him in a ground floor cell.

He shook off his reflections and approached Karen and the besuited guy. Turned out the little twerp – he couldn't be more than twenty five – was photographer-cum-reporter for the *Courier*. Bryan told him crisply exactly what he thought of his most recent effort, then turned away again. His new wheelchair was proving a godsend in terms of making a swift exit from conversations in which he no longer had an interest. Figured he'd christen it 'the party animal' and use it for all such future occasions.

Then the Mayor made an entrance. She was so short and broad she was almost a cube on legs. Her regalia clanked as she moved: a great, gold chain dangled round her neck, at the end of which reposed, on the awesome plateau of her bosom, a big badge of office. A small nobody of a female followed this personage. Someone from the Town Hall's Committee Secretariat, Bryan decided, noting the short, mousey hair, the spectacles, the hand-knitted, bobbly sweater and the drooping skirt the colour of dung. Daresay the Mayor couldn't get her proper secretary to turn out out of hours; especially for an occasion as piddling as this.

And here was the creative writing tutor who had lasted only one session at the Centre. Bryan wheeled gladly up to her.

'Hi, Jill.' She didn't stand over him, but dumped herself on a chair so they were both at the same height.

'Hi, Bryan. Marion tells me you're hooked on whodunnits.' She tugged nervously at the pocket of her jeans. 'Am I allowed to smoke in here? Given it's a party.'

'Bet your life you're not. I was. Hooked, I mean.'

'So which sleuth would you be? Supposing you could?'

'Hercule Poirot. He doesn't rush around following up clues, detecting things. He just sits back in his chair and lets his little grey cells do the walking. That's me. Can't do anything else but sit, can I?'

'How come you've stopped being hooked?'

'These days I'm planning my own crime.'

She didn't get a chance to respond to that. Because the Mushy Pea Company erupted – tumbling, juggling, somersaulting – into the Activity Room. They were singing some sort of jolly song which, as far as Bryan could gather, was about the joy of picking flowers. It was a pity John had missed this, he reflected. Actually, it was the other way round, Bryan was missing John, could have done with his levity to puncture the seriousness with which the occasion was taking itself.

Certainly the Head of Centre was taking it very seriously indeed. He called for silence. He ushered the Mayor into the centre of the assembled company. He waved to Marion and she began to marshal all the Centre users into a group behind the Mayor.

'For the photo opportunity,' she informed Bryan. 'Come along, get in line.'

'Not on your life.' Okay, so only a hack from the *Crandon Courier* was here and few of Bryan's friends from his past life would ever come across that rag. But suppose they did? A chilly frisson stiffened the hairs on the back of his neck. Christ, imagine them seeing what he, successful Bryan Greyshott, was reduced to these days. No way would he let that happen. He made his excuses. And though Marion reproached him, said he ought to join in, there were too many other cripples lining up for the honour for her to have the time to persist. And his new wheelchair made a speedy getaway a doddle.

The tableau was quite a set piece in its small-time way. The photographer was making a big deal about taking light readings, setting up his equipment. The Mayor opened her mouth to begin, but he silenced her. First he had to set up a sort of silver umbrella behind her. All utterly unnecessary, thought Bryan, who had seen decent photographers at work in the past.

At last the Mayor began. With a load of smarmy, do-goody stuff about the value of the Centre to its users, what wonderful work was being done here and so on. She pointed out that – on the downside – decisions on funding applications weren't made until the end of the financial year, but that on the basis of what she had seen so far today . . . Not that the Grants Sub Committee hadn't a difficult choice to make. They'd be looking at applications from the Bengali Action people, the Afro-Caribbean Alliance, the Asian Community Federation, The Irish Pensioners Group, the Senior Citizens' Forum – all eminently worthy causes. Bryan's mind wandered.

He watched Marion. She was still standing beside the other cripples, behind the Mayor, holding them in readiness for when they might next be called upon to smile sweetly or to say their piece. Stupid, patronising cow!

'Not that they haven't competition, too,' the Mayor was saying. She paused and adjusted her badge of office to a more comfortable position on her ample boobs. 'The Gay Men's Woodworking Centre. The Lesbian hang-gliding project.' Bryan blenched. 'And on a personal note . . .' she beckoned her nondescript female acolyte to her side. 'For the benefit of the media,' the Mayor went on, addressing its one representative, the photographer from the *Courier*, 'Maureen and I are partners. Lesbian partners,' she added. 'And though I've been married for twenty-five years, this is the occasion of our coming out.'

Nice one, John, thought Bryan. Inspired guess, mate. Then, no accounting for taste, he added to himself. On either side.

The photographer was cock a-hoop. It was a local news coup, no less. He tried to persuade Ms Dung Skirt and the Mayor to a) hold hands b) put their arms around each other c) gaze into each other's eyes. He couldn't care a rap about the cripples now.

But the Mayor quelled him with one upraised hand.

'Parasites,' she said.

'Pardon?' The photographer was homing in for a closer shot.

'The media. The press. All you're interested in is dirt.' Her face turned grim. 'This is a serious announcement and my partner is Chair of the Media Consultative Committee of Crandon Council,' she reached for Maureen's hand, 'so if you don't get it right, you'll be looking at a court appearance.'

The Mayor paused for a moment. 'You'll be looking at damages,' she continued, still clutching Maureen's hand. 'I've struggled with this for years. Joel is ten now, and old enough to understand. And my husband, Phil is, well, Phil is,' Maureen visibly squeezed her hand. 'Phil isn't . . .' The Mayor stopped.

There was a seriously uncomfortable hiatus. The Mushy Pea Group ended it by taking centre stage. First they sang another jolly song. Then they introduced each improvisation with a brief history of its genesis and of the background of its

123

performers. Bryan watched a smiling Karen ('rarely ever offered an opinion of her own before our drama therapy,' vouchsafed one of the green-clad mob) enact a sequence which was incomprehensible without John to give it its salacious tinge. Then it was his and Kenny's turn.

'Bryan came to us,' intoned one of the Mushy Peas to accompanying background music of a vaguely oriental turn, 'in the aftermath of a serious accident which put paid to a promising career.' What was this? How the fuck did they know that? Who had decided that records which surely should be confidential were now a matter of public knowledge? Marion, of course. He shot a look at her. She stood, smiling smugly. Not for much fucking longer if he had his way.

But in the meantime he couldn't disappoint Kenny. Kenny was already well into his version of being the sea. So well into it that a particularly exuberant wave (Kenny) smacked sundry pebbles (Bryan) hard on the cheek and left him smarting. He fingered his cheek, wondered whether pebbles could retaliate and . . . all hell broke loose. The Centre was full of kids.

Dawson wasn't making much progress with Hindmarsh. Tried to put him at his ease by asking him how he was finding the work, then gradually bringing him round to a few friendly questions about his family, that sort of thing. But it was no go. The lad refused to express any opinions at all and kept his lip tightly buttoned about his personal life. Dawson thought that perhaps he was overawed by the presence of so senior an officer and redoubled his efforts. But whatever the enquiry, Hindmarsh replied only in the most formal of police jargon. Guy sounded as though he'd swallowed a training manual whole. In the end Dawson decided it was a form of defence against his youth and inexperience. Bet his bottom dollar he was being bullied in the nick. Par for the course and he'd have to learn to ride the storm.

They all had to go through it; Dawson himself had many years ago.

'Are we due at the Community Centre yet?' Hindmarsh nodded and turned the car in its direction.

'Anyone in particular making it hard for you in the nick? DC Banks for instance?'

They were in the mall now, the steel-grilled shops on either side.

'Well, sir, he is in command, isn't he?'

Which was news to Dawson – *he* was in command, but he let it ride.

At which point a small figure erupted out of the dark, with something clutched in either hand. Looked like a couple of bottles, could be a couple of weapons. For a short second the figure was silhouetted in the glare of the car's headlights. Then it took off.

'Worth investigating, sir? asked Hindmarsh, pressing his foot on the accelerator.

'Absolutely. Everything is worth investigating. Good police work leaves no stone unturned. Stop!' And Hindmarsh jammed on the brakes, flung open the door and hit the ground running. Dawson followed more slowly.

Lee was legging it. He'd found Aunt Suzy's flat in darkness. There was no one there. Still clutching the wine and the perfume, he set off back across the estate. He was going home. There was nowhere else to go. But he desperately needed to show someone – anyone – how powerful he was. He ran on, faster and faster; that, in itself, showed how powerful he was. If Mum, if Aunt Suzy, if Uncle Jack could see him now they'd know he could run his way out of anything. He was running so fast he ran directly into the beam of the headlights of a car. A police car, he realised, as he saw by the dim streetlights the stripes along its sides. He accelerated to a sprint. Didn't matter whether they had anything on him, he wasn't waiting to find out.

It took Bryan no more than a few seconds – the reflexes in the parts of his body that still worked were as good as ever – to realise that the gang of kids who'd invaded the Centre weren't here to applaud Kenny's efforts to convey the roll and swell of the English Channel to his audience. To note, too, that they weren't little kids like the ones who usually sat on the wall outside the Centre. These were great louts of boys almost as big and certainly as strong as men. Some wielded impromptu weapons: a thick chain, the neck of a broken bottle, even a shotgun which Bryan was fairly sure was a replica, but whose butt end could still do serious damage. And they were headed not for him, not for the able-bodied either, but, as though they had been given instructions, for the most vulnerable people in the room: for Kenny, Mr D and Laura. Bryan watched in sick horror as Kenny went down, squealing and flailing in a forest of punching fists and kicking feet. He turned his eyes up to the able-bodied people; they were retreating, as fast as they could, to the Pottery Room, the Gardening Room, the Art Room. He could expect nothing from them, when could he ever?

And the photographer – cruel, callous bastard – was actually taking pictures of Kenny and Mr D as they fell.

No one ever knows what they'll do in a situation like this, when they're face to face with violence, violation. You can discuss it all you like, ask a police officer like Dawson what he'd recommend. But when it comes to the real thing, theory and reason both fly out the window and your reaction is the instinctive, unthinking reflex of a wild animal under attack. Bryan's reaction was one of pure, ungovernable rage, rage which impelled him to act. He couldn't reach the phone – the Centre's office was on the far side of the mêlée. Instead he spun his chair away from the gang, all the way to the further wall of the Activity Room, then spun again and paused. The fracas had moved on towards the door of the Pottery Room. Only two youths – the ones battering Kenny – stood in his path. He launched himself towards them, hands working furiously on the wheels of his athlete's chair, gaining momentum so fast that to the able-bodied watchers his wheels seemed no more than two blurs of speed. Until the last second he had surprise on his side, but in that second his mouth opened and emitted the furious, red roar of a baited bull. He was still bellowing as he cannoned into the shins of the two youths. They both went down with a startled 'Ouf!' Bryan nearly lost his balance, nearly fell forward from his chair, recovered himself with a strength he hadn't thought he had, sashayed round the two boys in an instant, was in the Centre's office, had slammed and locked the door and punched out 999 on the phone. He managed to steady his voice enough to order an ambulance and the police. He returned to the fray.

There wasn't one. The youths had retreated, swept out of the Centre the way they had entered, and the able-bodied guests were creeping out of the various rooms in which they had sheltered, like voles from their holes. Bryan's fury was unabated, now it was directed at them. He sat, panting and swearing, bellowing, incoherent. Marion started to make soothing noises and he struck out at her with the back of his hand. She side-stepped. Only Jill had the sense to start removing debris from Kenny's prone form, to check his pulse and to direct the others to lift Mr D back into his chair and to see if Karen had been injured by shards from her shattered silver screen.

'Oh dear.' Marion was shaking, ineffectual, 'I'll call an ambulance.'

Bryan wasn't about to tell her he'd already done that. He still couldn't speak clearly through the choking phlegm of anger which clogged his throat. And he wanted to make her sweat. He dogged her footsteps to the office. But it was already occupied, the phone was already commandeered, by the photographer.

'News desk,' the guy was saying into the phone. He drummed his fingers impatiently on the Head of Centre's desk. 'Give me the desk editor. Yeah. Sure. Been stringing for him for years.' He paused and waited. 'Lew? Got a great story for you. Pics as well. The unacceptable face of hooliganism. Not much else to run with have you, this time of year? Make a great contrast to the usual Christmas crap. Sure, I've got a close-up of the bruising on the old guy's face.'

Trash, thought Bryan, that's what this guy was. The utter, fucking pits. Marion totally lost her cool and started screaming at the photographer.

'I have to use the phone. To call an ambulance.'

'Piss off,' he responded. Marion grabbed his arm and shook it like a terrier worrying a shoe. He shrugged her off. 'They're holding the front page, you silly bitch. This is the big time for me. I'm on to the nationals.' He shot her a venomous look. 'Go find your own phone.'

She looked helplessly at Bryan.

He could manage – just – to speak real words now. He could have reassured her, but he didn't. He saw that his opportunity had come. Not to achieve a perfectly planned, cold-blooded, bloodless crime. Not to indulge in any arid, academic exercise. But to satisfy the lust he now felt for revenge. Against everyone who could walk. Against the nurses in the hospital. Against his friends who'd visited him there. Against Edward. Against the Mayor, the Head of Centre, the Mushy Pea mob. Against anyone who was concerned, compassionate, patronising, dismissive, anyone who treated him, them – the Centre users – as some form of lower life. And particularly against the physically perfect, stupid, silly Marion.

'Do what the bastard says,' he growled. 'Forget what he's done for the moment. The police'll get him for it eventually. There's a phone in the mall, isn't there?'

She took off at a run, rust-red fabric flying back from shapely legs.

Bryan threaded his way swiftly back through the debris in the Activity Room. Jill appeared to have organised everyone and was administering the best she could do in the way of first aid. Kenny – thank God! – was now sitting up, bleating, blood pouring down his face. Mr D was being supported in his chair. Two of the Mushy Pea people were cradling Laura in their arms. No one noticed as Bryan scooped up a discarded crutch and pursued Marion outside.

Chapter Seven

Constable Paul Hindmarsh was the arresting officer. Stood to reason, given he was the first one at the scene of the crime. Could hardly believe his eyes. A guy in a wheelchair wielding an offensive weapon and at the guy's feet – Constable Hindmarsh clocked what was there, turned aside and gagged, then turned back to do his duty. The body on the ground was that of a young woman, but the face was no face at all. It had been smashed in.

Paul knew the drill from umpteen procedural practices, but he'd never carried it out for real. He stumbled over the words of the caution. Then he unsnapped the handcuffs from his belt with shaking fingers. The murderer laid down his weapon, offered his wrists and Paul imprisoned them in the steel ringlets. There! It was done. Paul looked around him a little wildly, wondering what came next.

Two cars screeched to a halt. The CID Guvnor leapt from one, DC Banks and Dosh from the other. Paul consulted his notebook – in which he'd had no time to make any notes – then tried to give a coherent account of events so far.

But DCI Dawson wasn't waiting to hear him out.

'Get the area sealed,' he instructed Paul. 'Get onto SOCO. And the pathologist. Get me more troops. And an ambulance.' At which point one drew up.

'Not a bad response time after all,' said the guy in the wheelchair. 'I can't have called more than five minutes ago. Same goes for you lot. I'm really quite impressed.'

'*You* called?' DC Banks was incredulous. He was all for taking the guy in then and there. But DCI Dawson shook his head. No false starts this time. He wanted an absolutely watertight case before he made his move. Besides which, this was the guy who'd been so clued up the day Dawson'd given his talk at the Centre. Probably knew his rights inside out.

Certainly he was now dismissing the patrol car with a wave of his hand and demanding to be taken to the station in transport which would accommodate his wheelchair.

'Could have got there under my own steam,' the man informed them, 'but I've given my carer a couple of hours off. He's taken the car. Though he should be back,' he consulted his watch, 'in another couple of minutes.'

Dawson overruled Banks's attempt to bully the suspect into being hefted from his chair into the car. He listened, concealing his impatience, to the man's questions about disabled access at the station, whether there was an adapted loo and, finally, to his suggestion that, as he was unlikely to be able to flee the country, they allow him to return home for the night and question him further in the morning. The suspect added that he would be perfectly prepared to put up any reasonable amount of bail, should that be deemed necessary. Dawson made a swift decision. It was true the guy was hardly likely to be going anywhere. Better by far to interview him after he'd heard what any witnesses had to say. When he had the facts at his fingertips. Better too, not to risk causing offence to a vulnerable member of the community – you never knew to what action group or other an articulate guy like this might take his grievance. So, to Banks's disgust, Dawson ordered Hindmarsh to remove the cuffs and told the suspect to go home, stay there and be prepared for an interview the following morning.

'Fine by me,' said the guy in the wheelchair, then added as a four-wheel drive drew up, 'there's my carer. Bang on time as usual,' and trundled away towards the vehicle.

Dawson turned his attention to the rest of scene. He had already realized from the number of paramedics tumbling out of the ambulance that he could expect more than one casualty this evening. Banks filled him in on the 999 call they'd taken at the station. They left Hindmarsh and Dosh beside the body and headed for the front door of the Centre. It was going, Dawson thought, as he stepped inside

132

and saw the mayhem there, to be another long night for Crandon CID.

As soon as Bryan was home he dismissed Edward and phoned John's shared house. It was late, the staff wouldn't like it; they could lump it.

'He's watching TV,' said the woman who answered. 'It's a repeat of *ER* and he's laughing every time they pull in another casualty. No matter how harrowing the scene is, he's laughing. It's upsetting the other residents,' she added as though Bryan was to blame for John's behaviour. Which he was, though she couldn't possibly know that.

'Get him to the phone right now.' Bryan was as forceful as he had been in his previous, active life. 'Tell him it's Bryan and it's urgent.'

She protested, but disappeared. Sounds of life in the shared house ensued. Someone shouting incoherently at someone else. Soothing noises from one of the staff. The volume of a TV rising and falling according to the dictates of the drama it portrayed.

And then there was John. 'Hi, mate. Get my prezzie? Edward said he'd stick it in the back of your chair.' John's voice was slurred. It sounded as though he was floating. Evidently Edward had, as Bryan had instructed, scored some very high class puff indeed and John had probably smoked the lot at one sitting. Great in the normal run of things, but not too clever now.

'You sound high as a kite.'

'Higher. Completely off my trolley. Figuratively speaking, you understand.' John emitted a long, meandering giggle.

'You've got to come down. Right now. It's about Marion.'

'Ah, the lovely Miss Shaggable.'

'Don't call her that.' Bryan's tone was sharp.

'Why not? Don't tell me! Someone's got into her knickers. Bet it's that poncy policeman. Hardly going to be the likes of you or I, is it?' John choked on yet another giggle. 'That'd be hot news, wouldn't it? Send out a press release, I would, if I were giving her one. Broadcast to the nation, no less.' He adopted a plum-in-your-mouth accent in imitation of the Queen. 'My husband and I,' he pronounced, 'have great delight in informing you . . .'

'Shut up,' said Bryan. 'She's dead.'

'Oh well, I guess it was too much to hope for. Still, a dead Marion would be almost as good as a live one. I always say beggars can't be choosers. I do say that, don't I?'

'John, get a grip. She's really dead. Her head's bashed in.'

There was silence on the other end of the line.

Then: 'So you really did it? You said you were going to.'

'Are you crazy? Me kill anyone?' Though it was true that when Bryan left the Centre he had been in the grip of a crazed black rage. 'I might have thought I could,' he admitted. 'I was in one hell of a paddy.' He paused, then sketched in what had happened to Kenny and Co. John remained silent.

'Anyway, when I got outside I found her lying there with her head split open. And it turned out that . . . well, she wasn't perfect after all.'

'She wouldn't be if her head was split open,' John pointed out.

'No, I mean before she was killed.'

Bryan shivered as he recalled the moment when he discovered her. She was lying just outside the phone box – presumably she hadn't made it to the phone. Her head was a broken, bloody mess, her halo of soft gold hair had been driven into the flesh and bone of her skull by the blow that killed her. Her eyes were wide, her mouth was open, as though she had had time to feel fear but no time to cry out. How could her beauty have been destroyed so completely in the minute or so it had taken him to seize the crutch and pursue her? He shook his head. He shifted his gaze from her poor, battered head to the rest of her. Her red dress was rucked up around her waist, her perfect legs led in their two slender columns to a perfect rounded bottom. No, a decidedly less than perfect bottom.

134

From the centre of one plump cheek ran an angry, red, puckered birthmark in the shape of an elongated comma. She lay sprawled on her right side, so he could see that the mark trailed up beneath her stark-white bikini briefs, mounted the projection of her hip, then dipped, like the finger of an intrusive hand, under laundered cotton fabric, towards her genitals.

Had he been able to stoop and put the dress to rights he would have done so, out of pity. Instead he sat there, for endless seconds, in the dark, dirty mall, as though mounting a vigil. He felt empty, like a deflated balloon. His initial fear of the louts, his adrenaline rush, his rage, his furious headlong action; they'd dissipated as though at a pinprick. What the fuck did he think he'd been doing lately, harbouring – no, worse, fostering – murderous thoughts about another human being, simply because she irritated him? And then sending her to the phone box and so to her death. Okay, he couldn't have known that some psychopath was lying in wait; but he sure as hell should have known that it wasn't kosher for a woman who looked like Marion, dressed like Marion, to be out alone after dark on the streets of Crandon for more than a nanosecond. He felt disgusted with himself. Christ, had his accident snapped some inner core of humanity as effectively as it had his spinal cord? He had been utterly insane for the past year. But now, whatever the current state of his physical disability, his mind was, sure as hell, back to normal. It was as if he had been drunk or stoned for months, and now he was sober and straight. He tried to order his thoughts, to convey some of what he'd felt to John. And was relieved to find that John, too, was coming down from his high.

'See what you mean, mate. Wouldn't have talked to her the way I did if I'd known she was going to cop it. But there again,' John added, with one of his sudden flashes of insight, 'we cripples all say things we don't mean. Because we know – they all know too – that we're harmless. The only freedom we have is in what we say. We can't actually *do* a thing.'

Bryan thought for a moment. 'Sometimes we can.' And he gave a brief, self-deprecatory account of his furious onslaught on the two kids who'd battered Kenny. He played up the manoeuvrability of his new chair, played down his role in manoeuvring it: but when he'd finished John still muttered,

'Awesome.' There was a moment's silence. 'So what are we going to do?'

'We? Do? What d'you mean?'

'We owe her one. And you've just proved we *can* do stuff. Plus you've solved umpteen fictional murders over the last months. How about getting your head around a real one? Especially if, as you say, the cops aren't likely to look further than the most obvious suspect – that's you, mate. Do the honours for Marion and save your own skin at the same time. Otherwise,' John gave a sudden cackle and relapsed into dope-induced idiocy, 'you won't have a leg to stand on. Either that or it won't stand up in court. Same difference.' He made an audible effort to control his voice. 'You on?'

It took Bryan only seconds to decide. 'Yes. But before we get cracking, there's a little matter of a story we need to agree on. That is if you as well as me – not to mention Edward – are to stay out of custody. Oh and get your arse over here tomorrow. I'll send Edward for you in the car.'

Dawson had detained everyone who'd attended the social – everyone, that is, apart from Bryan and the injured – at the Centre until he'd questioned them all. He'd sent officers to the hospital to interview the casualties. He'd sent out an alert about a gang of kids and specifically about the one kid with the bottles in either hand. Now, the following morning, he was bringing the team up to date with absolutely everything that, between them, they had got. First he dismissed the three injured people: because although none of them had suffered broken bones, only bruising and lacerations, they were all incommunicado. The old man was reported incapable of doing anything but nodding, the young woman couldn't communicate without some complex gadgetry which had been smashed and would apparently take thousands to replace and the able-bodied young man with a mental health problem was simply incoherent with terror.

'Might mean he did it himself, Guv,' said Banks. 'You never know with some of these care in the community people. Weird how it takes them.'

'I'm well aware of the issue.' Dawson frowned. 'I'm also aware that . . .,' he consulted his notes, 'Kenneth Harker was either under violent attack or lying bleeding on the floor during the entire time in which we are interested.' He wondered, though, but not out loud, where said Harker had been when Julia Stone was killed. That had certainly had the stamp of a loony's motiveless crime.

'On the evidence of many witnesses,' he went on, 'the three disabled people in question along with all the others in wheel-chairs – bar one – can be excluded from any direct, physical involvement in the death of Marion Charteris. That's as much firm ground as we have under our feet at this moment in time. We don't know whether this was an opportunist killing committed by someone unconnected with the Centre. We don't know whether it was a planned killing perpetrated by someone similarly unconnected. We've got feelers out on both those possibilities. In the meantime we'll start with what we've got: the people who attended the Christmas social (whether invited or uninvited) and the incident that took place there.'

He paused, indicated the flip chart on which he had written the names of the guests and began to read them aloud. 'The Mayor; her partner, Maureen Clegg; Jill Rush, creative writing tutor; the Head of Centre and three staff; four members of the,' he gave a small grimace, 'Mushy Pea Community Arts Group; a photographer from the *Courier*, name of Jim Hepworth; a community librarian, Raji Balasun. Other than that it was mainly friends and relations of the people who use the Centre, all of whom can be ruled out. The pathologist's preliminary report is quite clear that death was instantaneous and took place only minutes – maybe as little as one minute – before Constable Hindmarsh arrived on the scene. At that time all the guests and the users of the Centre were inside the building recovering from the aftermath of the unprovoked attack by youths whose identities remain unknown. We've questioned all the guests several times as to who was where, when, and no one is unaccounted for.'

'Bar one,' put in DC Banks.

'Bar one.' Dawson nodded. 'I'll come to Bryan Greyshott in a moment. He's our prime suspect and I imagine most of us believe he's our man. For what it's worth, I certainly do. But police work isn't about belief, it's about evidence.'

'We've got more than enough to make a case against him,' objected Banks.

'I'm not interested in "making cases". That's a recipe for overlooking evidence which could be crucial in court. From what I've seen of Greyshott, he may be in a wheelchair, but he's no mug. Cobble together a "case" which relies on what we believe and he's a dead cert to run rings round us. What we need are hard facts. And we need to look at them objectively, not merely as a means to getting our man before the bench. Is that clear?' They all nodded. 'So,' he flipped over the guest list on the chart to reveal beneath a timetable of the previous evening, 'let's get on with it.'

The sequence was clear. The social had begun at 6 pm. Everything had gone according to plan until the Mayor's surprise announcement of her sexual orientation.

'Does that have any bearing on the case?' queried Dawson. 'Anyone here have any local knowledge as to whom such a revelation would be a minus? Or a plus?'

'The Opposition on the council,' offered Banks. 'Tories have been spoiling to pin something on her for years.'

Dosh disagreed. 'It works the other way round these days. Coming out is very fashionable. Gets you in the papers too.'

'Guv.' Banks had been perched on the edge of a desk for the duration of the briefing. Now he shifted his heavy buttocks impatiently on the surface. 'Is this really worth bothering about?'

'Anything untoward is, as you put it, worth "bothering about". To continue. The Mayor finishes her speech at approx. 6.45, the photographer takes his pictures. It is now approx. 7.15. The Community Arts Group introduce a drama perform- ance by the Centre users. The first sequence is a solo – and a pretty peculiar one, by all accounts. It's a solo because John Garnet, also confined to a wheelchair, has been banned from attending the Centre. On account of his extremely hostile atti- tude to the deceased and, I may add, to me. I observed him on the day I addressed the Centre users and consider him not only unbalanced but easily provoked and highly volatile. As you know, we'll be making enquiries shortly in the house where he lives as to his whereabouts at the time in question last night. After the solo Kenneth Harker and Bryan Greyshott put on their performance. In the course of it Harker hits Greyshott. That was at about,' he consulted the flip chart for confirmation, '7.25 pm. We have no idea why this altercation took place, but it is worth bearing in mind that it did happen and that something might lie behind it. Perhaps Harker wanted to curry favour with Charteris – she was, after all, an extremely attractive woman – and thought Greyshott was getting more than his fair share of her attention. Not that there's any evidence to support that supposition; but who knows what goes on in the minds of these people? Greyshott recovers from the blow and continues the performance. Then the gang of kids arrive.'

'Do we know how they got in?' asked Dosh.

Dawson nodded. 'It seems the victim herself left the doors unlocked. Entirely against accepted procedure, according to the Head of Centre. She was hoping some other journalists might turn up. And wouldn't be able to get in if they were late.'

'Wanted her picture in the papers,' was Dosh's opinion.

'The gang single out Harker, Derry and Cousins for the brunt of their attack. Greyshott, instead of showing the

139

normal fear of the vulnerable in such circumstances, takes on two of the gang and calls the emergency services.'

'Great stuff,' applauded Dosh. 'Guy must have quite a nerve.'

Dawson frowned at him. 'The call is logged in the station at 7.36. Constable Hindmarsh who is in pursuit of an IC1 male, aged approx. eleven years old, comes upon the victim and the suspect at exactly 7.43. He checks the pulse of the deceased and finds that life is extinct.' Dawson paused and searched the room with his eyes for Hindmarsh. 'Good work, lad,' he approved and nodded at Paul. 'Constable Hindmarsh cautions the suspect.'

'Then *you* let him go,' complained Banks.

'He won't go far. Now we come to the evidence against the suspect.

'He is found at the scene of the crime holding a heavy crutch. We don't yet have confirmation from Forensics that it was the murder weapon, but it seems more than likely it was. Throughout the evening he was extremely hostile to the victim. He was curt with others of the guests. Many of them testify that he appeared preoccupied. We also have testimony that he has harboured a grudge against Charteris for some time. Possibly has some chip on his shoulder about being disabled – it appears he had a highly successful career before that happened.'

'Thought that when we questioned him,' Dosh put in. 'Said he sounded more Kensington than Crandon.'

'Questioned him? When?'

'The night Julia Stone got done in. His flat overlooks Carleton Park.'

'A point to bear in mind,' Dawson noted, then swept smoothly on. 'For reasons which are unclear he goes to the rescue of Harker – that shows Greyshott has the nerve and the strength to act on his aggressive impulses. He conceals from the other guests – why? – that he has phoned for assistance, he abuses Charteris, tries to strike her and, under

140

cover of the disturbance, follows Charteris outside with his weapon.'

'Open and shut case,' said Banks.

'There's more. I mentioned the photographer. Nasty piece of goods. Actually took pictures of the injured people, intending to sell them to the newspapers. When he gathered there was another incident outside, tried to push past us to get pictures of that. Soon stopped him. But the point is: Greyshott was in none of the photos. All the other users of the Centre were lined up, smiling, behind the Mayor for the official shots. Why not him?'

'Something to hide?' suggested Dosh.

'Whole thing's a foregone conclusion,' said Banks.

'Not quite.'

Paul Hindmarsh piped up from the back of the room. 'Sir, can I ask a question?'

'Go ahead.'

'Has anyone identified any of the gang that broke in?'

'No. At the moment, not even the Mayor is admitting to any knowledge of who they were.'

'Sir, is the photographer to be considered entirely free of suspicion?' asked Paul. 'Wouldn't it be in his interests to reveal what he knows? Wouldn't it be a coup for him in his career?'

Dosh shook his head. 'He's a Crandon man. Wouldn't do to finger them. Same goes for everyone else.'

'Exactly,' said Dawson, 'which brings me to a point of strategy. We urgently need to get the community on our side in this one. We need people to come forward with what they know. Any bright ideas as to what will make them do that?'

'In Crandon, Guv?' Banks was dismissive. 'Fuck all. They're scared shitless.'

'Exactly. Fear is their motive for remaining silent. Fear will be an equally powerful incentive for them to speak out. Are any of you familiar with policing experience during the reign of Jack the Ripper?'

141

The roomful of blank faces told him that they were not.

'According to Chief Inspector Abberline's records of events in the 1880s,' he informed them, 'as soon as it became common knowledge in the East End that a sadistic murderer was at large, that he might strike at any time, that no woman was safe, there was a fundamental change in attitudes towards the police. People who under normal circumstances would have run a mile if they saw a constable – prostitutes, pickpockets, thieves, all the usual low life of London – were queuing up at the station in Whitechapel Road to give whatever evidence they could.' Dawson, sensing that Banks was about to intervene, held up his hand for silence and went on, 'There were two reasons for this. First was the obvious one that their fear of the murderer was greater than their fear of the police. The second – a more telling one in our case – was that they didn't believe this was an East End crime. They accepted petty crime, wife-beating, mindless one-off brutality, as the stuff of daily life. But gratuitous mutilation, skilled, purposeful dismemberment were entirely outside their experience. Thus, the perpetrator could not, to their minds, be a local. This *increased* their fear that he might attack them or their women – his crimes appeared to be completely random – but *decreased* the fear of reprisals, he wouldn't know any of them from Adam, however much they squealed. The result was a major influx of information to both the Aldgate and Whitechapel stations.'

'Interesting historical anecdote,' sneered Banks. 'How's it supposed to give us a handle on what we're up against?'

'I'm issuing a statement to the press,' Dawson said, 'implying that the murders of Stone and Charteris might be connected, might have been committed by the same man. It's feasible – after all, both women were struck on the head. And implying that the perpetrator hails from outside Crandon and simply comes here to do his dirty work. No, no,' he raised his hand again, 'I am well aware that we have a confession for the Stone homicide. We're talking here not about what we know,

142

but about what we tell the public. About what would prompt them to tell us more. Any questions?'

No one asked him a thing, but he could just hear Constable Hindmarsh's whispered enquiry to Dosh as to whether Jack the Ripper was ever caught.

Dawson drowned out the reply with his own voice.

'A couple of other loose ends before we get to work,' he said. 'Why did Greyshott call the emergency services, then pursue Charteris *after* he had done so? Why did he call the emergency services in the first place? I want these loose ends tied up. Because it's clear to me that if the crime was committed by anyone who was at the social, then that someone must be Greyshott. But there are other avenues to investigate. We might, just possibly, have a quite different killer on our hands. I doubt it, but we must be certain. And if it is him,' Dawson paused and surveyed his troops, 'I sure as hell want him nailed.'

Because Marion, Dawson reflected as he summoned Banks to accompany him on his interview with Greyshott, had not deserved to die. Sure, there had been no spark of chemistry between the two of them the night they'd spent together, but she was an attractive young woman with years of life ahead of her. But in Crandon, as he knew to his cost, what you deserved and what you got were entirely different matters.

Bryan was more than ready for his interrogators. Last night, after he'd spoken to John, he'd typed his own summary of the case so far on his PC. Decided what he would tell the cops. And made his own plans for future investigations. Figured his softly-softly approach would get a lot more out of people than would the crude, bully-boy tactics of the police. Not that Dawson was a bully-boy. Man had a deal of subtlety about him, witness the way he'd backed off last night. Witness, not the least, the speed with which he had appeared at the scene of the crime; but, then, Bryan had expected

143

Dawson to be a bit of a hot shot when it came to action. Don't underestimate the guy, he warned himself. But Bryan was much better placed than Dawson to get to the bottom of things. Okay, so Dawson had legs, but he didn't have the in that Bryan did with Crandon's underclass. Nor with the other Centre users. And Dawson didn't – crucial point – have Bryan's certainty that neither he, nor John, nor Edward had committed the crime. He stopped and reconsidered that last thought. Edward was at this moment in the kitchen, clearing up the mess Bryan had made after an ambitious but rather cack-handed attempt at doing Eggs Benedict for breakfast. What did, he, Bryan, really know about Edward? He knew he was unfailingly kind, caring, that he ministered to Bryan's every need. Why? What kind of job was that for a healthy young man? Not the sort of job he'd have wanted were he in Edward's shoes. Of course, Edward had come with impeccable references, but what did that mean? Fuck all. Bryan hadn't followed up on any of them, not in the state he'd been when he left hospital. He paused in his thoughts, hearing Edward clattering dishes, running the waste disposal unit, and chided himself for his suspicions. But why chide himself? Everyone – if you looked at things objectively – was a suspect until things were cleared up beyond all doubt. Except himself and John. Bryan switched on the PC and looked at his other pointers to the future of the investigation. No names of any suspects, not as yet. Only leads to follow up.

'Re-interview Mrs Corke and Gerald Tozer,' he had written. 'Enquire into their daily routines. Find out more about Marion's life away from the Centre. Was she in a relationship? A job? Was her money – she must have money, given her clothes – earned or inherited? If inherited, who were her parents? Who were they anyway? Investigate what sort of network the kids have in this area. Maybe hang about the school gates when they come out and see if you recognise anyone?' He deleted that idea with vigour. No call to be branded a pervert as well as a murderer. 'Talk to Jill. Ask John for ideas.' He closed the file. It wasn't much to go on, but it was a start.

Then he summoned Edward to help him dress for the fray.

Bryan was at his most urbane when the pair of policemen arrived.

'How can I help you gentleman?' he asked, ushering them into the living room.

Dawson looked around him. 'Our enquiries may take some time. Please have some chairs brought in.'

'I don't have any. Except my old wheelchair.' Bryan gestured to the cumbersome monstrosity. 'You're welcome to sit in that.'

'He didn't!' exclaimed John that afternoon when Bryan relayed the events of the morning to him.

'You bet he bloody did after half an hour shifting from one foot to the other. Bit like a form of torture the Japanese used to go in for, kept people standing on exactly the same spot for twenty-four hours. Only they weren't allowed to shuffle their feet.'

'Christ, I wish I'd been there,' exulted John. 'Must have been a real treat seeing that bastard in a wheelchair. Not even a new wheelchair, either. Daresay you were a cut above him, eh?'

Bryan nodded. 'By a good few inches.'

'What about his sidekick?'

Bryan gave a bark of laughter. 'Wandered about the room, trying to hitch his buttocks onto the windowsill, the edge of the desk. I asked him – I was polite as all get out – not to put his weight on the desk, it wasn't built for it. God, that man has an arse the size of a hippo's. Anyway, at one point I actually thought he was going to give up and sit on the floor. But eventually he came to rest on the coffee table.'

'So you were looking down on both of them?'

'Yeah.'

'What about the interview itself? Are you still Public Enemy Number One? The prime suspect?'

'Yes and no. Wouldn't let on whether they'd got forensic evidence yet, but as and when they do, they'll know that crutch I had hold of hadn't been anywhere near Marion's head. And if I read Dawson right he won't make an arrest until the thing is watertight. As for the rest of it they asked all the right questions. Clearly done their homework the night before with everyone who was at the social. Had the timing of events down to a tee. Far as I could gather I was the only one present who had both motive and opportunity.'

'Well, if you will tell all and sundry you're planning to do someone serious damage . . . Actually, who did you tell?'

'See what you're getting at. Someone could have taken advantage of my big mouth to direct suspicion at me.' Bryan thought for a moment, then counted on his fingers. 'You, Raji, Jill, the creative writing tutor – I saw her at the social. And Edward must know, of course, though I didn't actually tell him. He knows pretty much everything about me, damn it.'

'Incidentally, where is Edward?'

'In the kitchen making a cake for tea – madeira, I decided. That should keep him out of our way for a while.'

'Since when did you start having tea and cake in the afternoon? Not exactly your style, is it?'

'It isn't for me. Nor you for that matter. Mrs Corke's coming.'

'Hang on a tic. Stop introducing new characters before I've got the gen on the old ones. Did they question Edward?'

'Bet your life.'

'What did he say?'

'What I'd told him to.'

'Thought he would. As well to be sure though. It's my skin at risk on this one.'

'Said he went, on my instructions, straight to collect you. Explained – as I already had – that I wanted to give you a night out, given you weren't welcome at the Centre. Started

146

off very precise about the pubs you visited. Gave names, times, what you drank, what the landlord looked like, etc. Said, of course, he wasn't drinking, he was driving. But you insisted on going to so many different places – you hadn't been on a pub crawl in years, you were determined to make the most of it – that he eventually lost track. You give the same story?'

John nodded.

'What about the staff in your house? Could they back up any of it? Did they see Edward when he brought you back?'

'You bet. I was so out of my skull, Edward could hardly keep me in my chair. Told you last night I thought I was floating, didn't I? Anyway we made a right commotion just getting through the front door. Had a real reception committee. Should have seen the faces on all of them, Shelley included. Expected better of her. By that stage I'd decided I had wings and I was flapping my arms up and down like all get out. Didn't even get a rise out of her when I knocked an umbrella out of the hall stand and said not to worry, if she was getting into a shower, she'd better get into it with me. Have a suspicion I accompanied the remark with a rather suggestive gesture. Then, between the lot of them, they practically manhandled me into the living room. Very disapproving, they were. Went on and on at Edward about bringing me back in what they called "that condition".'

'Point is, did they believe you were pissed, rather than stoned?'

'Sure did. And now for this Mrs Whatsit of yours. How's she fit into the picture?'

Bryan relayed the contents of his interview with Mrs Corke in her fourteenth floor flat.

'You tell the police all that?'

'Enough of it to start the bright bastard on the track of making a connection between the two killings. Wouldn't be surprised if he has second thoughts, pretty sharpish, about the guy they've nabbed for the Carleton Park murder.'

147

'How's that going to help us? More to the point, help you?' John paused and sniffed the air. 'Christ, that cake smells good. You are a jammy bugger, having a carer like Edward. Though with your dosh you could just as well have had him buy a cake. Run to some lavish Sarah Lee number. Would have done your old biddy just as well.'

'I wanted him out of the way,' Bryan explained. 'It's not exactly suspicion, more elimination. I don't want him to know every move I make, every breath I take. He doesn't need to these days. I've got the hang of the hoist for the bathroom, I've conquered the cooking. Pretty soon I won't need him around at all.'

'In your dreams, cripple!'

Bryan shifted a little, uncomfortably, in his athlete's wheelchair. 'Well, yes, there are other reasons. In a word, the less Edward knows the better. That way I have the scope to determine surer, sooner, whether he's in the clear.'

'Christ, you're paranoid! You think your carer knocked off two women?'

'I don't think anything. That's the point. It isn't time to think yet. It's time to gather facts, evidence, details.'

'Which is where your Mrs Clarke comes in?'

'Corke.' Bryan glanced at his watch, 'She'll be here soon. One other thing I should tell you – though I didn't tell the police, didn't want them to think I was doolally.' He explained about Mrs Corke's ramblings concerning sundry people living, undetected, on the fifteenth floor of the tower block. 'Could be nonsense. And you're right, I should have had Edward buy a cake. The one he's made won't have time to cool. Though I did get him to buy a rack to turn it out onto.'

'You're mental. You're under suspicion of murder and you're worried whether a cake will be cool. Next you'll be insisting on doilies.'

'Her mother used to have them,' said Bryan, laughing. 'The other thing we've got to think about,' he went on, 'is these kids. The ones who attacked Kenny, the bastards. The police didn't seem to have a clue who they were, which strikes me as extremely odd. I'd certainly know them if I saw them again. Identify them like a shot. Said so to the plods. Completely motiveless and mindless – still makes my blood boil.'

'Talking of which,' John pitched in, 'you've missed out the most vital thing in the whole shebang. Why did someone want to kill Marion? Assuming someone did specifically want to kill her and it wasn't just some sicko who gets a kick out of doing women in.'

'We can't dismiss the sicko angle.' Bryan nodded. 'It wasn't a straightforward sexual attack, though, there wouldn't have been time. It could have been a jealous boyfriend – perhaps he found she was seeing someone else and flipped his lid. But why would such a person be hanging about outside the Centre? He could hardly expect Marion to run to the phone box. I just don't see how the thing could have been premeditated.'

'More likely someone took advantage of the unexpected opportunity. Probably been on the lookout for some time.'

'Who'd do that?'

'Well, you did.'

'Ha, ha. If that was the case it'd mean it was someone who knew exactly where she was going to be that evening and who, what's more, was watching her. A stalker in fact.'

'Got it in one. And given he was gone by the time you arrived, it's a fair bet that he has the use of his legs.'

'What other motives? Come on, John, give it some welly.'

'One brainstorm coming up. In no particular order. She wasn't killed for money because she wasn't robbed. Or if she was killed for money the killer didn't have time to rob her. Did she have a bag with her?'

'No.'

'So mugging's an unlikely motive. Someone was jealous of her because she was so perfect. That means a guy – or a woman – who hates beautiful women.'

'Except she wasn't entirely perfect,' Bryan pointed out.

'They weren't to know that. To continue. One of the gang might have dashed outside and done it. Given they were already in the mood for bashing in heads. Only this time they bashed a bit too hard. Or one of them could have been outside all the time. That would make sense if they saw her heading for the phone box, she'd be bound to be calling the police. Or, supposing someone – someone who wasn't on the scene – but who was the leader of the gang of kids, was there? He'd sent them to give the Centre a doing over. In fact, that was all a cover. What he really intended was to do Marion in and let the kids take the blame. Alternatively it might be that something illegit was going on near the phone box that Marion saw and the guy she saw doing it topped her. Or she might have seen something incriminating on an earlier occasion and he'd been looking for the chance to silence her ever since.' John paused. 'Hey, a round of applause is in order, I'm really excelling myself here. To sum up,' he raised one hand as though he were calling for silence from a large audience, 'Marion was either killed by someone who knew her and didn't like her, knew her and didn't like what she knew, or didn't know her from Eve and was simply looking for a young woman to do in. Or a combination of all three. Is that masterly or what? You'd think it was me who'd been reading the detective novels.'

'It'll do. And it's pretty much as far as we'll get without more facts. Which brings us to Mrs Corke. Not that she can help us with Marion, but you never know, she might have more to say about Julia Stone. Might make some sort of connection between the two deaths. Only, I warn you, she's not always easy to follow.'

The doorbell went. 'That'll be her now,' Bryan added, but they could both see through Bryan's picture window that Mrs Corke was not alone. In front of her on the path stood a small, skinny boy much younger than the ones who'd attacked Kenny. He had a wedge haircut and a face like a terrier who'd been caught piddling on the carpet. As Edward made his way along the hall, the boy side-stepped swiftly in an obvious effort to dodge around Mrs Corke and take off. Not swiftly enough. One of her gnarled hands shot out and pinched his right earlobe firmly between two fingers. He squirmed in pain, but she wasn't letting go. Instead she shoved him in front of her and he disappeared from view into the now open door of Bryan's flat.

'Couldn't risk bringing him in,' Dawson announced to his troops, 'not given the forensic evidence.'

It had turned out that the crutch Bryan Greyshott was holding when Constable Hindmarsh found him was not the murder weapon. The shape of the wound did not match with the business end of the crutch. Or the other end, for that matter. Forensics'd tried it every which way and couldn't get a fit. It was a serious setback.

'So, he could have done it with something else, Guv,' suggested Banks.

'Thrown the real weapon away,' added Dosh.

'Sir!' Paul Hindmarsh was raising his hand at the back of the room. 'What about the juvenile I was in pursuance of shortly before the time in question? Could he have been an accomplice? Could the suspect have handed the weapon to him?'

'Good thinking.' DCI Dawson nodded. 'Any results on the search for the kid?'

Everyone shook their heads.

'Redouble your efforts. Think schools. Make enquiries with the head teachers. Ask the mothers at the gates. Think truants. Where do the kids go when they bunk off? Try Carousel, the amusement arcade. I want the manor combed for that kid. I'll re-interview the old lady in the tower block. It was shoddy police work not getting her story out of her in the first house-to-house, but I'll deal with that when the investigation's successfully concluded. Given Greyshott's statement we can't

151

afford to rule out a connection between the deaths of Charteris and Stone. Banks and myself will be questioning Green further. And I want some results on all the stuff that was found in Carleton Park after Stone's murder.'

'Sir,' Hindmarsh piped up. 'We've had a result on the request you put in to the council. For employees who might have seen something in the park. Would have come through before, but the street sweepers were on strike. Work's been contracted out to a private company the last couple of weeks.'

Which might account for why the mall had been looking a damn sight cleaner, Dawson thought wryly. 'So what have we got?'

Hindmarsh read aloud the notes which, on this occasion, he'd had ample time to make. 'Cleansing operative Bill Curtis was returning to the depot after completing his shift on the Carleton Park estate on the afternoon in question. He reached the main gate of Carleton Park at 4.20 pm. The duty roster maintained by the Works Department Supervisor confirms that this would have been correct within – say – five minutes either way. Operative Curtis's final task of his shift was to sweep the tarmac path which runs west to east in the park.'

Which task Curtis had shirked that day and probably every other, Dawson surmised.

'On nearing the vicinity of the park shelter,' Hindmarsh continued ponderously, 'Curtis became aware of a dispute in progress inside it. The dispute was being conducted at some considerable volume and appeared to involve two people. Curtis did not attempt to intervene, nor indeed, did he take further steps towards the shelter. As I'm sure you're aware, sir, a number of employees of Crandon Council have recently been the subject of vicious attacks by members of the public. Their instructions on encountering any potentially violent incident are to proceed with all due caution to a senior officer to whom they should report the incident in order that appropriate action can be taken. Curtis therefore continued to propel his barrow along the path rather than deviating across the path in the direction of the shelter.'

'For Christ's sake get on with it, who do you think you are, Dixon of Dock Green?' muttered Banks.

'On reaching the small, eastern gate of the park,' Hindmarsh pressed on, 'operative Curtis considered himself sufficiently distant from the disturbance to permit him glancing back. Issuing from the shelter at some speed was a man.'

'Description?' barked Dawson.

'Yes, sir,' responded Hindmarsh. 'I questioned him on that point.' He proceeded to read. 'An IC1 male, aged approximately thirty-five. Heavily built, dark hair. Wearing a bulky, black leather jacket, a white shirt, dark pullover. Jeans – very clean, Curtis noted – and brogues polished to a shine. As the person in question walked past him to the gate Curtis was at sufficiently close quarters to be able to detect a gold signet ring on the subject's right hand.'

'Well done. Good, solid police work,' approved Dawson. But Hindmarsh hadn't finished.

'Bill Curtis,' he intoned, apparently gratuitously, but with an admirable attention to detail, 'is not a Crandon resident. His known address for the past thirteen years has been that of a council flat in Camden where he lives with his common-law wife and five children.' He proceeded to furnish flat number, name of estate and postal code.

'In other words,' judged Dawson, 'he wouldn't be backward in coming forward with information like the denizens of Crandon are. Well done.'

Hindmarsh pocketed his notebook and sunk into his seat. Dawson took centre stage again.

'The evidence is that whatever we think of Julia Stone, we now have to accept that the two murders may have been connected. May even have been committed by the same man.

'As for Charteris,' the sudden sharpness in Dawson's voice made everyone sit up a little straighter, concentrate a little harder, 'we're not talking a local tom here. We're not talking some sleazy back street domestic between a couple of Crandon losers. Charteris was an outsider. She was also an entirely respectable citizen whose background is an open book. Not because she had a record either. Marion Charteris,' he paused and referred, as he had in his previous briefing, to a flip chart, 'was twenty nine years old. She was born in a village in Clwyd, where her parents still live. They are by any standards fairly wealthy. Independent means, I gather, supplemented by judicious investments. All entirely above board. Her father is a Justice of the Peace, her mother goes in for various charities. Charteris married three years ago into more money; her husband, Jonathon, is in the City. They shared a garden flat in Downshire Hill, Hampstead. She had worked as a secretary in a merchant bank, but gave up her job on her marriage. On a personal note, she had no close friends of her own, the people with whom she socialised tended to be couples, the male half of whom her husband had met through his work. She entertained these couples to dinner parties and holidayed abroad with them twice a year – skiing in the winter, sunbathing and sightseeing in the summer – with the occasional weekend accompanying her husband on business trips to . . .' Dawson consulted his notes, 'New York, Brussels, Paris, Luxembourg. And so on. There was no one particular couple with whom the Charteris couple remained in close association over the years – these people came and went according to Jonathon Charteris's latest business deals and the demands of what appears to have been a fairly meteoric rise in his career. I infer that his wife's role was primarily to look decorative in expensive designer outfits. She employed a cleaning woman – a Hampstead local from one of Camden's council estates – who came to the flat three mornings a week. Occasionally she attended up-market cookery courses or evening classes in interior decoration. I gather she had just completed one such in rag rolling. Otherwise she was free to spend the bulk of her time,' his mouth narrowed in disapproval, 'shopping. She held charge accounts at . . .' he again checked his notes, 'Harrods, Habitat, John Lewis etc., etc. '

'So what the fuck was she doing in Crandon?' Banks demanded.

'Along with money, Charteris had inherited from her mother the notion that it was her duty to do voluntary work.'

'Sure, but why in Crandon?' Banks persisted. 'Why not go for the sort of glamorous stuff with kiddies that Princess Diana went in for?'

'Land mines aren't glamorous,' protested Dosh.

Dawson intervened. 'We've had all that checked out. Charteris contacted a volunteer bureau, said she particularly wanted to work with disabled people who were also disadvantaged. According to the records at the bureau she was keen to help them "realise their full potential". Apparently stemmed from her having taught some village boy on crutches to ride her pony when she was a kid. Any rate, the bureau were most impressed with her. Said she even took a couple of courses – paid for them too – to get herself clued up on the latest techniques for dealing with these people. People with disabilities, that is. So they gave her the most difficult assignment they had. Crandon Community Centre. Presented it to her as a worthwhile challenge. So she took it on. She'd been attending the Centre three times a week, Tuesdays, Wednesdays and Thursdays for the past eleven months.' He stopped and referred to his notes once more. 'One final thing to complete the picture. The Charteris couple owned a fifteenth century thatched cottage in the village of Green Haddock in Kent at which they spent most weekends. She generally drove there – late on Thursdays after her session at the Centre – in their Range Rover. He followed her on Friday afternoon by train and she collected him from the station.'

Dosh whistled between his teeth. 'Not kidding she wasn't your average Crandon tom,' he muttered.

'How the other half lives,' responded Banks.

And Dawson himself marvelled silently that, given Marion's background, she had been so keen to come back with him that evening to his loft. But perhaps her husband had been away

155

on a solo business trip and she was lonely? He dismissed his speculations and confronted his troops.

'Any questions? Any ideas?'

There were plenty.

'How much do we know about the husband?' asked Banks. 'That's always the guy to start with.'

'Good point. Far as we know he's entirely kosher. Seems devastated. Cast-iron alibi for the evening in question. He was dining with the Minister of Agriculture in Brussels. But we'll be keeping an eye on him.'

'Could the motive be something to do with money?' Banks persisted. 'Anyone in Crandon might have thought they had more than their fair share.'

Dawson made a note of his comment.

'Why didn't they have kids?' Dosh piped up with what Dawson could only assume was a prurient curiosity about the mores of the moneyed classes. 'They could afford to.'

'Probably an irrelevance,' he responded, 'but that did occur to me too. They were planning to start a family in about two years' time, in fact. Jonathon Charteris told me that off his own bat. Said it would give them time to move from a flat to a house and for her to supervise the interior decorations. They intended to have three children.'

'Sir?' Paul Hindmarsh was drawing attention to himself again. 'Could I enquire how long the suspect Greyshott has been attending the Community Centre?'

'Polly?' Dawson turned to WPC Jones for the answer. She leafed through the notes she had taken the previous evening of the Centre users' details. 'Eleven months, sir.'

'Could be something, could be not.' Dawson nodded at Paul. 'You're thinking there's something in them both turning up at the same time?'

Paul nodded. 'Good thinking, lad,' said Dawson. He looked round at the rest of them, but they had dried up. They were as clueless as ever. He felt anger rise against them, anger rise against the mindless violence which pervaded

Crandon and which its inhabitants accepted as a fact of life. But not this time. Never mind building bridges with community leaders, paying lip service to a lot of mealy-mouthed, politically correct guff. Solve this murder and he'd show them all – community and villains alike – that he was a force to be reckoned with. He gathered his breath for his final speech of the briefing, a speech designed to motivate his troops, to make them think beyond the ways to which they were accustomed.

'This young innocent woman,' he began, 'had a full and happy life ahead of her. She had a husband, she had money, she had a decent background, she had everything to look forward to. Now she's dead, killed by a single vicious blow – weapon unknown – to her temples. At the time of her death she was engaged in voluntary work, helping people less fortunate than herself. As I intimated at the outset, her death is not the stuff of your average Crandon killing. She has friends, family, connections. They won't let our investigation slide into obscurity. We'll be – make no bones about it – in the spotlight. We can expect to be under the media's microscope. Not to mention the Met's.' Dawson shifted from one foot to the other as he had in Greyshott's front room, but this time to give them a moment to let his words sink in.

'Which may be no bad thing,' he resumed, allowing his voice to increase in volume. 'Here's our chance.' He swept his eyes around the room. 'All of us. Our goal is simple. To be seen to have brought the perpetrator to justice.'

'It's you!' The skinny kid's expression changed from truculence to excitement the instant he set eyes on Bryan.

But Mrs Corke's eyes were fixed on the tea table. 'Goodness, no bread and butter, just cake. And home-made if I'm any judge. You are spoiling me.' She settled herself on the canvas chair which Bryan had had Edward buy that lunch time specially for the occasion. One way or another he'd had Edward buy quite a few things today.

'Help yourself.' He turned to the kid. 'What do you mean, "it's me"?'

'I saw you last night. You was awesome.'

'Still warm? Fresh from the oven?' Mrs Corke crammed a large portion of crumbling cake into her mouth. 'Haven't tasted anything like this for years. Not since Mother passed away. What is it you want to know this time?

'Not about the old days. Who's he?' The sulky, skinny kid – like a rabbit, not a terrier, Bryan decided – perched himself on the edge of the coffee table – as the bulldog policeman had this morning, but with far less threat to the table's stability.

'Oh, he lives near me.' Mrs Corke shook her head of grey hair. 'My mother would wonder what life was coming to.'

'How was he awesome?' asked John.

'What did you see?' asked Bryan.

'You in the Community Centre. The Mandela Estate gang. For years,' the child's expression was suddenly that of a wizened, world-weary, old man, 'they've been taking the mickey. Can't hardly go nowhere without finding they've been there first. Beating on the little kids. Trashing cars. Emptying the machines in Carousel. Smashing shop windows. Duffing up old gits. Wherever we've been we've found they've already been there, done that.' He paused. 'But last night was something else.'

'In what way?' asked John carefully.

'You should of seen it! I was coming back across the estate from Aunt Suzy's. Only she weren't in. Saw lights in the Centre. Stopped for a look in. Okay, so the windows have bars but it's easy enough to see what's going down through them. Man, he had Wolf and Hunter on their knees. You wouldn't believe it. Specially as he's in a wheelchair.'

'Wolf and Hunter,' Bryan interposed quickly. 'You know them?'

'Course I know them. Call themselves after the guys on *Gladiators*. All the guys in the gang do.'

'Could you identify them to the police?'

Lee wriggled his buttocks on the coffee table. 'I don't have nothing to do with the old Bill.'

'But you could tell me. They didn't see you, did they, when you were looking in the window?'

'Me? Nah. Course not.'

'How about it then?'

'Nah.'

'Did you see anything else last night?' Bryan persisted.

'Saw you standing over the tart outside. With a crutch. 'Spect you gave her a seeing-to as well.'

'No I didn't.' Bryan was sharp. 'See anyone else? Anyone running away?'

'Nah.'

Mrs Corke, apparently overcome by the hospitality to which she was being treated, butted in with a long, rambling tale of how, when the missus's husband returned from the War, he brought umpteen friends with him who all needed a good square meal.

'Very gay, they were,' she commented.

'In the old meaning of the word, I assume,' commented John.

'Just out of interest,' asked Bryan, 'why did you bring . . . what's your name?'

'Lee,' replied Mrs Corke on the boy's behalf.

'Why did you bring Lee with you today?'

'Knocked on my door once too often. Always doing that and running away. This time I caught him. Been wondering what to do about him for weeks. Needs a father's hand, you know. A man's influence. That's what Mother used to say about our Frank. But, of course, he'd felt the back of her hand more times than he'd had hot dinners. This lad never has. If it's all the same to you, I wouldn't mind a refill. Tea isn't as strong as I usually make it.' She beamed as Bryan poured, then returned abruptly to his question. 'You seemed like a nice young man. Thought you might be able to talk some sense into him.' She looked down at Lee sitting quietly on the coffee

159

table. He was still regarding Bryan with open admiration. 'And I was right. Didn't catch what you were saying, but it's worked a treat. Butter wouldn't melt in his mouth. I wouldn't say no to another piece.'

Bryan turned his attention back to Lee.

'Just for the record,' he explained, 'I don't give people "seeing-tos". And the only reason I went for those two kids was because they were attacking a friend of mine. Who couldn't protect himself.'

Lee nodded in a knowing way. 'The weirdo,' he said. 'We always chuck stuff at him.'

'He isn't a weirdo,' Bryan protested angrily, 'he's just . . .'

'Differently abled,' said John with a grin.

Bryan had been about to embark on a little lecture about how everyone was different, had different strengths and weaknesses etc. He had been about to turn as po-faced and PC as Marion herself. He had even been about to deliver a Kiplingesque homily on how the strong should always protect the weak. What a load of crap! Besides, who exactly was weaker than whom here? Kenny was as strong as an ox, but far too gentle to fight back. Even Lee was a hundred times more agile than he was himself and – when not sitting on the coffee table – topped Bryan by a good few inches. But Kenny had looked to Bryan for help and Lee was looking up to him now. He'd consider the implications of this later. In the meantime all he managed was a noncommittal, 'Um.'

He changed his tack. 'Did you see the fire in the park too?' he asked and was startled to see the sudden gleam of unshed tears in the boy's eyes.

'That was his mum,' said Mrs Corke in a conversational tone. Having apparently satisfied her appetite for cake, she was now loading her third cup of tea with several spoonfuls of sugar. 'No better than she should be, mind you. Always said she'd come to a bad end.'

'She was all right,' muttered Lee fiercely. 'And I didn't see the fire, I started it, so there.'

160

'I know you did, dear. And very naughty it was too. You and the two bob-a-job boys. I expect you thought it was Guy Fawkes night. I'm forgetful about dates myself. My, the fun we used to have! Couldn't afford fireworks in those days. But we had a Guy all right. Stuffed with straw. He had an old tweed cap Frank had found down by the river. And potatoes roasted in the embers. That would have been just after the Great War. Let me see.' She paused and gazed unseeing into the now dark park outside Bryan's window. '1918? No, 1919. Of course, silly me. Just after my fifth birthday.'

'She's raving, the silly old bag,' grumbled Lee.

'Call her that again and you'll get a kick up the arse,' Bryan told him.

'With whose foot?' asked John.

'Pedantic sod. If I can't kick I can sure as hell paddle.' And he seized the cake slice which had been yet another of Edward's purchases and waved it in mock menace in Lee's face. But Lee merely dodged, his green eyes watchful. He had no intention of challenging his new-found hero. His only desire was to impress him. How, though? He trawled his mind for when he had ever come across men like Bryan: on daytime TV movies, that's where. *Robin Hood, Prince of Thieves. Sergeant Yorke.* The defenders of the Alamo. *The Magnificent Seven. The Dirty Dozen.* Douglas Bader – he'd had no legs either. What made guys like that give you some respect? They weren't like Uncle Jack, they didn't care a toss about money. Also they had screwball ideas about being soft on deadbeats: women and children first, that kind of crap. Beat up on the deadbeats was Lee's creed, but it wouldn't wash here. Guys like Bryan Greyshott were into being brave, they were into action. But they were also – Lee recalled *The Great Escape* – into information. Information about the opposition.

'I know something you don't,' he announced.

'Yeah? What?'

'Harry didn't kill Mum. But I know who could have. Who'd have had the bottle. And I know why they did it. The Mandela Estate lot.'

'The kids at the social?'

'Yes. But he didn't say to bash their faces in, just to rough them up a bit.'

'Who did?'

But Lee wasn't saying another word.

Jack Noble pulled Banks a pint in person, and suggested he cool it.

'But he's getting too close for comfort.' Banks kept his voice low, though there were only two other people in the Icicle at this hour, and they were out of earshot at the other end of the bar. 'Lucky for you it was me he sent to make enquiries.'

'I don't need luck.' Noble leaned back against his bar. 'I've got you to protect my interests.'

'It's not quite like that.' Banks lifted his glass to his mouth. 'He's turning the whole fucking place upside down.'

'So stop him.'

'You don't realise the difficulties.'

'And you don't realise that you're not exactly delivering the goods right now.'

'What d'you mean? Dawson could be for the chop, what with the murder of the rich bitch and the people in wheel-chairs getting done over.'

'That's not down to you though, is it? The photographs in the Centre would have been quite enough to convince the media – and then the Met – that their blue-eyed boy hasn't an earthly about policing Crandon. Coming on top of Julia getting topped and the fire in the mall, would have been enough to make him look like your original incompetent. But the Char-teris murder was over the top. Gives him the chance to make all the right moves.' Noble stopped and took a sip of his drink. 'Saw a fax of his press release at the *Courier* today. Kind of stuff he's talking about making streets safe for decent people, hunting down villains and stamping out organised crime – enough to turn your stomach. Bound to get public opinion on his side, though. Which doesn't exactly mean hitting pay dirt for me. You should have nipped that in the bud.'

'What? Stopped her getting topped?'

'Yeah. If necessary.'

'How was I supposed to do that? It wasn't down to me that she got done in.'

'Which shows how far you're losing it. It should have been down to you that she wasn't. Isn't that what the police are paid for? To stop innocent people copping it?'

Banks tried to gather his thoughts. He tried to regain some semblance of control of an interview which was swiftly becoming a disaster.

'We're pretty close to nailing the main suspect,' he said. 'Had my way I'd have had him in custody well before now.' And he told Noble, with an air of imparting official secrets, everything he knew about Greyshott.

'And another thing,' he added, offering the information as a sop, 'he's got one hell of a personal computer in his flat. And damn all in the way of security. Could get into his place with no more effort than sticking a credit card in the Yale. Guy can't put up a fight, he's in a wheelchair.'

'Thanks, but no thanks. I'll decide what I steal and what I don't. Besides, I've got bigger fish to fry. Added to which, no way I'm touching a murder suspect, that'd be asking for trouble. In the meantime you know why you get your cut, don't you? To keep the Bill off my back. I pay you good money for it, so get on with it.'

'Sure. Yeah.' The strain in Banks's muscles from the work-out at the nick returned a hundred-fold. He felt as though his entire body had been chewed up and spat out.

'So that's the score.' Noble smiled and clapped Banks on the shoulder. 'No hard feelings. No cause to fall out over a little hiccup like this. Daresay you'll soon have things kosher again. Get yourself another drink, why don't you? No, no,' Noble raised one hand in a gesture of refusal. 'Haven't the time to join you. As I said, I've got bigger fish to fry.' And he left.

Banks gazed after his retreating back. In all their dealings Noble had never been the first to leave. Christ, what a come-down! He pulled himself together. He braced his sore body. Because he could turn things around, of course he could. But first he'd have that drink.

He approached the bar. Tanya, Noble's woman, was serving, filling in during the early evening hours when punters were few and far between. He ordered a double whisky.

'That'll be two pounds forty-nine,' she said.

Banks had never had to pay for drinks at the Icicle before.

Bryan and John were in Bryan's living room. Mrs Corke and Lee had left, Edward was to return later to deliver John to the shared house. 'So what did you make of that little lot?' Bryan asked apropos of what Lee had said.

'Weird. Not that it gets us much further.'

'It might do. Calls for a spot of the Hercule Poirot approach.'

'Which is?'

'Sitting back in our chairs and letting our little grey cells do the walking. Know what might help.' He glanced at his watch. 'Sure, why not? Sun's well over the yard-arm.'

'What the fuck are you on about?'

Bryan trundled wordlessly into the kitchen, returned with a bottle of malt and two of the six cut-glass tumblers which had also been on Edward's shopping list that day. 'Straight or on the rocks?' he asked, ejecting a couple of ice cubes from the tray he'd brought from the fridge. One of them missed his glass, slithered across the coffee table and landed on the floor. Nothing he could do about that. Dammit, he might be able to afford whisky, to pour it into glasses, but he still couldn't manage to bend down to retrieve an ice cube; or to put dead Marion's dress to rights. He scowled.

John appeared not to have noticed. 'Whichever,' he said as he took his glass. 'Christ, you've got it made. Catch the staff in my house offering us a drink of an evening. Or going on about yard-arms for that matter.' He took a sip, smiled, then looked around him. 'Place is a bit bare though, isn't it? Would have thought you could do better than that.'

Bryan scowled again. 'No one ever comes here.'

'Pull the other one. That is, if I had a healthy one to pull. Told me yourself you had the police here at the crack of dawn. Then Edward. Then me. Then Mrs Corke and that apology for a child. Can't kid me – you've got the social life of Tara Palmer-Tompkinson.'

'Not quite. And that was today.'

'So what's to make tomorrow different? What you could do with is some pictures. Brighten the place up. Which reminds me. Did you like my prezzie?'

'What?'

'Told you about it.' John wheeled himself behind Bryan. 'Told you I'd had Edward stick it in the back of your chair.' He returned to face Bryan and thrust a flat object wrapped in cheap Christmas paper at him. 'Go on, open it.'

It was a magazine. Called *Page Four*. The cover featured a bare, big busted woman hoisting her boobs towards her chin with her cupped hands. Her nail varnish was chipped, Bryan noticed, and the nails beneath looked as though they had been bitten.

'Sometimes, John, you are utterly over the top, What am I supposed to do with this?'

'Cut out the cream of the crop and stick 'em on the walls. That's what I do.'

'In your room?'

'Yeah. Drives the staff bananas. Wouldn't allow it in the communal rooms, of course. Not a lot they can do about it in mine. Censorship stops when my door closes.'

Which was what it was all about, Bryan realised. It wasn't so much – wasn't at all, he guessed – that John wanted to feast his eyes on naked women. Umpteen acres of exposed, pulchritudinous flesh probably left him cold. What he cared about was the fact that his choice of whether or not he wanted

165

to look at women in the buff – a simple choice for most men – had, because of his disability, his lack of privacy, become a privilege for which to fight. It was his front line, the limit beyond which he was not prepared to go. He looked up and saw John watching him, the black pupils of his eyes waiting for Bryan's reaction.

'The rest of them have the same sort of stuff in their rooms?' asked Bryan.

'Nah. Old Joey has cuddly toys. Teddy bears mostly, the place is packed out with them. Crawling all over the pillow. And Laura has Little Pony stuff. Posters and all.' John was still watching.

'What I really want to know,' said Bryan, 'is how do you manage to reach the top shelf? In the newsagents.'

He'd struck the right note. He was rewarded by a quick grin. 'Get the other punters to give me a hand. The one they're not using at the time.'

'Why's it called *Page Four*?'

'Because it goes further than any pic you'll ever see on Page Three.'

Bryan began to leaf through the repulsive thing.

'See what you mean.'

The pictures weren't just of breasts and bottoms. It was all a good deal more intimate than that. And it turned his stomach rather than turning him on. Looking at photos of the fleshy folds of female genitalia wasn't at all his cup of tea. He flicked the pages faster, then stopped.

He was looking down at the anatomy of a woman whose head was obscured in shadow. Her naked body was young and beautiful, almost perfect. Except for the angry, red puckered birthmark in the shape of an elongated comma. She lay sprawled on her right side so he could see that the mark began in the centre of one plump cheek of her bottom, mounted the projection of her hip, then dipped, like the finger of an intrusive hand, towards her exposed genitals.

Chapter Eight

'Christ, if I have to put up with any more of those little buggers sticking chewing gum inside my helmet,' Dosh told Paul Hind-marsh, 'I'll bash their fucking heads together.'

The two of them were returning from their fourth school visit of the morning. Like many others of the uniforms they had gone, under DCI Dawson's instructions, from classroom to classroom – ostensibly to introduce themselves to the children as friendly, local, neighbourhood policemen and to encourage efforts to produce home-made hats for the Fun Day – but also to see whether they could uncover the identities of the boys who had invaded the Community Centre. Dosh and Hindmarsh had uncovered nothing apart from their heads, with predictable results.

'I did reprimand the last juvenile to offend,' Hindmarsh reminded his colleague. 'Told him that although his behaviour towards an officer of the law was of insufficient gravity to warrant a caution, any repetition of the incident would, if notified to the police, be bound to be viewed with serious concern.'

'What did the little bugger say to that mouthful?'

Hindmarsh looked rueful and for once spoke normally, 'Said to f . . . off' – then reverted to studiously stylised type. 'All the same, the Guvnor cannot fail to recognise that in spite of many such incidents this morning we have carried out community policing duties to the best of our ability.'

'With zero results,' Dosh pointed out as they rounded the corner by Crandon nick. 'We'll get nowhere with the kids. "Police" is a swear word to them. Mind you, got to hand it to the Guv in terms of psychology far as the adults are concerned. People coming out of the woodwork with what they think might be evidence or might be the murder weapon. Christ,' he added, clocking the long line of people – many

167

clutching heavy objects – which straggled outside the front door of the station. 'Looks like a scene from *The Antiques Road-show*.'

Inside the nick, the shuffling queue of people were being processed with painstaking care. Dawson had given strict orders that he was to be notified of absolutely anything which was out of the ordinary, however apparently trivial. As a result he had so far officiated at interviews with six different members of the public who had seen a stranger 'lurking' (as they all put it) in Carleton Park on the day of the Stone murder. All agreed he was 'acting suspiciously', but couldn't put their fingers on what made them think so. Nor did they agree about what he'd been wearing: their descriptions varied from a smart suit to baggy street gear. One said he had a limp, another claimed he had a 'sinister' beard, a third refused to be shaken from his conviction that the man had an 'evil' glint in his eye. Only the testimony of a young woman with greasy rat-tails of black hair and a snarling baby in a buggy gave any hint of confirming the sighting made by the road sweeper of a well built man. But it turned out she had only seen him from behind and was clueless as to further details. Hopeless!

On the plus side, a number of the objects found during the search of Carleton Park had been returned to their rightful owners. And a number of petty crimes had been very nearly tracked to their source. Time and again the name of Jack Noble had come up. In connection with the pink conch and the metallic tubes, both of which, it turned out, were the property of a young woman who was into *feng shui*. She turned out to be a trainee solicitor living on a low income while she got her articles. The sort of woman, Dawson thought, appraising her neatly cut hair, neatly cut black jacket and short black skirt, who would be a prime candidate in due course for one of his lofts. So he was right. There were decent, upwardly mobile people who wanted to live in Crandon.

168

Dawson had also listened to a woman describe – with considerable relish – a series of high-pitched screams she had heard on the night of Charteris's death, but the timing didn't tally, it had probably been nothing more than a cat fight. A couple of drinkers at the Carleton Arms said they'd stepped outside for a moment (to piss in the street, Dawson surmised) and had seen a kid running past. But again they could give no detailed description, and they hadn't a clue as to when the sighting took place only that it was 'early on'. He was beginning to despair of getting anything concrete when Banks hurriedly summoned him yet again to an interview room. The room contained an old man wrapped in a huge scarf and a scruffy mongrel on a lead. It also contained, on the table in front of the man, a heavy metal object, wrapped in clear plastic. It was part of a car jack, and Dawson was certain that it was the murder weapon.

The address on the back cover of *Page Four* turned out to be on the edge of the Mandela Estate in a dirty, congested street lined with decidedly down-market shops. The pavements were cluttered with an overspill of cheap goods: dingy, second-hand furniture; chipped, grimy fridges; tables on which remnants of garish fabric tumbled in the confusion wreaked by desperate, bargain-hunting hands; and plastic laundry baskets full of toilet rolls and tins of Chappie.

'Must be the wrong address,' commented John, as Edward double-parked outside a plate-glass window which, according to the sign above it, was the office of the *Crandon Courier*.

'No.' Bryan was checking the magazine. 'This is it. Get us out, Edward.'

Edward undertook the clumsy procedure – lowering the ramp at the back of the people carrier, getting them both into their wheelchairs – involved in Bryan's instruction, to the accompaniment of blasts from the horns of angry motorists at the obstruction he was causing. Bryan checked swiftly that access to the *Courier* office involved no steps.

169

'Keep driving round the block till you see us come out,' he instructed Edward.

They trundled inside, one after the other. A dirty carpet. Walls which had once been white. A portable screen, on which were tacked curling displays of extracts from the *Courier* from what looked like the year dot, separated a small reception area from what was presumably the editorial side of things; at any rate Bryan caught a glimpse of several people at work there. This side of the screen a sharp-faced girl was tapping at a keyboard with the speed of a snail. The only other occupant of reception was an elderly black guy whom Bryan supposed, from the fact that he wore a dark uniform, must be 'Security'; not that he looked capable of ejecting anyone from the premises should the need arise.

The girl looked up from her keyboard, then lowered her eyes to wheelchair height.

'Can I help you?'

'We're looking for the offices of *Page Four*.'

'It's out back.' She jerked her head towards a door. Bryan and John headed for it. Behind them he heard the security guard say, 'Would you believe some of the sickos they get in there?' The girl giggled in response; a giggle, Bryan thought, which was tinged with nervous disgust.

Hardly surprising, given the scene inside the door. It was dark, black paper covered the windows. In the centre of the room was a large brass bed with stained black satin sheets pock-marked by cigarette burns. A woman lay on it, legs spread wide. She was lit from the front by lamps on tripods. Behind her was a silver, umbrella-like affair. Between her legs was the head of a man, dark, slicked-back hair curling on his none too clean collar. At first Bryan thought that he was witnessing a simple act of cunnilingus. Then he realised the guy was clicking away with a camera. He was taking photographs.

'It's no good if you don't show all you've got,' the guy complained. He shifted position, moving closer as though he were penetrating the woman with the zoom lens of his camera. He stopped and withdrew. 'Turn over,' he commanded, 'and let me get a shot of your arse.'

She was a young woman, not much more than a girl. Nineteen, at a guess, Bryan thought. Long black hair streamed in a river across her white shoulders, trailed down across the small of her back to her buttocks. Beautifully smooth, beautifully cut, beautifully tended, black hair. Her wiry pubic hair was black too.

He shifted his gaze to take in the rest of the room. Two other women sat on old kitchen chairs, wrapped in old dressing gowns, smoking and waiting their turn to be humiliated.

Bryan cleared his throat.

The photographer turned and faced them. 'You got an appointment?' he asked.

Bryan recognised him. He was the man who had taken pictures at the social of Kenny's bloodied face as he fell.

'Wrapped it up myself,' the old man told Dawson proudly, pointing to the jack, 'in case of fingerprints. Like they do on *The Bill.* Found it in the bins at the back of the Carleton Park Estate tower block. Tell the truth, Henry found it.' He bent and patted the dog. 'Forever getting into rubbish.' The dog cocked a leg and peed on the leg of the table. 'Henry, leave! Still, just as well he did this time, eh?'

Dawson nodded brusquely. 'Have one of the uniforms in to take a full, formal statement,' he instructed Banks. Seconds later, Hindmarsh entered with his notebook, saw the thing on the table, and recoiled.

'That's mine!' he said.

There was a pile of back issues of *Page Four* on the low table between Bryan and John. To pass the time till Hepworth was prepared to speak to them, Bryan picked one up and leafed through it. God, some of this stuff was seriously sick. This particular issue had a 'Speciality Section' called '*Shaving Ravers*'.

171

'Oh they often have specialities.' John was blasé. 'As I said, *Page Four* tends to go a bit further than your average "Readers' Wives". Podgy pussies, tattooed tearaways, bondage babies, pets win prizes. That sort of thing.' He sounded so matter of fact that Bryan gave him a searching look.

'Not the kind of thing I go for,' said John quickly. 'That's strictly for the pervs.'

'Look who this is,' said Bryan, pointing to one of the pictures. 'It's Julia Stone.'

At which point the photographer turned and gave them his attention.

'Now what can I do for you two gentlemen?' His eyes slid down to their wheelchairs. 'Looking for something in the speciality market, I expect?'

There was silence for a moment. Then:

'God,' said John, the penny dropping seconds after it had as far as Bryan was concerned, 'the guy thinks we want to look at pictures of naked cripples. Now that really is sick.'

But once Bryan produced a twenty pound note – from a visible, thick wad of notes in his wallet – Hepworth told the women to get themselves a cup of coffee. They melted away and Bryan and John soon had the interview going along the lines they wanted. Though Jim Hepworth denied all knowledge of Julia Stone.

'After all, loads of us do a bit of work here. Most news photographers on the up do a bit of freelance. Only way to pay the bills.'

It was a different story when Bryan produced the picture of Marion.

'Her? Oh, sure. Everybody knows her. Made quite a reputation for herself.'

'Where did you first meet her?'

Hepworth's eyes strayed to Bryan's wallet.

'None of my business why you want to know all this,' he said. 'But do you realise how little I earn in a month? Plus there's the expenses. Camera cost me a bomb. Film doesn't come cheap either.' He pocketed a second twenty pound note.

'It's not that I wouldn't like to help,' Hepworth went on, 'but we're planning to go public on the whole affair in a few days. Got the lawyers crawling over the story at the moment. Can't afford to risk a libel suit. Don't want the cops getting hold of it either. They'll only insist we keep it under wraps. Spill the beans to you, what's to stop you selling it to a rival paper?'

'The *Courier* is the only paper in Crandon,' Bryan pointed out.

'We're not talking locals.' Hepworth was indignant. 'This is bigger stuff. And you bet your life I'm not putting the kibosh on my exclusive.'

'It wouldn't hurt to tell us where you met her,' persuaded Bryan, producing another twenty pound note. He could see that Hepworth was torn between the possible prospect of big money in the future and the absolute certainty of a smaller – but still worthwhile – killing now of hard cash from a gullible guy in a wheelchair.

'We're not interested in the media,' Bryan assured him. 'And we won't go to the police.'

'We were friends of hers,' added John: which, now she was dead, was in a way, true.

'Strange choice of friends is all I can say.' But Hepworth, accepting another bank note, was weakening.

'Met her up the West End,' he said. 'Do a bit of paparazzi stuff on the side.' Most of Hepworth's 'work' appeared to be on the side, Bryan reflected.

'Movie premiere, it was,' the photographer went on. 'Must have been nearly a year ago now. She was there with her other half. Got a shot of Leo DiCaprio. Al Pacino. Mike Douglas. Christ, she was dressed to the nines. Practically smell the money she was wearing on her back, dress must've cost a fortune. Gold watch, gold necklace, gold bracelet. Expensive tan. Had whatever she wanted in the way of material goodies. Couldn't give her what she really wanted though, could he?'

'Which was?'

'You really friends of hers, you ought to know. Gave her one in the toilets, didn't I? Told her if she wanted more to get her arse down here.'

'And she did?'

'Sure as hell. Every Tuesday, Wednesday and Thursday. From around twelve till just before two. Said she had to be somewhere else at two.'

The Centre, thought Bryan. She was at the Centre by two. So that's what she'd been doing every day before she turned up in her expensive clothes to do her Lady Bountiful act. Christ, he thought, then amended his thought to 'Poor kid!'

'I imagine,' he said carefully, 'that it's not simply a matter of taking pictures here.'

'Course not.' Hepworth jerked his head upwards and to the right. 'There's upstairs. Plenty of bedrooms.'

'And did Marion go upstairs?'

'You must be joking. Can't keep a good woman down.' Hepworth chortled.

'And then you took her picture?'

'Sure.'

'Wasn't the . . . um,' Bryan paused, 'the birthmark a bit of a deterrent? I mean, didn't it put the punters off?'

'Oh, so you *were* friends of hers. Thought you was playing me along. Mind you, never have crossed my mind she'd go with a guy in a wheelchair. No accounting for tastes, is there?'

Bryan saw that John was about to make a comeback to that remark and quelled him with a swift wave of his hand.

'As I said,' he said, 'we were friends. Family friends. I've known her since she was this high.' He gestured at the wheel of his chair. 'And before I was in this.' He gestured at the chair again. 'Used to go down to the beach together,' he lied. 'Couldn't help knowing what she looked like without her

174

clothes. Even little kids,' he persisted, 'wear bikinis. So why didn't it,' he pressed on, 'put the punters off?'

'Quite the other way round. Turned them on. See the way that birthmark pointed to you know what? Came back time and time again, they did. And she was always ready for all and sundry. Quite a nice little earner for the boss.'

'Why d'you think she did it?' asked John abruptly.

'Search me. Some sort of compulsion, maybe? As I say, she didn't need the money. Which reminds me, you got any more dosh where that came from?' Bryan peeled another twenty pound note from the wad in his wallet.

'Ask me, it was because of the birthmark. Looked so perfect on the outside, like a package done up in a Harrod's box. Unwrap the thing and you find you've been done. Think that's what she thought. But none of the punters did. On account of when she got going she went like the clappers. She was anybody's. Grateful for the attention, I'd say.'

In other words, no different from me and John, thought Bryan. In other words, no different from anyone.

'Just one last thing,' he said. He palmed another note in his hand. 'Who runs this magazine?'

'Can't tell you that. I were you, I'd take a look at the incoming mail in reception. See who it's addressed to. And now I'd better get back to work.' He clapped his hands and the two women materialised and shed their dressing gowns.

'Let's get a close up on those tits,' he said.

In the outer office Bryan and John dallied, trying to get a sight of an envelope in an in-tray.

'What's the matter?' asked the security guy sarkily. 'Didn't get what you were after?'

'Sickos,' muttered the receptionist, stabbing at her keyboard with two angry fingers. Boyfriend trouble, thought Bryan.

'Don't get many guys in wheelchairs passing through,' the elderly black guy went on. 'Quite see you might have been disappointed.'

Which was when John erupted.

'What's the matter with you people with legs?' he shouted. 'What d'you think we are? Why d'you think we want to feast our eyes on other cripples? If we want to look at women, then we want to look at perfect women. Like everybody else.' He caught Bryan's eye and escalated his fervour, gesticulating with his hands. 'Equal gawping rights, that's what we want.'

John had distracted the attention of the security guy and the receptionist. Bryan had time to inspect the contents of the in-tray. And to note that all the mail was addressed to J. Noble. Some had been sent to the man at the *Courier's* offices and some to a private address on the Mandela estate. He memorised the second address swiftly.

They were outside. The air seemed clearer here. It was raining quite hard, so they sat in the porch of the *Courier* building.

'So that's why she came to the Centre three times a week,' said John. 'It wasn't to "help" us. It was a fucking cover for sleeping with him.'

'Not just him,' Bryan reminded. 'And anyway we didn't want her help.'

'Still and all. Turns you off a bit, doesn't it? You reckon she slept with everyone she met?'

'Is what the man said.'

'Except guys in wheelchairs.'

'Christ, if we'd known.'

'Yeah, all those months.'

'You know what?'

'No. What?'

'One thing looking at pictures of naked lovelies for a laugh,' said John. 'Quite another matter when you're brought up against the reality. Hey, here's a thought.' He tapped his forehead with the palm of his hand. 'D'you suppose she slept with Edward?'

'Which reminds me. Where the fuck is Edward? I told him to drive around the block, not the entire borough. He must

176

know we could be getting wet. Mind you, it is easing off a bit. Let's see if we can see him.' Bryan left the protection of the porch and began to move across the wide pavement. The pair of them were so engrossed in their conversation they hardly noticed that they were bumping into reconditioned fridges, stacks of loo rolls, plastic boxes full of biros. 'At any rate she must have slept with this man Noble. Finding him has to be our next task.'

Bryan propelled himself past an old sofa towards the kerb, still talking, his head turned to the right where John, behind him, was negotiating his way round the back of a gas cooker which stood on the edge of the pavement. So neither of them saw the car leave the road at speed and mount the kerb. First thing Bryan knew was the impact as it struck the wheel of his chair. He heard the sound of an engine screaming under full acceleration and was hurled backwards out of the chair onto – thank God! – something soft. He was only winded. not hurt. He'd landed on the sofa. There was no sign of the car – not that he knew what it looked like – but he reckoned the driver had scarpered into the traffic. Meanwhile his chair had careered across the pavement and collided with John's, which in its turn collided with a stack of plastic cartons of washing-up liquid which rolled into the road, where they squished, foaming in the drizzle, under the tyres of passing cars.

An Asian shopkeeper emerged, took no notice of Bryan lying on the sofa, but said mildly to John, 'If you don't want to buy, then please don't destroy.'

'Sorry, mate,' said John just as Edward appeared and rushed to Bryan's aid.

Getting Bryan back into his wheelchair and getting the pair of them into the car took a good deal longer than the disembarkation had. Horns were hooting in earnest this time. A traffic warden materialised, looked with disapproval at the sudsy surface of the road and began to lecture Edward about restrictions on loading and unloading; for all the world, thought Bryan, as though he and John were a cargo of supplies from the local Cash and Carry.

Turned out – Forensics were as quick as all get out with the results – that the car jack fitted the profile of the murder weapon. Also turned out that Hindmarsh, in a disturbing lapse from procedure, had been carrying the thing about all day under the seat in the back of the squad car on the date of the Charteris murder. Came up with some garbled tale of doing a favour for a friend who'd lent his own jack to another friend who'd . . . and so on ad infinitum, thought Dawson wearily. For what it was worth, he believed Hindmarsh's story. Every last vestige of pompous correctness had disappeared from the constable's speech, he was obviously scared stiff. So he should be. More so, given he hadn't reported the loss of the object on the night in question. Even more so because he couldn't recall when it had gone missing. There had been too many other things happening that night. He had attended his first incident. He had mounted his first solo pursuit. He had confronted his first corpse. He had met his first murderer. He had made his first arrest. And he had bottled out. Knew full well he shouldn't be carrying a potentially lethal object around in a squad car. And when he realised it had gone – not till the next morning, he'd simply forgotten about the jack in all the excitement – he was too frightened of repercussions to mention it to anyone. Took refuge, Dawson surmised, in an even more dogged devotion to chapter and verse of police procedure. Now he was just a young lad whose lower lip was quivering like the nose of a frightened rabbit. Dawson reprimanded him sharply – but not too sharply, no point in upsetting the boy too much, every point in letting him see his Guvnor as a man who tempered justice with mercy. Besides, Dawson had other fish to fry; the check on all known villains in Crandon had thrown up Noble time and time again. Jack Noble whom so far only Banks had inter-

178

viewed. This time Dawson would be along as a third party. And Hindmarsh – Dawson summoned him with a peremptory gesture – would have the chance to redeem himself by taking notes which were the epitome of correct police procedure.

'You know my spare room?' Bryan asked John. Edward had dropped them back at Bryan's place and they were finishing the cake left over from yesterday's tea, their knees comfortably tucked under the specially designed worktops in Bryan's kitchen.

'What about it?'

'Wanna move into it for the duration? So you can be on the spot for further investigations?'

'No, thank you,' said John, stiffening with resentment at even such a minor hint of patronage. 'I'm perfectly well cared for where I am.'

'Wasn't that. Until other people move into the rest of the flats in this house I'm on my own. Okay, so today might have been an accident, but on the other hand it might not.'

'Don't see how it could have been. Cars don't mount pavements unless they're driven there. And they don't take off at speed unless the driver's got something to hide.'

'Are you sure you didn't see anything?' Bryan asked for the umpteenth time that afternoon. 'If not the number plate then at least the make. Or the model. Or the colour?'

'I told you. I was behind that sodding cooker.'

Bryan returned to his earlier subject. 'So what d'you reckon on my spare room? Thing is,' he added, 'place isn't exactly secure. Told you what that policeman said the other night about the neighbourhood. He said I ought to have a Chubb on the door. Window locks too.'

'Well, why haven't you? You could have got Edward to buy them yesterday. You sent him to buy enough other stuff.'

'Had my reasons. So are you on?'

'Shelley and Co won't like it.'

'Tell them to go piss themselves.'

'Can't do that. If they think I've got some place else to go I might lose my room.'

'So what's so special about your room?'

'Nothing. But it is a room. Look, it's one thing for people like you who've got the money to pay for a decent place of your own. But I waited years to get that room . . . any room. Now I've got security. I'm what you might call,' he grinned, 'a sitting tenant.'

'You think I'd be about to throw you out? The room's yours for as long as you want it. And honestly, you'd be doing me a favour.'

'Oh yeah? So you think two cripples equal one able-bodied attacker?'

'No. I just think two cripples are better than one.'

Dawson swiftly established that Jack Noble's alibi at the time of Charteris's death was watertight. He was interviewing him in the small office at the back of the Icicle Club. Noble sat in a leather chair behind a leather-topped desk. He was wearing a gold signet ring on his right hand, Dawson noted. He, Dawson, sat in front of the desk. Banks hovered uneasily. Hindmarsh stood to ramrod-stiff attention, notebook at the ready.

'Ask anyone in the club,' drawled Noble in answer to Dawson's question. 'Must have been at least a hundred punters here. I was visible all evening.'

'I've checked, Guv,' Banks intervened. 'In fact he was making a speech at the time of Charteris's death. The whole place was listening. He'd given them all free drinks.'

'Announcing my impending nuptials,' said Noble with a smile.

'How very convenient,' said Dawson.

He knew the man was a villain, he'd seen his type before. Okay, so his record was for minor offences and they were all some years in the past. So what had he been up to since? More

180

to the point, given he would hardly have gone straight, why hadn't he been charged with anything in recent years? Dawson shot a look at Banks who was moving uneasily around the room, and put two and two together. He thought for a moment: no harm in letting the suspect wait while he, Dawson, put his thoughts in order. He'd never been one to rush things in an interview situation. Decided best to keep a watchful eye on how the pair of them behaved during the remainder of the interview. There'd be plenty of time to open up that line of questioning later. But for now:

'Were you acquainted with Marion Charteris?' he asked.

'Sure.'

'In what capacity?'

Noble laughed. 'You really want all the intimate details? Let's just say she used to come here – to my flat upstairs – of an afternoon. Tuesday, Wednesday and Thursday afternoons, in fact, before she went to help at the Centre.' He paused and leered. 'That is,' he added, 'when she wasn't otherwise occupied.'

So she'd slept with this jumped-up, over-confident, smiling bastard of a villain? Probably with the same enthusiasm with which she had slept with him. And the implication of Noble's last remark was that she had sex with other men too. Dawson was visited by a sudden wave of disgust so tangible it was as if vomit had risen in his throat. Thank God he'd insisted on using a condom that night in his loft.

He swallowed, feeling his Adam's apple convulse with the effort of holding the bile down. No point in persisting with questions about the Charteris murder, the man had a water-tight alibi. He changed tack.

'Were you acquainted with Julia Stone?'

'Sure.'

'In what capacity?'

Noble grinned. 'The same.'

'The flat above these premises is given as her last known address.'

181

'That's right. Got a bit down on her luck and moved in for a while. Don't usually have them living on the premises. Cramps my style, if you take my meaning.'

'The flat is also registered as your permanent address.'

'That's right. I live here. Over the shop.'

'Are you aware that a man of your description was seen in Carleton Park early on the afternoon of Julia Stone's murder? We have a witness who will confirm that he heard an argument take place in the shelter, the scene of her death.'

'So what?' Noble shrugged. 'Julia and me often got into a bit of a barney. What is all this? Thought you'd got a geezer banged up for topping her.'

Dawson changed tack again.

'Are you acquainted with Harry Green?'

'Yeah.'

'In what capacity?'

Noble laughed out loud.

'Got me there, squire. Can't say it was in the same "capacity" as the two broads. In fact, I bought stuff off him.'

'Stuff?' Dawson was on the alert. 'What kind of stuff?'

'Keep your hair on. It was all legit. Dresses mainly. He gets them out of skips in the West End.'

Banks interrupted again.

'You wouldn't know, Guv,' he said, 'but Green has been quite a character in the manor for years. Makes his living out of other people's rubbish.'

Came too pat, thought Dawson. Banks was clearly trying to protect Noble, and not with any particular success. Was it his imagination or did he catch the suggestion of a frown on Noble's face and a slight shake of his head in Banks's direction? But facial expressions weren't evidence. Dawson remembered Green's worry about the dresses he had with him at the station and thought: they must have been above board, otherwise Green would have disowned them soon as look at them.

Time to see what Noble knew about the other unsolved crime in Crandon.

'You're aware of the fire which took place in the mall two weeks ago?'

'Who isn't?'

'Are you aware of any motive anyone might have for setting the Patels' shop alight?'

'Racial harassment? Vandalism? Mindless hooliganism? Shocking what kids get up to these days.' Noble paused and shrugged again. 'Search me.'

Dawson would have loved to, but that wasn't on the cards. He had nothing concrete on the guy yet. He pressed on.

'Are you acquainted with the Mayor of Crandon?'

This time Noble's laughter was a derisive bark. 'You think I might have slept with her? Barking up the wrong tree. She swings the other way. Thought you would have known that by now. It has been in the *Courier*.'

'That wasn't always the case. She has a ten year old son.'

'Nothing to do with me, squire.' He shifted his plump buttocks comfortably on his leather chair. 'Now, if there's nothing else you want to ask, I have business to attend to.' He rose to his feet.

Dawson had no option but to do the same.

'I do hope I have been of some use,' Noble went smoothly on as he ushered them to the door with overdone politeness. Dawson made a point of going first. Hindmarsh followed at his heels like a dog. Banks was behind. At the threshold Dawson turned sharply, and caught the look which Noble shot at Banks – a look which promised serious reprimand if not something more.

Between them they cleared out the room. It was stacked high with piles of stuff. Who'd done the stacking? Edward must've when Bryan first moved in. And what was the stuff? All sorts. CDs. Expensive suits of clothes on hangers. Bryan's cut-glass Waterford tumblers. A couple of deco table lamps in the shape of scantily draped women which John thought very tasty. Half a bottle of whisky. Quantities of books. Wedgwood plates.

Some Lalique glass. And Bryan's watercolours – mostly of cities, but some of country landscapes – which he had collected from around the world.

'Venice, from the top of the Campanile,' he enumerated in response to John's queries, 'the Camargue, Manhattan Island from Brooklyn Heights, a pine forest just outside Luxembourg, the bridge over the Garonne in Bordeaux, the Sydney Opera House, the French Quarter of New Orleans.'

'That's the one I'd go for.' John was pointing at a depiction of an almost improbably blue sea fringed by a deserted white beach with green palm fronds beyond. 'Where is it?'

'Barbados.'

'My idea of paradise,' enthused John, 'always assuming a few topless lovelies basking on that beach.'

'There were.' Bryan backed sharply away from the picture, collided with a haphazard pile of books and knocked the whole shebang sideways onto the floor. 'And it was hell.'

'All right, keep your hair on. What happened? Did a particularly luscious one give you a knockback?'

Bryan shook his head, then confessed the fact which he had admitted to no one else in Crandon. 'It was where I broke my neck.'

'Whoops, put my foot in it,' said John, then added with the abrasiveness which never failed to bring Bryan back from the brink of self pity, 'assuming I could put my foot anywhere except on the foot board of my chair. You really been to all these places?' he hurried on.

Bryan nodded.

'How come? Expense account trips in the name of work? Or holidays?'

'Some were holidays. You get pretty stressed out in our job. Used to get my relaxation in a way which, with hindsight, was practically criminally insane.'

'Don't tell me. Pulling gorgeous birds night after night.'

'That too. But mostly it was the old eighties cliché of going for the max. White water rafting. Paragliding. Bungee

184

jumping. Off-piste skiing. Abseiling. Rock climbing. Deep sea diving. Solo parachute jumps.' He paused. 'And hang gliding,' he added.

'That was how you broke your neck?'

Bryan nodded again.

'What d'you do it for?'

'The buzz. The excitement. As I say, as a release from the tension of work. But mostly, I suppose, to convince myself I could. I've always been like that. Have to over-achieve at everything I do.'

'Christ, you must have been earning a mint to pay for umpteen holidays like that.'

'A fair whack.'

'So what – don't mind my asking, do you mate? – exactly did you do?'

'I was in the oil industry. Mainly I negotiated contracts.'

'Is that it?' John was incredulous.

'Well, yes. There's a lot of money in the oil industry. If you're tough enough, clued up enough to get the best deal from smaller rivals, then you can fairly rake it in. It's a bit like the City,' he added, 'wheeling and dealing for high stakes. Lots of people burn out. Only in my case I crashed out.'

John shook his head. 'I don't get it. Hang-gliding in a wheelchair, I can see that might be a few sandwiches short of a picnic. But negotiating ought to be a pushover. For a guy like you.'

'No.'

'Why not?'

Bryan flourished at his useless lower limbs with an extravagant gesture worthy of Sir Walter Raleigh spreading his cloak for Good Queen Bess to cross a puddle.

'I still don't get it.'

'Who'd respect an opponent in a wheelchair?'

'Come on, that's not what life is about these days. Remember what Marion – poor sod! – used to tell us? We're not disabled, we're differently abled. In other words, your brain is as good as theirs. Good as any in the field, probably.'

185

'I know,' Bryan conceded. 'Actually,' he admitted – for the first time, even to himself – 'it was nothing to do with them. It was me, my own attitude. I didn't feel I could compete. To start with, it was months before I got the hang of a wheelchair. Then I had a load of people visiting me in hospital. Looming over me, walking in and out like it was no big deal to get around on your own two legs. I couldn't face the fact that I 'd been cut down to size. I couldn't go back to work. '

John shrugged. 'It's your life, mate,' then changed tack. 'You miss all that? The jet set stuff?'

Bryan thought for a moment. 'Actually, no.' He surprised himself with that realisation. 'I've got enough on my plate these days to occupy my mind. And, after today, enough danger to boot. Plus,' he added, knowing it was time to lighten the mood, 'I have the serious problem of where the fuck to put all this stuff.'

'Stack it back against the walls. I'm used to living in far more cramped quarters.'

'Uh-huh.' Bryan shook his head. 'Space to turn your wheelchair is the bottom line. And room for Edward to get you into bed. We'll have Edward over for an hour every evening for the duration so he can do the necessary.' He forestalled an objection with a wave of his hand. 'Won't make a blind bit of difference to us communing far into the night if we feel so inclined. I'm well used to getting myself to bed these days. And the loo's a doddle with the hoist. Show you that later. In the meantime, let's get on. Most of this crap can go in the cupboard in the hallway.'

Dawson was back in his office. He wasn't happy with the progress of today's inquiries. Not at all happy. He knew, sure as Hell, that Noble and Banks were in something together. But what? Best let it ride. He'd figure it out when he got home to his loft. He thought of his loft with longing. That calm, simple, comforting space with the uncurtained windows opening onto the black velvet of the night. If only everything could be so uncomplicated. He was interrupted in his longing by a scratch at the door.

'Come,' he commanded.

It was Constable Hindmarsh, still cowed.

'We did the collection for the prize for the best home-made hat on the Fun Day sir,' he said, 'just like you told us to.' Hindmarsh's officialese seemed to have deserted him for good, Dawson reflected. Which was fine. But what did the lad want? The boy stammered and blushed. 'We've collected nearly seventy quid. Dosh said to come to you to top it up to a hundred, said that's what you'd want. In the interests of good community relations.'

Dawson sighed. He reached for his wallet. He forked out. If only everything could be solved by so simple a gesture.

'So somebody's out to get you, mate,' John said to Bryan. 'Who d'you reckon?'

'That's what I didn't want to say before. It could be Edward.'

'Christ, you're paranoid. Edward's the best carer out. Fucking lucky to have him.'

'You realise that neither of us got a sight of the car that headed for me?'

'Yeah.'

'So it could have been my car. Could have been Edward. He turned up pretty sharpish afterwards.'

'Yeah, but it could have been anybody. Specifically, it could have been this Noble guy.'

'Why?'

'Didn't want us poking about. Heard that's what we were doing.'

'From whom?'

'Could be your child friend. Could be the old woman who lives on the fourteenth floor.'

'Who else could have done the dirty?'

187

'Could be Lee's mystery man. The one he said had the bottle to kill. Or it could be – think about it – someone in the police.'

'Come off it, John. Not in real life.'

'Crandon isn't real life as you know it. Didn't you say that guy Banks wanted to pull you in the instant he clapped eyes on you?'

'I was sitting next to a corpse at the time. And waving a crutch. Besides, it's a big step from wanting to make an entirely legitimate arrest to wanting to do me in. Anyway, why would he?'

'Obvious. The person who's trying to do you damage either knows who killed Marion or did it themselves. If the first, they're protecting the killer. If the second, they're protecting themselves. Arrested or dead, it's all the same to them. Either way'll shut you up.'

'If that theory's right, then it rules Edward out.'

'I don't know why you keep banging on about Edward. Why would Edward want to kill her?'

'Which brings us back to why would anyone. With what we've found out today I incline to the jealous lover theory. I can quite see someone being thoroughly pissed off at discovering what she got up to when she was supposed to be doing charity work.'

'Maybe someone just wants to land you in it. Has got a grudge against you. Which would put Edward back in the frame.'

'How d'you mean?'

'Well, you're hardly the world's most sensitive employer. If I talked to the staff at the shared house like you do to him, they'd have me out.'

'But you swear at everybody.'

'No I don't. I swear about them, not at them. There is a difference.'

'Well,' Bryan was on the defensive. 'I pay him enough money.'

'Money isn't everything. So what do we do next?'

'I thought I'd cook us a meal. Then an hour or so in the living room. Put what we know onto the computer. Sort out our thoughts. Get into a few heavy duty ideas about suspects and motives, that kind of thing.'

'Cook what?'

'I thought avocado vinaigrette for starters. With plenty of garlic. Then lamb cutlets with rosemary. Accompanied by roast potatoes and braised cauliflower.'

'Christ. You can really cook all that?'

'Used to be able to. Watch this space.'

Bryan was pleased that the meal turned out exactly as planned. The chops were crisp on the outside, pink within. The roast potatoes were satisfyingly crunchy.

'Sorry that I don't run to dessert,' he apologised, when they'd both finished.

'Are you kidding? Haven't eaten a meal like that in years.'

'So what do you eat in the shared house?'

'You know. The usual. Fish fingers. Egg and chips. Sausages. Jelly and ice cream when it's someone's birthday.'

'Nursery food,' pronounced Bryan in disgust. 'Not fit for adult consumption. We'll stick this lot in the dishwasher, then it's time for some brain work.'

They wheeled into the living room. It was even barer than usual.

'Bloody hell!' exclaimed Bryan. 'My computer's gone!'

'Jesus,' said John, 'and it must be worth a fortune.'

'It's not that,' said Bryan, 'it's insured.'

'What is it then?'

'The stuff that's on it. The directory I opened on how to commit a perfect crime.'

Chapter Nine

'You should have installed that Chubb lock I advised, sir,' said Dosh.

'I will now.'

'Bit late, if you don't mind my saying so, sir. Bolting the stable door and that. Lost a valuable asset there.'

'It's insured.'

'It's what?' Dosh looked as though he had never heard of such a thing being done to household contents except perhaps on TV. Probably no one did in Crandon. The premiums would be so high they'd never be able to afford them and they'd lose their no claims bonuses within weeks. Besides which most of them probably didn't possess anything worth stealing. Except that one of them did – now.

'Can't hold out much hope, sir,' Dosh went on. 'Knocked-off stuff changes hands in a flash on the streets of Crandon. But of course I'll put in a report.'

After the policeman had gone:

'We'll have to make do with pen and paper,' Bryan told John. 'We could share a spliff first. And have a glass of malt each.'

'Count me in. What exactly are we going to do with pen and paper?'

'Make notes. Try to work out what the fuck's going on.'

'In what way?' John was watching Bryan peel cigarette papers from a green Rizla packet.

'Put it like this.' Bryan paused, licked the gummed strip on the paper and rolled his joint. 'Yesterday I'm damn near arrested for a murder I didn't do. This afternoon I'm nearly run over. This evening my computer is stolen.'

'Yes, well,' said John, 'they always say that calamities come in threes. Which might mean,' he added, brightening, 'that with any luck you've had your quota.'

191

'Stop talking luck and start talking logic. Who knew I had a computer in my flat?'

'Me. But aren't you making assumptions? Couldn't it be that someone just broke in on the off-chance?'

'Chance is as unlikely as luck in the circumstances. Who else?'

'Mrs Corke and the kid.'

'Mrs Corke wouldn't know what to do with a computer, never mind how to lift one. The kid is another matter. What I'm getting at,' Bryan went on, 'is that list we made earlier of people who had the motive for getting me out of the way and/or the opportunity to kill Marion. Lee had the opportunity to kill her. And Lee knew about my computer.'

'He's only a kid,' John protested.

'He could still have the strength to kill. Kids have.'

'He thought you'd killed her.'

'Classic case of self-protection. He's a smart kid, he could lie his ass off without betraying it by as much as a tremor of an eyelid. And he has no scruples at all about the morality or otherwise of topping people. After all, he admires me solely because I committed an act of violence.'

'You didn't?'

'Sure I did.'

'When?'

'John, don't be dense. When I mowed down the two kids attacking Kenny.'

'That wasn't violence. That was revenge. I'd have done it myself if I'd been there. And,' he added honestly, 'if I'd had the bottle.'

'We're getting off the point. Other people who knew about the computer: the police – DCI Dawson, the obsequious uniformed officer and the bulldog, Banks. The night they questioned me about Julia Stone's murder Banks took a serious interest in the computer. Stopped him in the nick of time from reading what I'd written. If ever there was a bent copper, I'd put my money on him. Dawson's out of it. He could afford to buy his own PC – probably has a laptop – in any case, he simply wouldn't do anything so blatant to jeopardise his career. The uniformed guy is an air-brain, couldn't pull off any sort of scam to save his life. And then, there's Edward. Edward knows I have a computer, he may even know what I was writing on it that night. Edward was driving back from his evening with you when Marion was killed. Edward might have a motive for getting me out of the way. Or incriminating me, showing the stuff on the computer to the police. Though, no,' Bryan paused and rubbed his temples, 'he could have copied the stuff from the hard disk to a floppy any time if that's what he was after. And,' the thought struck him suddenly, 'if Edward *was* fucking Marion – remember that throwaway remark of yours on that subject? – jealousy when he discovered what she was up to could be quite enough of a motive for killing her.'

John pooh-poohed the idea, but Bryan resolved to have eyes in the back of his head in future where Edward was concerned, and to check up on his background.

Dawson was in his loft. He was reviewing what today's enquiries had revealed. After interviewing Jack Noble he had collected the photograph of the Mayor's son which he had earlier instructed Dosh to obtain, he had detailed Banks to re-visit the Patels, then taken Hindmarsh with him to talk to Mrs Corke. Once she'd established that they were bona fide police, she welcomed the pair of them with open arms, insisted on making tea and said how delightful it was she was getting visits from so many nice young men these days, made her feel in quite a social whirl.

Dawson coaxed her into answering his questions. She confirmed what Greyshott had said: she had seen three boys setting fire to the park shelter shortly before the discovery of the body of Julia Stone. She added, 'Oh dear, I forgot to tell the young man in the wheelchair that I dialled 999 as soon as I saw the flames were out of control. Small fires you get used to around here, the children are always lighting them, but I thought that one was a bit much. I knew when he was here that I'd left something out, but I couldn't think what it was. Still, don't expect he'll mind, he really came to hear about the old days. Should have seen his expression when he heard about the fires we had then.'

'What fires?' asked Dawson sharply.

'In the kitchen, dear. The range. And the black-leaded grate with a marble surround in the lounge. That was when I was in service. Of course we didn't have anything like that at home, bless you no. Why, Mother was still cooking on an open fire when I left home. Had to carry all the coals upstairs herself. I often think about that when I hear people talking about Victorian values. Mind you, the old Queen was dead by then, but that's what nearly everyone had to do during her reign. It wasn't easy. Do you know, when I . . .?'

Dawson put a stop to her meanderings by producing a clutch of photographs.

'Snapshots? How lovely. Is that your little boy? she asked, inspecting a picture of the Mayor's son. 'Mischievous looking little imp. Can't say I've ever seen him before, but he reminds me of our Frank. D'you know when I was ten we used to . . .'

Dawson indicated the other photos with a swift gesture, hoping to catch her attention before she launched into further ramblings.

'Oh, is that your wife?' she asked of a blurred shot of Julia Stone.

'Do you know this woman?'

'Of course I do.'

'And this man?'

'She's Julia. He's Harry Green. And that's Mr Noble. My goodness, you do have some awkward customers in your family for a policeman. It must be quite a trial for you. But there,' she stretched out a blotched hand and patted the back of one of his, 'no call to go believing that saying about one rotten apple turning the whole lot bad. I'd put my money on you any day to turn the family fortunes round. More tea, dear?'

'No thank you,' said Dawson. He had an uncomfortable feeling that Hindmarsh was only just controlling a nervous giggle.

'Did you see Noble cross the park on the afternoon of Julia Stone's death?' he pressed on. 'The afternoon of the fire?'

'Of course I did. I see everything from up here. Except when he's at home.'

'Could you clarify that? When who's at home?'

'Mr Noble. Can't see him when he's upstairs, can I? That's where he lives.'

Which was palpably untrue. Noble's known – and verified – address was the flat over the Icicle. Besides which, Dawson recalled that Banks's report of the house-to-house at the start of the Stone murder inquiry had contained no interviews with anyone on the fifteenth floor of the block. Still, he knew better than to neglect any discrepancy however infeasible; he had Hindmarsh radio in an order to check with the council's Housing Department.

On the off-chance he showed Mrs Corke photographs of the two boys who'd been injured in the fire at the Patels. She identified them instantly as two of the three who had set fire to the shelter in the park. That was the end of his photographs. He didn't think there was more to be got out of Mrs Corke. He thanked her and rose to his feet.

'Before you go, officers,' she said, 'could you just check my security arrangements? I do like to be sure I'm safe up here in my little nest.'

Better oblige, decided Dawson, then raised his eyebrows at the number of locks on the front door. A Chubb, two Yales, a chain, a bolt top and bottom and another in the middle. The door itself was, like all the others along the corridor, made of a single piece of solid wood with a panel of reinforced glass at eye height.

'No need for you to worry,' he assured her. 'That should be quite enough to keep intruders out.'

The answer to Hindmarsh's query re: the Housing Department came through as they were in the car on the way back to the station. The entire top floor had been decanted, the last tenant had moved out over three months ago. And there was an extra piece of information volunteered by some diligent Housing Officer: the last tenant had been Julia Stone who'd lived there with her twelve year old son, Lee. She hadn't been decanted to other council accommodation, she'd made her own arrangements. Which, Dawson surmised, was one less headache for a Department faced with the fairly major administrative task of relocating all the residents of the block. So they would have asked no questions about where she went. Or what became of her child.

He instructed Hindmarsh to put in calls, via the station, to the Education Department and the Social Services Department. He also ordered a check on Lee Stone in police records of juvenile offenders. By the time he reached his office reports lay on his desk. The story proved a familiar one. Lee Stone was a disruptive pupil from an unstable home. He was a persistent truant. The Education Department's report cited many attempts to make contact with the mother, although Dawson suspected the matter had been handled with typical Crandon laxity. No real effort was ever made by the authorities to bring a miscreant to book, they simply took the easiest option.

The police files revealed no mention of Lee Stone ever having been in trouble. And as there had been no question of any sort of abuse by the mother, Social Services had not seen fit to place the child on the 'at risk' register or, decided Dawson, reading between the lines, to make anything more than a nominal attempt to keep tabs on him. In other words, the child had slipped through the net. Where was he now?

It was a question which continued to exercise Dawson as he sat in his loft, sifting the evidence. Hadn't had a chance to do much in the way of thinking in the office. First he had given a press conference to appeal for further witnesses re: the Charteris murder to come forward. The remainder of the day had been taken up with phone calls from various members of the Organising Committee of the Fun Day, and with assuring them that all necessary arrangements were in place for the festivities the following day. The Mayor wanted to know about road closures. Rashid wanted to know about the composition of the police presence in terms of equal opportunities. On the first Dawson had no problems, the second was a little more tricky. Young people and women were accounted for, Hindmarsh and WPC Jones would both be on duty. But, in spite of an urgent official request to the Yard for temporary secondments, he still had no members of the black and ethnic minority communities on the strength. It took all his powers of persuasion and a full reading of his official request to placate Rashid.

But now it was dark and silent and he had the peace he needed. So what had he got? As far as he could see, he had four crimes on his plate. The first was the murder of Julia Stone and the subsequent burning of the park shelter. The second was the protection racket. The third was the arson attack on the Patels' shop. The fourth was the murder of Charteris.

What did he know for certain about any of these? Mrs Corke's evidence, given her obvious senility, was always going to be suspect and any defence brief would have a field day with her in court. Still, he was inclined to believe, on the basis of the alacrity with which she had identified the pictures of the two boys, that she really had seen three children set the park shelter alight. If she had, what of the third child? Could it have been Lee Stone? He was the same age as the other two, he had recently lived – Dawson now knew – in the same tower block. They all had a record for truancy – he'd had the Education Department run a check on Rick Mason and Danny Angelo as well as on the Stone child. It made sense to assume that they might have spent their idle, directionless days together.

Then there was the second fire, at the Patels. Bank's interview with Mr Patel earlier today had yielded no further information. Which was, in itself, a cause for suspicion. Either Banks was concealing evidence – Dawson considered that highly likely – or Mr Patel had been silenced. Or both. Two of the boys who'd started the first fire had been injured in the second. Which left the third boy. He recalled how Mr Patel on the night of the fire had mentioned a complaint of which there was no record at the station. He recalled Banks's insistence that the Mayor's son was acting as a gofer for a protection racket. If Banks – who needed the 'if'? – was bent, then that statement could only mean that the Mayor's son was to be dropped in it and another gofer recruited. Who better than a child who had no parents and about whom no one cared?

It all added up. But if Lee Stone had torched the shop while his friends were inside, had torched the park shelter when his mother was inside, then the child was a monster.

Then there was, he recalled, the child who had been fleeing across the estate after whom Constable Hindmarsh had given chase. There were too many children unaccounted for in this business. Or perhaps there was just one.

He turned his attention to the protection racket. He was positive that Noble was at the back of it, and that Banks was taking backhanders. But, again, he had no proof.

What about the murders? He considered Julia Stone's first. Part of Harry Green's confession was untrue – he hadn't set the shelter alight – but what did that matter? Green was certainly a petty criminal and society – Crandon – would benefit from him being locked away. Added to which Julia Stone had been a no-mark of a tom. Hadn't even made a good job of keeping his loft clean. He raised his head and looked about him. He was going to have to do something about getting a new cleaner. The chrome shelves were thick with dust, there were kittens of fluff on the floor. And the entire place smelt a tad rancid. All in all it wasn't exactly an advertisement for the lifestyle in an improving area which he had envisaged would attract the middle classes. He switched his thoughts back to the crimes. Whether any case against Green would stand up in court was an academic question; he'd lied about the fire and the only other evidence they had against him was the remainder of his confession. The DPP would never stomach bringing a case against him on the grounds of that alone.

Dawson thought back to his appearance earlier on *London Tonight*. At least he'd managed to keep the media on his side. He put that small success down to the neatness of appearance which he always meticulously maintained, the calm resolution and authority with which he faced their questions, the stress he placed on the unpredictable, possibly volatile, character of Charteris's killer. Under no circumstances were members of the public to approach anyone acting suspiciously, he announced. Should they spot anything out of the ordinary, they should come to him, his door was always open. And the community was responding, he could at least take pride in that. As he had anticipated, they were scared shitless at the prospect of a mindless psychopath at large in their midst. After all, they had come forward in droves to report minor incidents which led to the solution of minor crimes. And there had been a record number of applications to the Crime Prevention Officer about how best to secure their homes from attack. Pretty soon most of the innocent people of Crandon would be as securely immured of a night as Mrs Corke was in her fourteenth floor flat. The extra business for locksmiths promised at least a small boost to the economy of the borough, he reflected wryly. For the prospect of murder prompted people to act as the daily fact of theft never had. Still, their co-operation with the police was a fragile affair; without a result on the Charteris murder soon he would more than likely lose it.

He returned to his reflections on the evidence and the suspects.

His money was on Bryan Greyshott: certainly for Charteris's murder, possibly for both deaths. For Stone's murder, Greyshott relied solely on his carer's alibi. The carer was in Greyshott's employ, was paid by him: therefore he could be lying. But it was over Charteris's murder that the evidence was most damning. The run-up to the event, the man's dishevelled appearance at the scene of the crime. The only sticking point was the failure of the obvious weapon to match the abrasions in Charteris's skull. Had Greyshott been your average Crandon resident – Harry Green, for instance – Dawson would have had no hesitation in pulling him in. But he was fairly sure – from Greyshott's accent, his car, the expensive clothes draped over his wasted frame, the fact that he could afford to employ a full-time carer of his own – that the man could pay for the best defence brief in town. Dawson racked his brains. If he couldn't make the connection with the murder weapon, might there be some other piece of evidence, as yet undetected, which would link Greyshott irrevocably with the crime?

For the moment he pushed that thought to the back of his mind. The other question mark was over Banks. Dawson was ninety nine per cent sure he was in Noble's pocket. But how to prove *that*? Christ, he thought, indulging, unusually, in a spot of wishful thinking, if he had Banks nailed he could bring every single copper in the manor into line.

What he'd got, he summarised, was most likely a child arsonist; a contemporary Fagin who commissioned children to commit his crimes for him; a bent copper; a petty criminal who got so out of it with drink and drugs he couldn't remember whether he'd killed someone or not; and a deformed member of the middle classes who was demon-strably violent and possibly seriously disturbed. But zilch in the way of watertight cases. He could have roared with frustration.

Okay, so he'd cautioned his troops to proceed entirely by the book in order to gain the trust of the decent people of Crandon. But these five weren't decent people, they were the scum who stood between him and his goal. Between him and his career. Between him and the success of his property deal. If he didn't move fast they would destroy him as his father had been destroyed a generation earlier. He had made a point all these years of keeping his hatred and his anger under wraps but now, with the prospect of failure staring him in the face, it welled up with all the ferocity of its first visitation. He recalled his father, head in hands, broken by the demands for protection money which had cost him the loss of his shop. And of the flat over it. He remembered the small, damp room in which all three of them lived after that. Crushed glass outside their door, graffiti, a pile of human faeces; these were the tamer of the landlord's tactics when he realised they couldn't pay the rent. After that he sent the bully boys. Men like Banks, men like Noble, who got a kick out of seeing the cringing fear in the faces of those they terrorised. Dawson recalled with a sharp, twisting wrench of his gut, his childhood self's impotent fury at being unable to help his father, unable to protect his mother. He recalled the sadistic pleasure with which the men removed every scrap of the broken-down furniture from the room and set fire to it in the street outside. And he recalled, once more, that terrible corpse swaying over the open, stinking toilet bowl.

Christ, he was damned if he was going to be defeated!. He felt a sharp pain in both hands, looked down and realised that he had clenched his fists so hard his nails were grinding into his palms. He unfolded them carefully. Then he unfolded the late final edition of the *Evening Standard* which he hadn't yet had time to read. He should check up on what was being said about his patch, he should do some more thinking, keep his cool, look to the future. But when he reached the third page he stopped short. The media had turned against him. Bastards! Some grubby hack was under the impression that he'd come up with new evidence into Charteris's death which the journalist claimed that he, Dawson, should have made public. It was only a small piece and its references were somewhat veiled but the overall import was clear. Marion Charteris was a rather different young woman to the respectable citizen Dawson had told the world she was. Worse, a feature length investigative piece on her past was promised for the following day.

Dawson's rage returned ten-fold. He ripped the page from the paper and flung it in the empty waste bin at his feet, dumped the rest of the filthy rag of a newspaper on top of it. He seethed with the need for action, but there was nothing he could do. Even an hour's exercise would, he knew, do little to cool his anger; the newspaper would lie there in the bin, a silent reminder that the tide had turned against him.

He couldn't tolerate having the thing in the place. He struck a match and tossed it into the metal bin. The paper flared. Within seconds the flames were high. Too high. Christ if he didn't watch it, he'd set the entire loft on fire. Already the bin was too hot to touch. He swiftly doused the fire with a saucepan full of water, then, with a towel around his hands, hauled the bin to the lavatory area and flushed its charred contents down the toilet bowl. He stepped back, and stood still, breathing hard.

Chapter Ten

It was past ten on the morning of the Carleton Park Fun Day and the Community Centre was once again festooned with decorations. Multi-coloured bunting hung outside and a vast blue banner with 'Carleton Park Fun Day' painted on it in white letters was draped over the façade of the building. Inside the Activity Room disco music blared from loudspeakers and two community artists in paint-splashed Oxfam shop clothes were covering the parquet floor with a vast sheet of tarpaulin so that kids could spill as much paint as they liked without causing permanent damage. In the canteen volunteers were heating water in the tea urns. In the Pottery Room a small bouncy castle was being inflated. In the Art Room the Pensioners' Forum were setting up their 'Down Memory Lane' display of the history of the Carleton Park Estate. The Garden Room was the territory of the black and ethnic minority groups all of whom had booked stalls for the day; they were busy laying out leaflets on benefits, equal opportunities, racial harassment. And in the Art Room a handful of over-early, over-keen amateur poets were waiting for the creative writing tutor to arrive.

'When's she due?' asked Naheed, who was looking forward to showing Jill the latest revision of her saga of a disastrous arranged marriage.

Reg Harris looked at his watch. He was equally keen to air his masterpiece on the joys of digging an allotment. 'Not for at least another hour,' he said dolefully. 'And she's always late. Should we get on with reading what we've done to each other?'

Everyone nodded.

'And you can get out of here,' added Reg to a small boy in an apology for a hat made out of last week's *Courier*. The boy skidded out into the Activity Room where a straggle of other kids were already knocking over jars of water and stabbing at each other's eyes with the handles of paintbrushes. The day's programme was to begin with the children's painting competition. They could paint anything they liked; the only rule was that all the people in their pictures had to be wearing a hat of some sort.

John was still asleep. Lazy bugger, thought Bryan who had dressed himself, shaved himself, cooked his own breakfast, washed up afterwards and wiped down the kitchen worktops. Edward was at the door. He came later these days now that Bryan was more independent. But Bryan still needed him to propel the heavy old chair across the park. No way was he getting the wheels of his athlete's chair covered in dog shit. And the washable gloves he'd had Edward buy were not a success. Okay, so they could be stuffed in the washing machine when he got home, but who wanted to spend the duration of an outing wearing gloves which stank to high heaven? So it was business as usual far as his seating arrangements were concerned. Once he was settled to his satisfaction he gave Edward the instruction that he wanted to be pushed around the park. He said no more than that.

Because Bryan still didn't know whether Edward was in the clear. Okay so his references were kosher – Bryan'd spent the hour between nine and ten this morning phoning them and the story was, in every case, the same. Edward was a kind, compassionate young man with a vocation for helping others; so much so that he'd braved his solicitor father's wrath that his son was not entering what he considered a proper profession. Bryan was swayed, but not completely convinced. Okay so being a committed carer seemed incompatible with being a murderer, but, supposing there were a motive of sexual jealousy, he couldn't rule it out.

It was a bright morning, far crisper than the preceding days. The sky was sharply blue with scudding white clouds whipped to a froth by a swift wind. Scraps of litter scurried busily along the pavement like commuters in a rush to get to work. It was cold, but it was a cheering cold, not the damp chilly murk which Bryan had so far associated with a Crandon winter. Indeed, in spite of the loss of his computer, the fact that he was under suspicion of murder and the likelihood that someone was out to do him damage, he felt glad to be alive. Or perhaps, perversely, it was these very facts – facts which had given him new interest – which made him feel like that. He took a deep breath as he sat stationary at the top of the ramp over the roadworks while, behind him, Edward closed the front door. The trench in the pavement showed no signs of being filled in or for that matter of anything in the way of pipes being laid in it. What was it for? He should ask the men working on it sometime. Not that anyone was working today. The trench stretched as far as he could see, cutting through the surface of the pavement like a crevasse through a glacier.

Edward's hands were on the handles of the chair, it began to roll down the ramp. The surface creaked and groaned beneath the wheels as usual. Not as usual. A sudden tilt. Bryan had just time to feel a stab of fear, sharp as a needle, before the ramp gave way. He was rolling, free-falling as he did in his nightmares. Then he was sprawled on the ground in a flurry of spinning wheels with yelps and anguished cries ringing in his ears. Was he making those sounds himself as he had when he fell from the sky?

No. He wasn't making any noise at all. He was lying, still as a mouse, his cheek on the tarmac, watching a bicycle wheel slowly revolve, then stop. He was seeing, at close quarters, Henry, the mongrel, stagger to his feet with a whimper. He was hearing angry accusations from the cyclist whom his wheel-chair, running full tilt, had struck down. And he was conscious of someone else who was fussing about, concerned in equal measure about Bryan and the dog. It was Gerald Tozer.

Gerald harried the cyclist into helping Bryan back into his chair. He dumped the still whimpering Henry into Bryan's lap. The cries went on. They came not from Henry, but from

Edward who lay awkwardly in the trench in the pavement. His face, which protruded above the tarmac surface, was ashen with pain.

'I think I've broken my leg,' he managed.

Bryan asked the cyclist to hop over the trench and use his phone to call an ambulance. He assured Edward that on past experience it wouldn't take long.

Gerald, after making sure that Henry was all right, bent to inspect the ramp which lay half-in, half-out of the trench.

'You could have come a nasty cropper,' he told Bryan. 'Mark my words someone shifted this on purpose.'

So whoever was trying to do Bryan damage, it wasn't Edward.

Dawson was giving orders for policing the Fun Day. He'd promised the committee that there would be a senior plain-clothes presence as well as the uniforms on duty; might be no bad thing given they still needed information from the residents, every single one of whom, according to the committee, would turn out for the main events of the day – judging the painting competition, the drama performance and reading the creative writing. Those would take place from 2.30 onwards and he'd make sure he put in a token appearance himself towards the end of the affair. Meanwhile it'd just be a trickle of people setting things up plus a load of kids splashing paint about. Just the kind of menial, tedious duty Banks would hate – keeping a watchful eye on all and sundry with little prospect of any action except chatting to the punters. Serve him right for turning up at the station late again this morning. He despatched him to the job, instructing him to mingle as much as possible.

The ambulance turned up in record time. But Bryan and Edward had to wait for what seemed ages in the Casualty Department before the fracture of Edward's leg was confirmed and the limb encased in plaster.

'You'd better have my old wheelchair for the duration,' Bryan said. 'It's lucky I've got two.'

By the time they arrived back at the flat the council had responded to the cyclist's second telephone call and reinstated the ramp. The ambulance driver stayed to lift Bryan into his athlete's chair and to put Edward into the old one. As the man was leaving, John put in an appearance, dressed but still unshaven.

'God, you are a slob,' Bryan told him. 'It's gone twelve. And I bet you've left dishes all over the kitchen.'

'A few,' John confessed airily. He took in Edward's situation. 'I see we have a new cripple in our midst,' then turned his attention back to Bryan. 'So what's on the agenda for today?'

'Getting my sodding computer back.'

Lee was crossing the park. He was going to the Fun Day. Not that he'd join in, nah, he was much too old for that stuff; but he'd read the leaflets and the posters stuck up all over the estate and there was going to be painting this morning. Chuck a few pots of paint at the littler kids, wouldn't he? and see how they liked that. But he was only half-way across the grass when Bryan and John closed in on him, one wheelchair on either side in a pincer movement. Bryan looked grim.

'Wossa matter?' asked Lee.

'Someone nicked my computer. You must know everything going on around here. Any ideas where I might start looking?'

'Um,' said Lee. 'If I say, would you tell I told you?'

'Tell who? I wouldn't tell anyone. I just want the thing back.'

'Uncle Jack's got it.'

'Uncle Jack who?'

'My Uncle Jack. Everyone knows Uncle Jack. He owns the Icicle.'

'You mean Jack Noble?' Lee nodded. Bryan and John exchanged an excited look.

'I think we'll pay a call on this uncle of yours. There's other things we want to ask him about.'

'Hang on a tic,' said John. 'Why would a guy like that break in, presumably on spec, and nick a computer?'

''Spect he knew it was there. My Uncle Jack knows everything going down in Crandon.'

'But why did he want it?' John persisted. 'I'd have thought he dealt in much bigger scams than that sort of one-off. Besides, doesn't he have a computer in one or another of his businesses?'

'Course he does. He has dozens. But he says word processing is for women, so he never had one at home. But Tanya needed one quick yesterday and he didn't have time to get down the Tottenham Court Road and buy her a new one. Tanya's his girlfriend. He gets her anything she wants.'

'Right then,' Bryan told John. 'We'd better take a taxi down to the Icicle.'

'It isn't there.'

'Come off it, Lee, you said he wanted a computer at home.'

'That isn't where he lives.'

'But it's his address. It's where people send his mail.'

'That's because Uncle Jack's clever. He's the cleverest man in Crandon. He says the flat above the Icicle is his cover. He says it's clean. But he really lives somewhere where no one knows anybody is living.' He stopped and thought for a moment, then added, 'You're clever too.'

'Thank you. Are you going to tell me where he does live?'

Lee shook his head. 'He'd kill me. Besides, you'd tell the old Bill.'

'Which I've every right to. It is my computer.'

'No can do,' said Lee, scuffing the side of one smart new trainer with the toe of the other. 'I've got to go,' and he legged it across the park.

'What now?' asked John. 'Go to the Icicle anyway and tackle the man there?'

'No point. He'd simply deny he had the thing. We haven't any proof and we can't rat on Lee. Better option would be another touch of the Hercule Poirot's. Sit still and let the little grey cells do the work.'

'Bit cold for that.' And it was true that, although the day was still bright, the wind had picked up.

'So roll around for a bit to keep yourself warm. Where could someone live that no one else would know about?'

'It's all very well for you in that designer athlete's number. This bloody chair of mine's pissing awkward to move. Plus, I'm not used to propelling it far on my own. Keep the rolling to a minimum is my philosophy.' John paused and added, 'A hole in the ground. A tree house. A derelict building.'

'You're a genius!' Bryan executed a swift 360 degree circle.

'Have to do something to make up for the lack of other physical equipment. So what have I been a genius about?'

'I told you what Mrs Corke said about people living above her. Bet you that's where Noble is. On the fifteenth floor of the tower block. Let's get cracking.'

'Hang on, cripple. I know you're the hero of the Christmas social, but don't go thinking you're Superman *before* he got into the saddle. This Noble guy sounds like a hard man. How we going to persuade him to cough up with the computer? When there's just the two of us in our wheelchairs?'

'I've thought of that. There won't be just the two of us. I'll explain on the way back to the flat. Thing is,' Bryan said as they both turned, 'we won't be dropping Lee in it by telling the police. Seeing we deduced where the man was likely to be off our own bat.'

'We can't be sure. Can you slow down a bit? You're getting as bad as someone with legs the way you race around. You should be making allowances for the less able among us. And if you think you'll get much joy out of the Crandon police, you must be joking. They've hardly covered themselves with glory the last couple of weeks. Besides which, they think you're a murderer.'

'Wouldn't trust most of them as far as your arm. But I would trust Dawson.'

'That poncey git!'

'That poncey git as you call him may be an arrogant bastard, but as far as I can tell he knows his stuff. And as far as I can tell, he's straight.'

'What makes you think that?'

'Main reason is I know he's pretty damn certain I killed Marion. But he won't arrest me till he's one hundred per cent sure. I call that integrity.' Bryan trundled up the ramp to the front door. 'I'm going to ring him and ask him to meet us on the fifteenth floor. That'll put the odds in our favour. Might be different,' he added, 'if we invited just any old plod. Might turn up, might not. And when they did, more than likely they'd side with this Noble guy.'

Edward was in the living room in Bryan's old chair. He asked if they needed him to make lunch and added that he'd done the washing up.

'No thanks,' said Bryan. 'We need food, we'll get it ourselves. We may be cripples. Doesn't mean we're completely helpless. Specially when you're in the state you are.' He realised that John was looking at him in some surprise, because it was true that he, Bryan, had hardly given a thought to Edward's welfare in the past. But he did now. Was it solely because Edward was in a wheelchair too? Or was it that, imperceptibly, his attitude to all other people was changing? Was he able, these days, to empathise as well as criticise? Whatever the reason, he told his carer, 'They gave you painkillers, you may feel a bit dopey. Have a kip if you feel like it. If you want something to eat, stick one of the M & S ready meals you bought the other day in the microwave. And if you want to look in on the Fun Day after that, feel free.'

The call to Dawson came in at 12.30.

'Bryan Greyshott asking for you in person, Guv,' said a uniform.

210

'Greyshott?' Could this be a breakthrough in the murder inquiries? 'Put him straight through.'

He listened. After he'd taken all the details:

'Don't go thinking you can take the law into your own hands,' he instructed. 'Whatever you may think and say about citizens' arrests, in practice you're hardly in a position to take on an able-bodied man. I can be there in,' he glanced at his watch, 'an hour from now.'

'You can't make it sooner?'

'Not in person. I'd have to send one of the uniforms. I can't give this top priority. Not when I have murder investigations on my plate.' Though, in fact, until Greyshott's call, he had been facing nothing more than a mass of paperwork and the prospect of putting in an appearance at the Fun Day.

He replaced the receiver. Could this be his chance, finally, to nail Greyshott? Plus the chance of catching Noble red handed, even if only in a minor crime, was too good to pass up. He left his desk and set off.

The Community Centre was filling up fast. Pensioners, single people, entire families had begun to pour down from the tower block in such droves that there were queues on each floor for the lifts. In their hands they held bulging plastic carriers, huge red and white checked laundry bags, or pushed shopping trolleys in front of them. They toted bundles of paper plates, six packs of beer; they clutched full casseroles, brimming salad bowls, plates of cake and dishes of dessert to their chests. Even the smallest of children balanced a Sara Lee gateau or a plate of sausage rolls swathed in cling-film on proud, trembling hands. The Fun Day looked set to be a serious success.

DC Banks was swimming against the tide. He'd had enough. Enough of directing stray members of the creative writing group in the right direction, enough of making reluctant conversation with sundry members of the black and ethnic minority groups, enough, most of all, of kids chucking paint about. He dabbed at a long smear of bright yellow on the sleeve of his black leather jacket. He'd nearly topped the kid who did that – restrained himself just in time. Now he shouldered his way through the throng. He thought, no one would notice his absence. Plenty of time to have a beer or two with Noble, put his feet up afterwards and have a kip. God, his feet ached. Didn't seem to have done anything recently except trudge about on them or stand about on them. He shoved a kid aside and a quantity of cream-drenched fruit salad spewed from the bowl in the child's hands, arced upwards, staining Banks's leather jacket one more time, then hit the deck. Christ, he couldn't be doing with this. He struggled into the lift.

Bryan and John had even more trouble getting into the lifts. Eventually Bryan went and fetched Constable Hindmarsh who was on crowd control duty just outside the block. Bryan thought it was decent of Hindmarsh to do as he asked, given the constable was clearly a committed member of the 'Greyshott murdered Charteris' brigade. Bryan and John settled in solitary state into a lift each. This time Bryan, having braved the heights before, had fewer qualms. It was only a lift, after all, not a hang glider.

The two of them arrived at the same time without mishap. The corridor on the fifteenth floor was much the same as that on the fourteenth. Long, gloomy, with a window at the end offering a vertiginous view of the grimy park. But here there were no bolted, Chubbed, Yaled, or even closed doors like that of Mrs Corke on the floor below. Instead there were gaping doorways with splintered frames.

'Looks like Mrs Corke was right about people taking the doors off,' said Bryan. He peered inside the nearest flat. Peeling linoleum topped with piles of dusty, reeking detritus, the sordid remains of some family's life. Christ, he thought with a sharp stab of pity, what terrible conditions some people had to endure. Overlaying the rubbish was an ocean of junk mail. Bryan saw movement under the mess and spotted the scaly tail of a rat as the creature scuttled beneath an envelope.

'Yeugh!' he said.

'Bloody wild goose chase,' said John. But it wasn't. Two smashed door frames later, two doors which remained boarded up and they found what they'd been seeking. Two doors side by side which were just ordinary doors with ordinary locks on them. Bryan knocked on the first of them. After a moment a young woman opened the door. She had gleaming waist-length black hair. He recognised her. She was the woman he had last seen having close-up pictures of her crotch taken on the premises of *Page Four*.

'What can I do for you?' she asked.

'We've come to see Jack Noble.'

'Jack!' she called and led them into an extraordinary, opulent living room. The walls were covered in heavy, embossed purple wallpaper, a huge, satin-covered, pink shell-shaped couch took up nearly half the room, there were other monstrosities of monumental furniture fashioned out of equally expensive materials. God, thought Bryan, recalling Mrs Corke's room below, the taste in interior decor of people in tower blocks seemed to come not merely from another continent but from another planet than that of people the foundations of whose homes rested directly on terra firma.

'You'll have to excuse me,' said the woman. 'I have to get on. Expect he'll be through in a moment.' And she crossed the room to the window, seated herself in front of a marble-topped table and began to type. On Bryan's computer.

Wasn't long before Lee was booted out of the Fun Day. The two young community artists were made of sterner stuff than most: had to be, given the number of school groups they'd worked with in the past. So, when a second pot of paint 'fell' on a small kid's head, Lee got his marching orders.

'Sure, you can come back,' said Lawrence, wiping his paint-stained fingers on the thighs of his seventies' flares.

'When you've decided to apply paint only to paper,' added Venetia, cleaning her hands on her fifties' floral dress.

Lee swore at them, long and loud. Didn't get a rise out of anyone. No option but to head back across the park, to home. There wasn't any hurry, he dawdled along, kicking cans.

'Okay, so what you want?' A vast bulk of a man loomed in the doorway of the opulent living room. The young woman leapt to her feet.

'Jack, I've finished it,' she announced.

'I expect you have, my poppet.' He placed a heavy hand on her shoulder. 'Finished what?'

'My poem. For reciting this afternoon. I'll read it to you, shall I?'

'Not this minute.' The man's eyes went from Bryan to John, then back again. 'Well, what have we here? A wheeled version of Hopalong Cassidy?'

John opened his mouth to respond, but Bryan silenced him with a gesture.

'You do really want to hear it,' the young woman pressed on. 'All of you. I wasn't expecting this many people to try it out on. That's quite a bonus.' She struck an attitude, hands on hips, and declaimed:

'Roses are red, violets are blue, pinks are pink,
I think of all of them when I wash dishes at the sink,
Flowers in a bright, colourful spray,
Flowers that you gave me yesterday.'

'Lovely, pet,' said the man who must be Jack Noble. 'Now you just run along and strut your stuff. You know I always say that whatever turns you on is fine by me.'

She pouted, her lower lip projecting like the bottom drawer in a chest of drawers which has jammed open on account of too many clothes being stuffed inside.

214

'I haven't finished yet. Jill says she's going to put the creative writing together in an anthology. It's almost like being in a real book. So I want to illustrate it. I've done all sorts of stuff in "Paint". But this PC you got me,' she shot an angry look at Bryan's computer, 'won't print it out.'

'No colour ink in the cartridge,' said Bryan.

'How would you know?'

'Because it's my computer.'

'Oh well.' She shrugged her shoulders. 'I'll just have to illustrate it myself.' And she settled down at the marble-topped table to draw flowers in lurid pink marker pen around her poem.

Noble told her a second time to cut along.

'Why should I? ' She smiled and added sweetly, 'You know, when I was getting used to the programme, I found some awfully funny stuff on here. All about murdering people.'

'Did you now? If you don't hop it you'll miss your chance to read your masterpiece to its real audience. People who'll appreciate a good poem when they hear it."

That struck a chord. She rose, clutching her poem and made for the door. She paused on the threshold. 'You will come and hear me, won't you Jack?'

'Of course I will.' He patted her behind. She left.

'So what's all this about then?' demanded Noble. 'How did you know I was here?'

'Never mind that. We've come to take my computer back.'

'You and who else, squire?'

'The police'll be here in a moment.'

'I've already got the police on the premises. In my pocket, so to speak.' And to Bryan's dismay, bulldog Banks wandered in from what was presumably the kitchen. He held a can of beer in one hand, his shirt was open at the neck and his hair tousled, his face flushed as though he had recently surfaced from sleep.

'What have we here?' he asked.

'Job for you, Banks,' Noble told him. 'Guy's mislaid his computer. Can't have that. Better get on the case.'

Banks turned his attention to Bryan.

'What makes you think it's yours? Can you prove it?'

'I reported it stolen. I gave the make, the word processing package, the type of printer. This is an exact match.'

'Doesn't mean it's the same computer. But of course we'll look into it. Meanwhile you can't burst into people's homes, accuse them of theft and attempt to remove without consent what may well be their legitimate private property. That's an offence in itself.'

'Oh, for Christ's sake.' That was John.

Banks rounded on him. 'When I want you to speak I'll let you know. Otherwise keep your mouth shut.'

He swung back to Bryan. 'If you could tell me why you suspected your computer might be in this particular flat?'

'Fucking pig,' said John.

'Cool it,' said Bryan, then added, 'I had information.'

'Whatever information you have it's your duty to impart it to the police. You could be charged with withholding evidence, you know that? As for you,' he took a couple of heavy steps in the direction of John's chair, 'abusing a police officer isn't exactly sensible for someone in your position.'

'Suppose it was his computer,' chipped in Noble, 'there's apparently some weird stuff on it. About murders.'

All in all things were looking pretty heavy, Bryan thought; when Dawson walked in.

'Thank God for that,' said Bryan.

'Never thought I'd be pleased to see the bastard,' added John; but quietly and without malice.

Dawson listened to Banks's story. Then, 'Let's get this straight,' said Dawson nastily. 'Mr Greyshott here reported the theft of his computer. And you're refusing to take his allegation of theft seriously.'

'He's got no proof, Guv.'

'I can identify it.'

'By what's on it I suppose,' sneered Banks. 'And that certainly is worth investigating. A lot of stuff about planning a perfect crime apparently.'

'Let's see it,' said Dawson sharply. 'D'you know what he's filed it under?'

Oh shit, thought Bryan.

Didn't take a candidate for *Mastermind* to figure that a directory entitled 'Crime' might be worth a look. And once Dawson saw what it contained he knew he had struck gold. A file on planning and committing the perfect crime, complete with lurid descriptions about the psychology of the murderer. A file on the murder of Julia Stone. And – even more damning – a lengthy file on his, Greyshott's, vicious hatred of Charteris and how he intended to give her her come-uppance.

Thereafter it was a simple matter to caution Bryan, handcuff him to his wheelchair, instruct Banks to find a floppy disk and to copy the material onto it. Dawson pocketed the disk.

'You still say this computer is yours?' he asked Bryan.

'Yes, but I can explain.' Bryan felt a complete fool. He was also flushed with the awful embarrassment of having his stupid meanderings about perfect crimes exposed, not only to the light of day, but to the eyes of a competent, active man who tackled crime for real every day of his life. Bryan had been cut down to size by his accident; now he felt as diminished as the bleeding dwarf of John's joke about conjuring tricks.

John looked fazed too. 'He didn't mean it,' he protested, 'he was only having a laugh.' But Dawson ignored him.

'I'm taking you in on suspicion of murder,' he told Bryan, 'and you,' he indicated Noble, 'for theft.'

Chapter Eleven

'Very nice,' said the Mayor, who was touring the display of paintings, 'and what is it supposed to be, dear?'

'My mum and my uncle in bed in their new house. The house we're going to have when they blow up where we live now.'

'And what's that on his head?'

'Uncle Joe's wearing a policeman's helmet what he nicked.'

'And why doesn't your mum have a hat?'

'She doesn't have one, does she? Couldn't afford to buy one special so I could paint it.'

The Mayor moved on. She politely admired a depiction of a gang of children in conical party hats playing on a great green field which one optimistic young artist had assumed would be a part of the Carleton Park Estate of the future. She pointed at some white blobs on the painted grass.

'Dear, dear. Has someone forgotten to pick up their litter?'

''Course not. They're sheep,' said a scornful girl.

'For our dogs to chase,' added a small boy.

Next was an idyllic scene of a pond fringed with reeds. Six huge white ducks on the water all sported jaunty expressions and back to front baseball caps. Then came a family scene in which five stick children wearing bearskins sat crammed around a small table eating yellow objects as stick-like as the kids: Chips? Fish fingers? Weetabix? The Mayor shook her head. After that was a scene of devastation, a vast building, recognisable as the tower block, but leaning to one side and with a mushroom shaped cloud of smoke issuing from it. Small figures wearing yellow hard hats gazed at the spectacle. The Mayor admired everything, made all the right noises, but her heart wasn't in it. She and Maureen had arrived arm in arm – after all they'd come out, so why shouldn't they? But now, after an hour, Maureen was nowhere to be seen. The last time the Mayor had caught a glimpse of her, twenty minutes past, she had been talking animatedly to Jill Rush, the young creative writing tutor. She knew what it meant when Maureen talked like that to a woman, it was how she had been when the two of them first met.

'Banks,' instructed Dawson, 'it makes sense to move the suspects to somewhere more secure. Until we call for reinforcements. It's too much of a risk for us to try to take the pair of them in between the two of us. Greyshott may be in a wheelchair but he's a tricky customer. And I wouldn't trust Noble an inch. We'll take them to the flat on the floor below. Decent old lady there, she'll be keen to help. And she's got enough locks on her door to keep them cooped up for hours.'

'What about the other one in the wheelchair? He's been seriously offensive.'

'We've nothing on him. He can go.'

'I'm not leaving, 'said John. 'Bryan, you might need a witness.'

Dawson shrugged.

'Shouldn't I radio in, Guv?' asked Banks.

'No. We'll get them downstairs first.'

Banks's turn to shrug. It wasn't correct procedure but he wasn't in a position to argue. Besides which, as they went into the corridor, there was a sudden diversion.

'Lee,' shouted Noble, 'scarper!'

But Dawson, fit, lithe, athletic, his reflexes finely tuned, spun on his heel, grabbed the boy by the collar of his puffer jacket. And held on tight.

'So you're Lee Stone, are you? There's a little matter of a couple of fires I want to talk to you about.'

The lifts arrived almost as soon as Dawson and Banks pressed the buttons. Dawson checked his watch. Just after 2 pm. He figured the entire block must be empty by now. Everyone would be at the Fun Day. Everyone bar Mrs Corke. She'd made it quite plain when he interviewed her that she thought the whole thing silly, said she'd rather sit and look at her view. While she had the chance.

On Dawson's instructions they divided into two parties. Dawson, Noble and Lee in one lift, Banks and Bryan squeezed into the other. John was left on the top floor.

They disembarked on the fourteenth floor. Dawson knocked on the red door embellished with the gilt numerals 85. A face at the panel of reinforced glass.

'Oh, it's you,' she said. 'The nice young policeman. I expect you want another cup of tea.' And proceeded to unfasten her bolts and chains and locks. They all entered.

'My goodness, it's quite a party.' She looked at Bryan and added, 'Lovely to see you again. Do you know, I've been taking a leaf out of your book and making a cake. But I don't think I've remembered the recipe aright.' She paused and sniffed the air. So did the others. There was a distinct smell of burning. 'And you've brought your little friend, she went on, smiling down at Lee. 'Quite the reformed character I bet, these days. Now do come in and I'll get the kettle on.' They trooped inside. As Jack Noble crossed the threshold: 'What's he doing here?' she asked. 'And why is he wearing handcuffs?'

'Police matter,' said Dawson brusquely. 'Nothing to worry about, madam, you're in no danger. This is Detective Inspector Banks,' he gestured in his subordinate's direction. 'He'll be taking charge for a few moments while I check out your security arrangements.'

'Just a minute.' John had caught up with them. 'I'm coming in too.'

'Are you, dear? That's nice. So many pleasant young men. What security arrangements?'

'Your keys. If I could trouble you to hand them over.'

She gave him the jangling fistful. 'It's so nice to feel that the police are taking an interest. Just like it used to be. The blue lamp, *Dixon of Dock Green* ,"Evening all", and all that. We slept safer in our beds because of it. Mind you,' she added, shooting a bright-eyed sideways glance at Banks, 'not all you young policeman nowadays have the same attitude. More's the pity, I say.'

Dawson hefted the keys.

He was still holding onto Lee. No cuffs to spare for him, Banks and he had just the one pair apiece. He dragged the boy along with him outside the flat into the corridor.

'What's he playing at?' Bryan wondered to John.

'Haven't a clue.'

'Surely you should radio in,' Bryan told Banks.

'Shut it,' said the bulldog.

'Daresay he can be bought.' Noble was still confident. 'Everyone has their price.'

Banks didn't think this was true of Dawson, but it was Noble's last hope of getting off scot-free. And once in the nick Noble could put him, Banks, squarely in the frame. Had no reason not to if Noble himself was at risk of getting sent down. Banks held his peace.

They waited, an odd assortment of people, all on edge for different reasons, while Mrs Corke fussed around with a teapot, then poured one of her trademark thick, black brews. No one lifted a cup to his lips.

'What the fuck's he doing out there?' asked Bryan.

'You know what you said after the Christmas social about people with legs,' said John. 'Go walkabout whenever you need them most.'

'Gives us time to work up a negotiating position,' Noble confided quietly to Banks. 'Have a nasty suspicion this one might be a "name your fee" scenario.'

A rattling of locks. Dawson appeared in the living room doorway. He was still, with his right hand, grasping Lee by the collar. But not by the collar of his puffer jacket, that had been shed. The GAP sweatshirt Lee wore beneath was stained with dark liquid. So were his tracksuit bottoms. He was inert with fear, a dead weight, his body limp, his feet in their sharp trainers trailing, toes down, across the floor. He was like a dog, dragged along by its collar, expecting a beating but unable to fight against it, and his eyes were those of a dog, cowed and terrified. Because the stain on his clothes – they could all smell it – was petrol. And because Dawson held in his free hand a cigarette lighter.

The Mayor was alone. Alone in a crowd. The Fun Day had exceeded all the Organising Committee's expectations. Absolutely everyone from the tower block, except Mrs Corke and the illegal occupants of the fifteenth floor, had poured into the Community Centre determined to make a day of it, and to have a whale of a time. Hordes of other people had turned up from the neighbouring streets. No qualms about kids interrupting these festivities, there were police in uniform dotted all over the shop ready to move in if anyone put a foot wrong. Not that anyone did. The worst crime on the horizon today, observed Dosh sagely to Paul Hindmarsh, was likely to be some kid snatching a mince pie or a cracker from some other kid. The two officers were standing in the canteen at the time, observing the behaviour of the crowd.

'Must be more than a thousand of them,' said Paul, amazed.

'Don't often get a chance to do anything like this,' was Dosh's opinion. 'Better than going to see the lights in Oxford Street, I reckon. And,' he added shrewdly, 'a damn sight cheaper, given what kids manage to spend once they get in sight of the shops.'

The tea urns were doing serious business. The throng had laid out their offerings on the trestle tables. Everyone seemed to have made an effort. Bags of Dorritos, piles of chapattis, trays of chipolatas. Sweet potatoes, sugared almonds, salads, a sumptuous array of cheeses. Fried chicken, vegetable samosas, puddings galore. People were poring over things and dipping into things. Stray children ran past screaming and hurling scraps of food into each other's faces. There was more than enough for everyone. The community had turned up trumps. They were all enjoying themselves. Only the Mayor appeared disconsolate.

'Wonder why?' queried Dosh. 'You'd think she'd be over the moon. Especially as she's behind the grant the council gave this shindig.'

But the Mayor was searching the crowd for a sight of Maureen's mousey-brown, bobbed hair and the white, lace-trimmed baby bonnet which surmounted it.

"Uncle Jack,' bleated Lee, tear-stained face raised towards the one person who would surely save him.

The big man took a step forward.

'Nobody move.' Dawson's voice was as cool and grey as steel. 'Or the kid,' he shook Lee by the scruff, 'goes up like a light.'

'Jesus Christ, Guv,' said Banks.

'Oh dear, what a terrible smell,' said Mrs Corke.

'You hurt him and you're dead,' said Noble.

'I think not,' said Dawson.

Bryan didn't say anything. Talk about barking up the wrong tree. Every last one of his deductions had been way off-beam. God knows how he'd live this one down. He glanced at John, half expecting a crisp one-liner which would cut him, Bryan, down to size. But John, for once, appeared not in the mood for quips. Like Bryan, he was silent, gazing at the terrified child. Oh sod it, thought Bryan, I got John into this. He cast a quick glance at the others. I got them all into it. Me and my stupid pissing about pretending to be a sleuth.

'Altogether now,' Dawson instructed. 'Take it slowly, over to the mantelpiece. You too,' he told Mrs Corke. 'Close as you can.'

'Do as the Guv says,' instructed Banks.

She did. But Bryan didn't shift from his position near the door. Not from bravery, not because he had some subtle plan of escape worked out, but because he was cursing himself. He was, as he had known before he embarked on this farce, the utter, stinking pits. Not just a cripple, but a cripple with delusions; a cripple who thought he could use his brain to compete on equal terms with able-bodied people. Above all, a cripple who didn't just make a balls-up of his own life, but who dragged other people into the shit. He was the lowest form of life on earth.

Dawson turned to him.

'You heard what I said, Greyshott. Move.'

Bryan still didn't. What was the point? Familar waves of self pity engulfed him. A sneer directed at himself curled his upper lip as he recalled his thought, seconds ago, that John would never let him live this down. He glanced again at the group by the mantelpiece. Live it down, be damned, what an arrogant turd he was. Because of him, what chance had they of staying alive at all?

Crack! His reverie was sliced in half by a searing pain in his right cheek. He reeled in his chair, saved from falling only by the handcuff which held him shackled to the arm of the thing. Cold pain, sharp as bone, spread across his face. He looked down and saw blood on his trousers. He looked up and saw Dawson, left hand held high, rock-steady, a silver ring on his index finger reddened with Bryan's blood.

'Fucking bastard of a pig!' Christ, John had found his voice. And not at the right time. Bryan slewed his chair swiftly and clocked that John was preparing, in his cumbersome wheel-chair, to have a go. No way! Bryan spun his own wheels, sped the few feet across the carpet and rammed John side on. The two of them bounced in their chairs at the impact. Then Bryan shook his head, three times, sharply at John – and John, thank God, stayed still.

'Good thinking, Greyshott,' came Dawson's cool voice from behind them. 'As I'd expect of a man of your intellect, you appreciate that I don't make empty threats.'

Bryan turned once more to face him. The blow and John's reaction had shocked him out of his paralysis. Christ, the one thing he should have learned from the last year – the one thing he should have learned from John – was that if you make one mistake you don't give up on life altogether. And, now that the mists of self-pity had cleared, his brain was functioning as well as it ever had before his accident. Perhaps better. It was telling him to play for time.

He sized up his adversary. A familiar buzz of excitement reduced the pain in his cheek to an irrelevance. He knew this game, he'd played it dozens of times over boardroom tables. Except then he'd been playing for money. Now he was playing for life.

Keep eye contact, he thought. Try to introduce subsidiary points on which to negotiate. And, above all, don't antagonise the guy.

'Intellect?' he enquired in a mild tone. 'Does this mean you've checked up on me? Well, of course a man of your calibre would.'

Dawson smiled. 'Down to the last inch. Paid off handsomely. Even supposing I hadn't all the other evidence, I've plenty of witnesses from your former life to testify that your accident unbalanced you. That you threw up everything to move to Crandon. Crandon! What sane man would choose to live here?'

'You have,' said Bryan.

'Because it won't be Crandon when I've finished with it. You,' Dawson pointed a finger of his free hand at Banks. Lee, feeling the movement, made a struggle for freedom. Noble took another step forward, then changed his mind as Dawson's grip tightened on the child. Bryan took advantage of the pause to wink at John. He was glad it was John at his side and not the usual piss-artist of a deputy negotiatior assigned to him on all his former confrontations.

'You,' continued Dawson. 'Don't think you're walking away from this. What happens to you will be a marker to all the troops. I'll tell you what the place'll be like in a year's time. Even six months, maybe. No one will take bribes. No one will smoke. Everyone will turn up for duty on the dot. Work-out classes in the station will be well attended. The force will be leaner and trimmer to a man. There will be no slouching around with hands in the pockets of leather jackets. There will be no intimidation. The uniforms' buttons will shine, you'll be able to see your face in their boots. They'll stand straight, jump to attention when I speak, and call me sir. And they'll put their noses to the grindstone and accomplish some good, solid police work.'

Bryan wasn't listening. He was reviewing his options. There was no hope of help – he'd made sure of that himself when he called Dawson to the scene. Their chances of survival were down to separating Lee from Dawson or, perhaps, separating Banks from the rest of them and persuading him to call for back-up – if he would. Slim chances! Meanwhile the only tactics were delaying ones, to keep the guy talking. And to put himself on the line if need be.

'There is no need for all this.' Bryan spoke slowly – and stiffly because of the already hardening gash in his cheek, 'You have the evidence you need. And I am quite prepared to sign a confession. Before witnesses.' He waved at the others. 'That I killed Marion Charteris.'

Dawson shook his head.

'Won't wash. The witnesses would claim duress. You'd renege on whatever you signed and hire an expensive brief and wriggle out of it. No. You can never rely on the courts for justice. So we'll continue with the original plan.'

'Why?' asked Bryan. Because, if Dawson was anything like the villains in fiction, he would welcome the chance to confess, to tell all before he despatched his latest victims.

'I would have thought that's obvious.'

'I meant, why did you kill Marion?'

'It was necessary.'

'Necessary?'

Dawson nodded. 'No reason why you shouldn't know the whole of it. After all, if you weren't,' he waved a hand at Bryan's chair, 'as you are, I daresay you could have been a credit to Crandon. I executed her. Killed her for the greater good.

'She was scum, of course.' Dawson went on. Bryan's mind was racing. He was dealing – nothing in his previous life had prepared him for this – with a madman. 'But I didn't find that out till later,' continued Dawson. 'Quite a little irony. The only way to bring the community together after the Carleton Park shelter killing was to have a second murder. It had to be brutal. It had to be savage. It had to be of someone so attractive, so decent, so respectable that the eyes of the community, of the media would all turn on us and stay on us to see how well we did our work. So I was on the lookout for a young woman on her own.'

Bryan held his breath. Was there any way he could divert Dawson's attention from Lee? Rush the man? Or was his only hope to keep him talking until people started returning from the Fun Day? He managed a surreptitious glance at his watch. Fuck, no chance of that, the festivities would just be getting seriously underway.

'Couldn't believe my luck . . .' Dawson went on. The man sure as hell liked the sound of his own voice, thought Bryan. '. . . when I saw Marion running across the mall in the dark. She was perfect. A young woman who devoted all her spare hours to caring for people less fortunate than her.' Could he use that to advantage? wondered Bryan. 'So I executed her. A pity in a way, that's what I thought at the time, but it had to be done. She made it easy – turned back and ran in my direction.' No, but it could give him time to think, decided Bryan. 'It was all over in seconds.' The crucial factor was how and when Dawson intended to set fire to poor little Lee. That would be the moment, Bryan concluded, for him to act. 'Put the jack back in the car and joined Hindmarsh at the scene of the crime. And it worked,' Dawson smiled. 'It brought Crandon to heel. Then I found she wasn't what she pretended to be. I could have killed her. Ruining my chances of clearing up a motiveless crime against a member of the middle classes.' He paused and added. 'Except she was already dead. She deserved to die.'

228

'What about Lee?' asked Bryan. 'He's only a kid.'

'Criminal in the making. Needs to be nipped in the bud. That's how most major villains start their careers. With arson.'

'I can see,' said Bryan carefully, 'that I'm by way of being a useful scapegoat. But what about Mrs Corke and John? They've done nothing wrong.'

'Expendable. Can't see them adding an iota to the economic future of Crandon, can you? Besides, he's volatile, not to say unbalanced. And she's senile. None of you is normal. But it's you,' he nodded at Bryan, 'that will really make my reputation. With you dead, the community'll realise I can deliver. Because all the evidence points to you, Greyshott. The small matter of making a connection between you and the murder weapon won't cut any ice without you alive to concoct fancy alibis for yourself. It'll be another case closed, and I'll be the one who did it.

'Plus,' he smiled unpleasantly, 'I'll rid Crandon of most of its organised crime at a stroke. With Noble out of the way there'll be no protection racket, the sex industry will have lost its baron, the incidence of burglary and handling stolen goods could be as much as halved.

'In a way it's a pity about you,' Dawson told Bryan. 'By all accounts you were a man with a future. Still, I suppose you did yourself a favour being in the wrong place at the wrong time. Because once I saw you there beside Charteris's corpse I knew I could have you on toast. And it's a kindness to you really, putting an end to you. What kind of life is it for a man like you, being confined to a wheelchair?'

Which had been Bryan's thoughts to a T a year ago. But fuck it, if he was going to top himself, he'd have done it then. Besides, if he was going to top himself, he'd do it himself, thank you very much. He opened his mouth to ask another delaying question, but Dawson wasn't having any. For Dawson, the time for talk was over, the time for action had begun. Action which had been stalled for so many years; since he was a child, clutching at his mother's skirt while the bully boys burned their furniture. Since he was a child, finding his father's body, swinging lifeless in the loo. Now he dragged Lee to the door, opened it and stood there, for a moment, looking back at them.

'Don't anyone move for the next five minutes,' he instructed. Then he was gone. They heard keys turning swiftly in locks. From the outside. They looked at each other in bewilderment. Noble started to say something, Bryan didn't gather what. Lee stood silent and shaken just inside the door where Dawson had deposited him. The letter box flapped. Which was when Bryan realised what was about to happen. He reacted with the same unreasoning, outraged anger, the same speed he had at the social when he waded in to save Kenny. With the same results. But this time, when Bryan floored Lee with a charge from the spinning wheels of his athlete's chair, he didn't leave his victim lying there. Instead, straining the newly toned muscles in his arms to the limit, he hauled the child by the scruff of his neck away from the door.

'Which room's the bathroom?' he demanded urgently of Mrs Corke, as the letter box opened wide and a flaming rag ignited the petrol-soaked spot of the carpet on which seconds ago Lee had stood. The bastard had planned to use the boy to fuel the fire.

The Mushy Pea Community Arts Group were dressed as low rise houses, great, bulky, swaying, red-painted polystyrene 'walls' obscuring their upper bodies. Their 'hats' were cylindrical chimney pots. Their green clad legs represented gardens and at the end of each bilious-shaded arm, emerald-stained fingers clutched a bunch of paper flowers. They sang a jolly song about the pleasures of leaving flowers *unpicked* so that everyone could enjoy the blooms in their neighbours' gardens. And they did a dance – rather more ponderous than their usual efforts on account of the encumbrance of the 'houses' – which was intended to celebrate neighbourliness. It ended with each of the 'houses'

230

kissing the 'house' next door on the cheek; then they linked arms and sank to the floor in a carefully choreographed symbolic rendition of a harmonious community settling down for the night.

Dawson set off down the stairs, well pleased with what he had achieved. Wouldn't be long before the fire in the flat took those inadequates out. He seized a couple of fire extinguishers, pressed the buttons for both lifts, descended to the ground floor and stuck the cylinders of the fire extinguishers in the lift doors to keep them open. So he'd cut off that line of escape. Wasn't enough to be certain, though. He laid a trail of petrol to the door of the block and stepped outside. The place was deserted. He continued the trail round to the back of the block where the rubbish bins were. He returned to the ground floor, deposited the petrol can, went into the boiler room and swiftly disconnected the smallest of the pipes from the gas boiler with the spanner he had brought for the purpose. He went back to the rubbish bins, ignited a scrap of rag, waited only to see that the petrol had caught, then ran. He sprinted for a hundred yards, then slowed to a walk. He wasn't even breathing hard. In a few seconds the block would go sky high. And once the fire escalated and reached individual flats, every single gas cooker, every Ascot heater, every gas appliance of any sort would go up too. From there it would only be a matter of minutes before electrical wiring caught all over the building. With luck the ferocity of the heat would melt the handcuffs on Noble and Greyshott. If not, what did it matter? There could be many possible explanations. The most likely – he would suggest it himself – was that Banks had arrested Noble, it was plausible enough; after all, the man was a known villain. The fire in Mrs Corke's flat might have been started by the boy, she'd complained enough times about kids making her life a misery. The boiler on the ground floor had a history of going on the blink. Even supposing Forensics discovered the seat of the fire and suspected arson, the finger would never be pointed at him. After all, he was the investigating officer, and now he had got a result. He curled his hand around the computer disk in his pocket. A posthumous conviction of Greyshott for the murder of Charteris was a certainty. He smiled. Crandon was well on its way to redemption. It was time he put in an appearance at the festivities.

Chapter Twelve

In the Centre the Mayor was judging the competition for the best home-made hat with ill concealed bad temper. 'Oh, no,' she said, her eyes on Maureen and Jill, who had their heads together, 'a clown's hat from a shop can't hope to win.'

She moved on past umpteen cowboy hats and witches' steepled crowns, then stopped.

'This is more like it.' A small child stood before her. Its head was wreathed in a complex, turban-like effect of green and yellow feathers with a plume at the back, like a peacock's tail.

'Except,' added the Mayor doubtfully, 'are any of those feathers from the plumage of an endangered species?'

They had the cold tap in the bathroom full on, the cold tap in the kitchen full on. Lee was in the bath, seemed the safest place for him. He was still fully clothed, Bryan reckoned he probably had so much petrol on his skin, it wasn't worth the time it would have taken to strip him.

Even without the incendiary stimulus of a burning boy, the fire was almost instantly fierce. Bryan ordered Mrs Corke to take John to the bedroom and help him strip the bed. They were to soak the bedclothes and fling them over the flames in the hope of depriving them of air. Not much hope that that would quench a petrol-based fire, but it might just give them breathing space. Mrs Corke surprised him. He would have expected her to be in tears at the destruction of her home but she said with considerable firmness to her lips that she'd been through far worse in the Blitz and got on with doing what she was told.

Banks was another matter. Bryan detailed him to turn off every gas appliance in the flat and to extinguish every pilot light; but he could see that the big policeman wasn't about to obey a cripple. Instead Banks turned his attention to the front door. In spite of the flames erupting around him he battered fruitlessly with one burly shoulder at its solid, impenetrable bulk. Defeated, he seized a chair leg and attacked the huge window which looked over the park.

Noble could have added his brawn to this mindless effort to achieve freedom, but instead, 'Cut it out,' he shouted.

John, returning with wet bedclothes snagging the wheels of his chair, did his bit to put a stop to Banks's effort to run a panic-motivated solo show.

'Don't you realise, you stupid bugger?' he bawled as he flung a damp blanket over the flames. 'Bryan's spent years in the oil industry. He knows the right way to deal with a fire like this.'

Banks took no notice. He continued his senseless battering. Until Noble crossed the room in a few swift strides, side-stepping the burning furniture and John's wheelchair.

'Shut up and do what the guy says,' he commanded. 'See the way he sat and sneered at that bastard and refused to move while we were all shit-scared? He's the goods and no mistake.' By way of emphasis he raised his handcuffed wrists and brought them down with serious force on Banks's face. The bulldog's nose opened like a bud in the summer sun. Blood flowed freely from the poppy-red bloom. The fight went out of him. He scurried to carry out the task to which Bryan had assigned him.

Bryan was thinking fast. Absolutely no point trying to break the window, the glass up here would be heavily reinforced to prevent accidents, suicides; it would probably take a pneumatic drill hours to make any impact. And they hadn't got a pneumatic drill. Or hours. Besides – Bryan glanced outside the window – the sun was still bright but the wind was immeasurably stronger at this height than it had been on the ground. Down there scraps of paper had hurried cheerfully along the pavement, here they whirled up and down at dizzying speed like demented doves. Who knew whether releasing a wind of that force into the room might not suck the flames into a tornado of conflagration?

He looked around the room. Not good. The fire had taken hold near the one means of escape available to them – the front door. In the interior, tea towels were curling in scorched festoons from the walls, there were spontaneous ignitions among the gew-gaws. John's efforts were sterling but they weren't having much effect. Bryan called everyone away from what they were doing and had them turn their attention to the burning carpet inside the front door.

'We need to get that put out,' he commanded. 'Pronto.'

Everyone, Mrs Corke included, formed a chain to slosh buckets of water over the spot on which a terrified Lee had recently stood. It still wasn't looking good.

'You get me out of these.' It was Noble who had spoken. Bryan turned to him. Noble was still standing by the mantelpiece. The man raised his wrists, shaking the cuffs which encircled them. 'And I'll get us all out of here.'

Bryan didn't trust him, but what had they to lose? They needed all the help they could get.

'Any ideas how?'

'Check out what tools she's got. Failing that, find anything you can that's metal and heavy, then beat the shit out of these things. Way you manhandled the kid out of the way you must have enough strength in your arms to deal with these. One thing, though,' he added, as Bryan set off to raid the kitchen drawers, 'try not to damage my fingers.'

Bryan rummaged desperately in drawer after drawer. Knives, spoons, a cheese grater. He was hampered by having only one free hand. There was nothing that would be of any use. He was looking in the wrong place. Even little old ladies must have heavier stuff somewhere.

'Of course I do.' Mrs Corke looked up from heaving a bucketful of water onto the now steaming carpet inside the front door. 'Workmen came round to fix the taps only the other week. Left something behind.' She disappeared into the bathroom and emerged with a heavy spanner. 'That do?' Bryan nodded.

Noble spread his hands wide and Bryan, taking careful aim, slugged away at the metal-encased space between them.

'Keep going with the wet blankets,' he yelled over his shoulder as he raised the spanner yet again. It had been worth concentrating on the blaze behind the front door, he realised. Their path to freedom – assuming they could get the door open – was almost fire-free. But the rest of the flat was close to becoming a cauldron. He coughed once, sharply, then re-applied himself to his task.

'Christ, the way you're going on,' said Noble, 'I almost believe you could have killed her. Killed both of them for that matter.' There was a gleam of admiration in the man's eyes.

'Keep still,' said Bryan tersely.

Behind him was a frenzied flurry of activity as the others fought the fire. He concentrated on the task in front of him, battering with all his strength. Several times Noble winced at the force of the impact of metal on metal. But, give the man his due, he didn't withdraw his hands. They were all coughing now from the smoke. Bryan hoped to God that the fire hadn't spread to the bathroom, to Lee. He smashed the spanner down again, and the handcuffs broke. Noble was at the door in an instant. He inspected the locks.

'Be better if I had a hacksaw,' he pronounced. 'But a bit of wire ought to fix the Chubb. You got a plastic for the Yale?'

Bryan handed over his Gold Card.

'Nice one,' Noble was once more at work. 'You must be worth a bob or two to be able to have one of them.'

'How come you know so much about locks?'

Noble looked up grimly from his efforts.

'Used to be a burglar din' I? Before I moved on to higher things. Won't take me more than a couple of minutes.'

The rehearsed reading of the efforts of the creative writing group was the highlight of the afternoon – in spite of the fact that none of its members had taken a blind bit of notice of the rules the Organising Committee had decreed. For a start, none of them was wearing a hat. Much more serious, none of them had written about hats. Only Tanya's effort, unheard by Jack Noble, was a serious, saccharine let-down. As for the others, bareheaded and with barefaced cheek, they sang the praises of the views from their high-rise flats which they would soon be forced to leave. Many ignored the issue of housing entirely and recited poems about the fierce, protective pleasure of keeping watch over the cot of a sick child; the friendly chatter which transformed the tedium and inhumanity of queuing for benefits in the grim, grey, local DSS; the stomach-clenching pangs of going cold turkey after years of heroin addiction; the racking sobs of a ten-year-old at the death of her hamster. An old lag took the mike and told of the ups and downs of life in and out of the nick. A little, lisping kid recounted her adventures – which included the consumption of vast amounts of ice cream, chips and chocolate cake – in a fiery land of dragons. A shuffling grandad read a riveting first-person account of how, as a boy, he almost drowned in the Silk Stream. Naheed said her sad piece on the violent husband of her arranged marriage. Reg waxed long and lyrical about the solitary pleasure of pulling parsnips from thick, damp, odorous clay. Between them they managed to strike a chord in every single one of the hearts of their audience; everybody had been there, done that – but they could never have put it into such wonderful words. Even the Mayor was diverted from her anxiety over Maureen's whereabouts. And, when the performance finished, there was a deep, appreciative silence of the collective experience which the creative writing group had summoned up.

But only for a moment. One person began to clap, then another, then another. The applause gained force, crescendoed to a storm. Feet stamped on the parquet floor of the Activity Room, voices cried out for an encore.

They were out! They were in the corridor. Noble swiftly freed Bryan of his handcuffs.

'One wheelchair to each lift,' instructed Bryan. 'The rest of you squeeze yourselves in around us.'

But the lifts were stuck.

'We'll have to carry them down,' said Noble.

'Count me out,' said Banks.

'Shut it,' said Noble. 'And get your arse into gear.'

The crowd in the Community Centre had clapped their hearts out. They had listened in silent respect to an encore: an affectionate eulogy to the idiosyncrasies of the old gas boiler in the tower block, an elegy about the effort of climbing – counting – umpteen cold, concrete stairs when the lifts packed up. They clapped again. And were eclipsed by a sudden, shattering, hollow boom. Too loud for thunder. Too close for a bomb – besides, what terrorist would ever bother bombing Crandon? The blast shook the walls of the Centre; in the Pottery Room and the Garden Room several windows shattered, sending kids running, screaming from the bouncy castle. Adults turned anxious white faces to each other. One little girl with a blonde pony tail and the face of an angel spoke for everyone.

'What the fuck was that?' she said.

Bryan was appalled at the prospect of having to rely entirely on the strength of a stranger's arms to see him through. John must be feeling as bad, given that he came up with a joke.

'What d'you call a cripple with a frigid girlfriend?' he demanded as Banks hefted him none too gently from his chair.

'Don't know. What do you?'

'Tell you when we get down.'

Which was when the explosion ripped through lower floors of the building. It shook the concrete beneath their feet. There was a dull rumble which seemed to come from way below.

'Jesus,' exclaimed John.

'Jesus Christ,' echoed Noble.

Most of them wore hats. All of them were running. Jill Rush and Edward had called the emergency services, Dosh and Constable Hindmarsh had summoned reinforcements and now everyone was on the way to find out for themselves what had happened. At top speed. Policemen's helmets, firemen's helmets, cycling helmets, hard hats, top hats, jockey caps, flat caps, baseball caps, bowlers, bonnets, halloween hats – they all bobbed across the mall as the people wearing this assorted headgear ran full tilt towards the epicentre of the noise, flanked by the uniforms.

'If we can't go down, we'll have to go up.' As Bryan spoke they all heard the crash and pop of further, smaller explosions below. Mrs Corke retreated, the fingers of one hand stuffed into her mouth.

'It's worse than the Blitz,' she managed through them.

They didn't have tower blocks in the Blitz, though, thought Bryan. Good thing they didn't. Because the place wasn't just on fire like Mrs Corke's flat, by the sound of it it was falling apart.

'Leave my wheelchair close to the bottom of the stairs,' he instructed as Noble and Banks stumbled hurriedly past the now glowing door of Number 85, their live burdens on their shoulders. 'It's the lightest of the two.'

The Mayor pulled her trilby from her head. She was running like all get out. She felt a warm hand lace its fingers into hers. She looked up and – thank God – Maureen in her dinky little baby's bonnet was running at her side.

'Where's that creative writing woman?' the Mayor gasped.

'Turned out to be a dyed-in-the-wool hetero,' Maureen gasped back.

Kenny was late again. He'd meant to be at the Fun Day hours before, had been looking forward to it, but on his way to the Centre he'd come across a cluster of plump pigeons picking at the rubbish around a grey paladin bin. He'd never really noticed before how many different colours each pigeon was. A lovely purple, a deep grey, a pale pink. Eyes as black as night and beady as buttons. He liked the way those eyes darted about, liked the way the birds cocked and dipped their heads. Funny how birds had one eye in either side of their heads. Did they get a different view from each, like having two TV screens going at once? Lucky birds. He sat down on the cold tarmac, waiting to see what they would do next. Gradually the pigeons became used to his immobile presence. They grew bold. They pecked all around him. One fluttered past his shoulder, its wing brushing his cheek. He wondered what it would be like to touch them, their feathers looked soft. But when he reached out a hand to try to do so the whole flock of them rose and retreated and settled down again several feet away. Kenny rose too. He was going to the Centre, he reminded himself. He particularly wanted to see the drama group. He liked drama. Would he be allowed to join in again, he wondered? That was the best bit. He didn't hurry. He'd left the shared house in plenty of time.

But when he reached the Centre, his excitement rising at the prospect of the colour and noise of the Mushy Pea Group, he found that it was all over, everyone had left. He peered in the windows of the empty Community Centre. The parquet floor of the Activity Room was bare.

'Doesn't it go quick?' he keened to himself.

But, just a minute, what was that? They weren't a performance any more, they were a procession. Because the Mushy Pea Company were pouring down the mall with the rest of the crowd, the 'houses' around their torsos lurching from side to side. Kenny took off at a run after them, clutching a schoolboy's cap to his head.

They were on the fifteenth floor.

'D'you know where the access is to the roof?' Bryan demanded.

'There's a ladder at the end of the corridor,' responded Noble. 'For when they need to get up there to do repairs. It'll be padlocked, but we'll soon have that open.'

Noble and Banks ran towards the ladder.

'Get into your uncle's flat,' Bryan told Lee, 'ransack the linen cupboard, drench as many towels and stuff as you can carry with water and bring them with you. And neither you or Mrs Corke are to go onto the roof until I say so.'

'Quick thinking, that, telling them I knew how to put out petrol fires,' said Bryan quietly to John.

'You do, don't you?'

'Who d'you think I am, Red Adair? I'm a back room boy. Never been near a flaming oil rig in my life.'

'So how d'you know what to do? Back in there?'

'Common sense.'

The heat was growing intense. They all clutched damp towels to their faces. Otherwise there was nothing to do but wait. But Noble was back in seconds with Banks in tow.

Lee and Mrs Corke stood together below a steel ladder, above which Bryan could see a rectangle of the still blue sky.

'What are we waiting for?' wailed Lee, but Bryan took no notice.

'Have you got any rope?' he asked Noble.

'Are you mad?' It was Banks who spoke. 'We've no chance of climbing down. And you must be completely off your trolley if you think you can do it in a wheelchair. What d'you think this is, some kind of fairy tale?'

Even John put his oar in. 'I bet you could do it when you had the use of your legs,' he assured Bryan loyally, 'but that was then. No point in being a hero if you're going to be a dead one.'

'There'll be no heroics. And I'm not proposing anything so ridiculous.' He turned again to Noble. 'Just get whatever you have. Really stout ropes capable of holding a person's weight. Or strong leather belts. Get as many as you can. Quickly.' Noble obeyed.

'Before you go up,' Bryan instructed, 'Each of you get one of those belts round Lee and Mrs Corke. Round the waist. Buckle it onto another belt and wrap that round your hand. Take a third belt when you get up there, don't let go. The wind will be blowing a bomb at this height. Get Mrs Corke and Lee tied to anything that you are certain is completely secure. A safety rail around the edge, for instance. Then come back for me and John.'

Another intolerable wait made tolerable only by John keeping up a steady patter, firing questions at Bryan, then answering them himself.

'What did the householder say to the one-legged burglar caught in the act?

'Hop it.'

'Think I'm on my last legs?

'Well, on my last legs I was a lot quicker than I am on these.'

'What's the connection between two guys in wheelchairs stuck in a lift and a couple of birds on a pond?

'Sitting ducks.'

'John,' Bryan managed through the damp towel, 'those must be your worst jokes ever.'

'Yeah, well, keep your mind off other things, don't they? Like not being able to make a run for it. Or, in our case, a roll.'

Noble was back.

'Are they safe?' queried Bryan.

The big man nodded. 'Good job you thought about the ropes and belts, though. Wind would have had them over the edge in seconds. Now for you.'

Bryan shook his head. 'Banks is to get John outside, get him lashed securely. You're to go back down and get my chair. Take one of the wet towels to cover your mouth.'

Noble didn't hesitate. He disappeared into the smoke. Banks lifted John towards the ladder.

'See you back in Blighty,' called John as he was manhandled up the narrow ladder.

Those were the worst moments. Bryan was sprawled, immobile, on the concrete floor through which he could now feel the heat of the conflagration below. If Noble didn't make it, he, Bryan, was for it. And so were the others. They were all depending on him, trusting that whatever plan he had made would work. Which given half a chance it would. For these were the best moments as well as the worst. He was alive again as he hadn't been in all those dreary, self-pitying months after his accident. He was facing physical danger again, but this time with a body which was not equipped to deal with it. He thought back to poor Marion and her facile contention that he was not disabled, only differently abled. He had to concede that in a way she had been right. Because now he had the courage, the mental capacity to accept what he was and to use his disability, the paraphernalia of his disability, to save them all. He grinned to himself at the serious, almost pompous turn his thoughts had taken. Better snap out of it. In the meantime, where the fuck was Noble? The floor was getting hotter by the minute. Lucky, he thought grimly, that he didn't have any feeling in his legs.

Noble was beside him, coughing furiously, dragging the light frame of Bryan's athlete's wheelchair behind him. His face was streaked with soot.

'Like hell, down there,' he said tersely. 'What next?'

'The magic marker from your flat. The one your girlfriend was using. Take the chair to the roof. Then come and collect me.'

'This had better be good, squire,' but Noble robbed the words of any animosity by promptly doing what Bryan said.

Negotiating the narrow steel ladder was a terrible ordeal. Bryan had never felt so helpless in his life, the inert cargo of a man whom he had little reason to trust. He didn't need to trust him, he reminded himself, he simply needed to go on giving orders with the authority he had so far. That way he would keep the upper hand.

243

The scene that met his eyes on the roof was terrifying, the noise of the wind even more so. The air was freezing cold. John was propped into a sitting position, firmly lashed to the railing at its edge, his useless legs trailing on the surface of the roof. Mrs Corke and Lee were tied beside him, their clothes all but whipped from their bodies by the blast which howled like a demon around them. Banks and Noble added Bryan to the row of trussed-up bodies.

'Now what?' screamed Noble above the din.

Bryan had his answer ready. Shouting for help would be no good. Waving would be no good. He gave his instructions.

The Crandon bush telegraph had done its work again. The mob had snowballed, attracting hundreds more people. The gang from the Mandela Estate, Lee's Aunt Suzy and her kids, hordes of people from all over Crandon had assembled to see the disaster. Jill Rush was pushing Edward in Bryan's old chair.

'It's very good of you,' he said. 'I'd never realised this thing was so awkward for the person sitting in it. I don't know how Bryan managed.'

'It's a pleasure. To be honest I was looking for an opportunity to get shot of Maureen Clegg.'

'The Mayor's partner? How come?'

'Um. In theory I've no problems about lesbians. But when one of them makes a hit on me it's a different matter. I just don't go for it. D'you think that's totally off beam?'

'Don't see why. It's a simple, physical preference. You might say the same about men who don't attract you. For instance you mightn't fancy men with brown hair.' He gave her a disarming, Hugh Grant grin. 'Or men in wheelchairs.'

'That's where you're wrong. I do go for men with brown hair. As long as they're in a wheelchair on a temporary basis.'

Kenny danced past them, absorbed in his practised interpretation of the English Channel. Jim Hepworth was taking pics like all get out.

And then they all saw it: the tower block in flames.

244

'Thank God no one's in there,' said Jill. 'Thank God they were all at the Fun Day.'

DCI Dawson, seeing the mass of people approaching, took immediate charge. He detailed the uniforms to crowd control duties, he radioed for more emergency services, he summoned officers to cordon off the area around the tower block. He called for a loudhailer.

'Get back! Get back!' he bellowed into the mouthpiece of the thing. 'There is no cause for alarm. For your own safety please withdraw beyond the tapes.'

Everyone stopped. Everyone except Kenny. He danced on, oblivious, immersed in his role of a raging, stormy sea. But where was the black rock he had learned to throw himself against? Where were the pebbles which rolled to and fro, hissing their reluctant song as he forced them this way and that? He didn't know. He could hear in his mind's eye the sounds of gulls crying, hear the flapping of their wings, see the shadows they cast over him as they flew between his eyes and the sun. And here came a huge one, screaming its way to the ground.

It wasn't a gull. It was a monster. Kenny tumbled to the ground as the thing sailed past him and broke up on the tarmac. A fragment of it rolled over and over, came to a shuddering halt.

'Christ,' said Edward, 'that's one of the wheels of Bryan's new chair.'

They all rushed towards it. On it were daubed, in bright, raspberry-coloured magic marker, the words, 'Help. We're on the roof.'

Chapter Thirteen

'All over bar the shouting,' said Bryan.

It was three days later, nearly midnight on Christmas Eve, and they were sitting in the bar at the Icicle. Bryan, John, Jack Noble, Tanya, Mrs Corke, Lee, Edward (still in Bryan's old wheelchair, plastered leg stuck out straight in front of him), Jill Rush, Kenny, Mr D, Laura, Karen, Gerald Tozer and Henry the dog. Banks hadn't been invited, the guest list for this evening had been down to Bryan.

The Christmas decorations above their heads were de luxe gold and silver affairs and in the corner of the room, lights winked on a huge tree. Everyone was drinking champagne. The drinks were on the house and there was a sign on the outside door which read, 'Private Function in Progress'.

'What d'you mean?' asked Noble.

'It's the wash-up, the finale. The bit when, if this were a novel, Poirot would explain all his deductions.' Bryan could afford to be flip now he had come through his last ordeal.

His suspension from the helicopter. That's how the emergency services got them off the roof of the blazing tower block. The experience was every bit as terrifying as his hang-gliding accident. The same crowd looking upwards at him with appalled, white faces. The same sense of helplessness as he spiralled down. Only this time the blue lozenge below wasn't a swimming pool but the banner which advertised the Carleton Park Fun Day. And this time John was there to welcome him to terra firma.

'So what do you call a cripple with a frigid girlfriend?' Bryan managed as he touched base.

'Roll and butter. Roland Butter. Geddit?'

'Uncle Jack.' This evening Lee had abandoned alcopops in favour of champagne. His elbows were on the table round which they all sat, it looked as though his head was about to join them.

'Yes, lad?'

'You would have given it back, wouldn't you? If I'd asked.'

Karen lifted a finger. Then she lifted a glass of champagne to Laura's lips. Laura sipped. They all waited for her reaction, then watched as a single word – 'Wow!' – scrolled across her new silver screen which Bryan, using his most up-market, executive voice had managed to con out of Social Services.

'Given what back?'

'The computer. You only needed it overnight so Tanya could type her poem. You said.'

'No point asking. The thing's gone the way of the rest of the block. But sure.' Noble looked at Lee, then at Bryan. 'I'll buy the guy a new one. Why not?'

John said, 'I still don't get it. Did Dawson kill Julia Stone as well as Marion?'

'Nah,' said Noble. 'Harry killed her. Or if he didn't he believes he did. Saw him earlier that day. Saw her too. Told her to steer well clear. He was too out of it even then to know whether he lit the fire or not. We all know he didn't. Even if we keep shtoom, there's no way enough evidence to convict him. Harry'll soon be back scouring the skips of Kensington, mark my words. Especially now that bastard policeman has been arrested for the murder of the rich doll. Who's to know he didn't do both killings? Harry never did have any luck.'

'How d'you mean?'

'In the nature of a punishment for him to stay out of custody. He was well ready for a spell in the nick. Been in and out of it all his life, s'where all his mates are. Quite a home from home far as he's concerned. Plus he doesn't have to earn a living. Fucking rest cure it is for him, spending a few years as a guest of Her Majesty. Won't be thanking anyone for getting off scot-free.'

'Talking of homes,' said Mrs Corke, 'you must all come to tea in my new flat. As cosy as anything, it is. You wouldn't believe the stuff I've ordered from the council's second-hand furniture store. All free, mind you. It's nice to have a clean sweep, a good clear-out, I always say. And it's on the sixteenth floor, so the view's even better. Said they'd move me to a house with a garden soon as they had one built and I said they had another think coming. They'll move me over my dead body.' And she puffed out her chest and looked as redoubtable as Bryan was sure she had during the Blitz.

'It's me for one of those,' said Gerald. 'Me and Henry. A garden'll suit Henry just fine.' He took a Twiglet from a bowl on the table and offered it to the animal at his feet. The old dog opened one eye and his mouth simultaneously, crunched briefly, then went back to sleep. 'She's finally decided to let me keep him,' said Gerald as though this were an honour.

'But if he did kill her,' Bryan persisted to Noble, 'shouldn't there be some sort of . . . well, not punishment but at least deterrent for the future?'

'Look, mate, it was only a domestic. Got stroppy with her because she was seeing other blokes. Probably only meant to give her a seeing-too, didn't realise his own strength when he was out of it. Could happen to any of us.'

Not to me, thought Bryan, then remembered his rage when he'd pursued Marion from the Centre the night she died.

'Harry's a loser,' Noble went on. 'She was a loser. Sure, it's difficult for the likes of you and me to know what goes on inside their heads. That's because nothing much does. Get short of money they go on the game or rob stuff. Get a few knockbacks, they take to dope and drink. Find their tart's having it off with someone else, they give her one. Simple as that. If she hadn't copped it from Harry she'd have snuffed it soon from the gear. Not worth worrying about. Whereas this lad,' he turned to a now sleeping Lee. 'You're not a loser, are you, son?'

Lee opened his eyes at the sound of his name. He shook his head.

'Attaboy! Haven't a clue who his father was. Must have had something in his genes, though. Lad's got what it takes.'

'To be what?' asked Bryan.

Noble laid a hand on the child's shoulder. 'Want to be a big businessman like me, don't you, lad?'

Lee raised his face to Noble. Then he switched his gaze to Bryan. Then he lowered his head once more onto his arms. In whose footsteps – or in Bryan's case wheeltracks – Bryan wondered, would Lee decide to follow?

It was Edward who spoke up next. 'What about those "accidents?"' he asked. Getting together with Jill Rush seemed to have given him a new lease of life, given him, at least, the courage to ask questions. 'The car mounting the pavement outside the offices of your, er, magazine and the ramp over the roadworks being sabotaged?'

'Hey,' interrupted Jill Rush, ' it okay if I smoke in here?'

'You must be joking. Punters would leave in droves if I tried to put them on a health kick. Feel free.' And Noble extracted a fat cigar from his top pocket, then made a great ceremony of peeling off its wrapper and sniffing the cylinder inside as though he were a Customs and Excise dog after a major haul of dope.

'If those are Silk Cut Ultra,' Edward ventured to Jill, 'I wouldn't mind one myself.' Jill handed him the packet.

'I had no idea you smoked,' said Bryan.

'I knew you wouldn't like it.' Edward lit up and inhaled deeply. 'And,' he added, reverting to his customary humility when dealing with his boss, 'I wouldn't have dreamt of asking.'

'Stuff,' said Jill. 'Don't ask, don't get. You soon learn that when you have to deal with publishers.'

And to Bryan's surprise Edward's free hand shot out, caught Jill's free hand and imprisoned it on his denim-clad thigh. Some guys in ancient wheelchairs have all the luck, thought Bryan without rancour.

'As I was saying.' Noble had lit his cigar, puffed a cloud of dense smoke into the atmosphere and was now calling them to attention. 'Both incidents were down to Banks. Thought he was doing me a favour. Afraid I gave him a rough time before that. Trying to get himself back in my good books by doing Bryan a nasty turn. Sussed Bryan was on my case, d'you see? Of course I'd never have given him the go-ahead for any of your actual violence. Not my style.' He shook his head firmly. 'No indeedy.'

'I really thought you'd killed Stone,' said Bryan. 'Possibly Marion too.'

Lee surfaced once more.

'I thought you might have, Uncle Jack,' he said in a slurred voice. 'After Bryan told me he hadn't done her in. I knew you wouldn't have killed Mum. Even though I told him that you could have. You could, couldn't you?'

'Me?' said Noble in surprise. 'I wouldn't hurt a fly.'

Lee looked positively downcast.

'But you sent me to torch the Patels.'

'Made sure they were all out first, din' I? It was their evening for the Cash and Carry. They go regular as clockwork every week. Kids and all. Besides, they're insured. Probably made a packet out of it. Doing them a good turn in a way.'

Bryan shook his head with a grin at this sophistry.

Tanya had disappeared a few minutes before. Now she returned with a pair of pyjamas and began to exchange Lee's street clothes, slowly and with infinite care, for striped, baggy trousers and top.

'Poor little sausage,' she commented, dropping a kiss on the kid's wedge haircut. 'Want your Auntie Tanya to read you a bedtime story?'

Lee shook his head and snuggled into her lap.

'Want to stay here. With Uncle Jack and you.'

Which meant, reflected Bryan, surprised at Tanya's hitherto unsuspected talents as a mother substitute, that Lee had fallen on his feet.

'What about *Page Four*,' demanded John with uncharacteristic seriousness. 'You can't tell me those women enjoy what they do.'

'Sure can. Take Tanya here.' Noble patted her thigh affectionately. 'Regular little exhibitionist, aren't you, poppet? As I always say, whatever turns you on is fine by me. Same with the others. Marion was a case in point, there was a woman who loved her work. Wouldn't dream of putting pressure on a doll to do something she didn't want. Matter of fact,' he added, 'worked up quite a nice little sideline recently, hiring the studio to lesbians who want to take pics of each other. Don't spread it around,' he lowered his voice, 'it's pretty hush-hush right now, but the Mayor's just booked the place for several sessions.' He winked. 'Private ones.'

Mrs Corke yawned discreetly. 'It's well past that child's bedtime,' she said. 'Never've been allowed to stay up this late when I was a girl.'

Bryan looked at Lee. 'What'll happen to him?' he asked. 'He can't go on living on his own. Besides, he's got nowhere to live.'

'No problem.' Noble paused and poured more champagne all round.

'Doesn't it go quick?' said Kenny, downing his glassful in one gulp.

Mr D. nodded. But then he'd been nodding ever since he arrived.

'Always told him I'd see him right,' Noble went on. 'He'll live upstairs with me, where else?'

Bryan turned to John. 'And where're you going to live?'

'What d'you mean? I'm staying with you, aren't I? You said I could.'

'Nope. I've got plans for my home. And they don't include you.'

'What plans?'

'Decorating the spare bedroom for a start. Then the rest of the place. Getting my house in order.'

'Got a couple of mates would do the whole job at a knock-down price,' Noble put in. 'Owe me a favour. Quality work, no rubbish.'

'No thanks. I'm going to do it myself. Thought I'd put a colour wash on the walls. Then get some proper furniture so I can entertain people who don't bring their own seating arrangements with them.'

There was silence. Bryan could see they were all wondering how a guy in a wheelchair would mount stepladders, spread dust sheets, shove furniture around.

'Okay,' he conceded, 'so I'll employ someone to do the heavy stuff. Got anyone on your books?'

Noble nodded.

'But I'll do the dirty myself. Buy brushes and a roller with long handles. Or have them custom-made if that's what it takes. Besides which . . .' he turned to John.

Mrs Corke intervened.

'Wouldn't catch the master doing a thing like that. Not with his own hands.' She emitted a sudden giggle. She was tipsy. 'He always had servants to do the rough. Reminds me of the day the under-gardener got his marching orders.'

'Why?' asked Bryan.

'That'd be telling. Can't say I remember myself. It was a long time ago.' Abruptly she sobered and sat up straight. 'The fourteenth of March 1928. 5.13 pm. You should have seen his face as he slunk out of the door. The back door, mind you. Went off by the tradesmen's entrance.'

Bryan looked at John, who twisted an index finger on his right temple. Bryan grinned. Sure, Mrs Corke was not exactly compos. But where was the harm in that? He looked around at everyone. A villain, several cripples, a senile old woman, an old man with a leaking rheumatic dog, a child arsonist; had anyone told him a year ago that he'd be spending Christmas Eve enjoying their company he'd have laughed them into the next county.

'What about Banks?' Noble interrupted Bryan's reverie. He was handing round a plate of stuffed olives. Gerald offered one to Henry, but the dog curled his lip, settled his nose between his paws and closed his eyes once more. 'You going to shop him or what?'

'Haven't got any evidence.' In his present, euphoric state Bryan felt there was even room in Crandon for a bent policeman. 'Daresay he'll tone down his activities in future, won't he?'

Noble nodded. 'If he takes my advice – which he will, mark my words – he'll lie low for a while.'

John had been silent for some time. Now he piped up.

'What did you mean about getting rid of me? Why do you want to get shot?'

'Easy-peasy. Because you're a slob. You get up late. You don't do the washing up. And you should listen to yourself sometime. You play music at a volume to send my neighbours up the wall. What's more you sing along, but with the wrong words. You should hear yourself at "Sit up for your rights". Or, for that matter, at "Sit by your man". Seriously not on, either for me or for them.'

'What neighbours?'

'Something wrong with your eyes recently as well as your legs? Was that, or was that not, a removal van earlier today? Delivering, as opposed to removing, furniture?'

'Disabled or able-bodied, are they?'

'Able-bodied. Young couple. First time buyers. Absolutely not on for them to be subjected to your renditions. The housing association'll have me out if you keep at it. Not supposed to have a lodger anyway.'

'So it's me for the street, then.'

'How come?'

'Lost my room while I was doing your dirty work, didn't I? Told you I might. People who run the shared house figured I had somewhere else I could stay. Moved in someone who needed it more.' He paused and giggled, then went on – the champagne was talking – 'Wonder what the new occupant made of the interior decor? Oh well,' he shrugged his shoulders.